When You Have to Go There

by

Kevin R. Doyle

When You Have To Go There

Cover Art by *Debbie Taylor*

The Wild Rose Press, Inc.
PO Box 708
Adams Basin, NY 14410-0708
Visit us at www.thewildrosepress.com

Publishing History
First Edition, 2021
Trade Paperback ISBN 978-1-5092-3939-9
Digital ISBN 978-1-5092-3940-5

Previously Published: MuseitUP Publications, 2018
Published in the United States of America

Dedication

To Monette M., the best department chair a beginning
teacher could have had

"Home is the place where, when you have to go there, they have to take you in."

—*Robert Frost,* "The Death of the Hired Man"

CHAPTER ONE

Everyone who worked with him, or met him in some way during the course of his life, considered Roy Michaels a good cop. Not an outstanding or excellent cop, but a good one. On the force for twenty years next February, he'd served as a patrolman for eight of those years and a detective for the rest. Most people destined for plainclothes made it in five years or less, and most of his colleagues considered the fact that it took Michaels a few extra nothing more than an indication of his methodical, plodding approach to his work.

Not a hot dog or superstar of any kind, Roy Michaels didn't go out of his way to horn in on the big collars, and had never been fortunate enough to be associated with a truly major case. But he went along, week after week and year after year, doing his job.

A good cop.

Though not great.

When he logged out at the end of shift, at four-thirty in the afternoon that Wednesday, Roy Michaels would not be a good cop for much longer.

He should have logged out at a quarter to four, the standard time. And for most of the day, he'd hoped to be out and home on time. But a mundane morning spent re-interviewing people in a three-month old case had included one of those witnesses having moved on, causing Michaels to spend most of the afternoon tracing through various lease agreements, forwarding addresses and employers before he managed to track down the eighteen-year old in question.

Upon finding his witness, zoned out after a night of bar hopping, it took every bit of effort and patience Michaels had to jolt the kid's memory and awareness long enough to fill in the blanks from the previous interview.

All of which left Michaels clocking out a good three quarters of an hour later than his shift mandated, but anyone who'd worked on the force more than a couple of weeks understood that shift start times, and especially end times, were more a matter of wish fulfillment than cold, hard reality.

At this point, Detective Roy Michaels had less than an hour to live.

He stopped on his way out of headquarters to check in with Sgt. Mulron in the patrol division, confirming their regular Saturday night poker game was a go. Mulron had been going through some sort of problems at home lately, though of what sort no one quite knew. Usually among the most talkative of the patrol guys, Mulron had kept fairly quiet lately. However, the sergeant perked up with the reminder of the poker game.

Maybe, Michaels thought, things had turned around for the sarge.

If only he could say the same for his own domestic situation.

Stepping through the revolving glass doors that fronted the Central Division building, doors which several members of the force felt a wee bit vulnerable in current times, Michaels took a deep breath. At the end of every shift, he never considered himself completely off duty until he could take a breath of clean, or as clean as possible in the middle of a major city, air. Breathing in, he could feel his muscles and tendons loosening, his nerves relaxing.

Standing in front of headquarters, Roy Michaels now had less than fifty minutes of life left.

Getting to the city parking garage and negotiating his Taurus out of the structure and onto the streets took another five and a half minutes. Making his way out of the downtown area and onto one of the main arteries that laced through the suburbs consumed eighteen.

Twenty-one minutes and change in the life of Roy Michaels, but by this juncture what's the point of counting?

In a relatively short time, he made it all the way to his house in Herndon, one of the moderate-classed suburbs linking to the larger city. It was the kind of community where you could find a lot of middle managers, union-card carrying blue-collar types, and the occasional once-higher executive on their way down the ladder. Roy and Lori Michaels had moved into this area during their fifth year of marriage, optimistically buying a four-bedroom ranch.

Years later, Roy had converted one of the extra bedrooms into a small study/ den while the other two still sat empty.

Lori had from time to time, and to anyone who would listen, complained that they should downsize a bit, since it had some time ago become pretty obvious that her yearning for children would never be met. She would tell friends and family, and now and then Roy himself, that they could sell the house and move into something smaller but fancier, closer to the city, or maybe even in the metro area itself.

Still, Roy had always found a reason to forestall moving, mainly because he didn't see any reason to give up such a comfortable and, more importantly, paid for home.

Pulling into his driveway, he now had less than two minutes to go.

His blood pressure ticked up a bit when he saw their mailbox, situated on a small pole next to the curb, canted at an angle. Roy pulled all the way into his garage. Then, rather than lower the door and head on inside, he turned and headed back down the driveway to see just how much damage some stupid kid had done to their property.

Thirty seconds, give or take, at this point.

The mailbox, though still hanging onto its post, had been nearly sheared off. A ragged tear no doubt, Roy figured, made from a ball bat or some other such club. Maybe a tire iron. Kneeling down, he peered closer, noticing it looked as if someone had ripped the box off completely, and then haphazardly positioned it back on its post.

But why the hell would a vandal bother putting the pieces back together, especially in such an obvious manner? Looking straight on, no one could possibly imagine that the homeowner wouldn't notice the damage. So why not just leave it lie?

Michaels bent down to inspect the mailbox closer (three seconds to death) and as he did so noticed a shadow hover on his right.

His instincts kicking in, he began to rise and twist around at the same time, but he had neither time nor skill enough for the move to succeed. Before he'd completed half the turn, a sharp, burning sensation hit his temple.

He never heard that first shot.

Or the second or third.

The shadow receded as the figure headed off, sauntering along so as not to call attention to itself.

Half a minute later, Lori Michaels, confused because she'd heard her husband's car pull up, stepped out of the front door and saw him lying on his side in the driveway.

Even from the distance, she could see the blood pooling out from under his head.

Detective Second Grade Roy Michaels had no time left in the world.

CHAPTER TWO

The information flowed outward in waves. At the sight of her husband's body, Lori collapsed screaming on her porch. Within moments, two of her neighbors, an elderly couple who lived next door, came rushing out of their house, and saw Lori throwing a fit on her front porch.

It took a few seconds for them to notice Roy farther down on the sidewalk. When they did so, the woman rushed over to Lori's side while her husband headed down to see what could be done for Roy.

Nothing, as it turned out.

Between coming to grips with the scene and trying to get Lori under control, it took nearly five minutes before the old man, leaving his wife to do as best she could, headed back into their home and grabbed his phone.

By this point, other neighbors had edged out of their houses, mutely watching the unfolding tragedy. There weren't that many, as most of the people in this neighborhood were either on their way or just getting home from work. But bit by bit, they appeared, some from two or three blocks over, all drawn instinctively to the scene of tragedy.

And while some of them may have wanted to help, through either shock or indecision they remained rooted in place, mute witnesses to the tragic scene.

Five and a half minutes, all told, before the call got through the 911 system.

The operator, efficient and controlled, did her job in the quickest manner possible, and less than a minute from the time the old man dialed his phone a call went out to the patrol division, and in four and a half minutes a cruiser pulled up to the Michaels' residence.

By this time, the neighbor lady had managed to get Lori back into the house. The first patrol officers appearing on scene saw only Roy's body crumpled on the drive.

The two officers, a rookie and a veteran, bolted out of their vehicle. The rookie stepped to the side and did a 360 survey of the neighborhood checking for either the shooter or shooters. He didn't see anything directly menacing, though the sight of several of the onlookers holding out their cell phones gave him some jitters.

Meanwhile, his partner, a gray-haired man with just the slightest bit of a paunch, approached the victim, snapping on a pair of latex gloves as he did so.

The older cop knelt down, careful to disturb the scene as little as possible.

Seeing no visible signs of life, he then reached out with his right hand and felt for a pulse.

The veteran cop was careful not to move the corpse, wanting to preserve the scene for the lab people. But when he detected no pulse, he stood up and walked around to the other side in an attempt to at least ascertain the victim's appearance.

Almost as soon as he knelt down to face the half-slumped form, the cop jerked back to his feet.

"Oh shit," he said to no one in particular.

His partner came over.

"What is it, Jeff?" the younger cop asked.

The veteran looked at his partner for a second before walking backwards from the corpse.

From opposite ends of the block two other squad cars were entering the scene.

"Get back on the horn," the older man told his partner, "and go to one of the special freqs. Don't broadcast over the regular air."

"What?" The younger man, seeing the expression of strain on the veteran's face, bulldozed backward, shaken.

Jeff lowered his voice to a near whisper, just enough for his partner several feet away to hear him.

"Tell them we have a cop down," he said. "It's Roy Michaels, out of Central."

Meanwhile, two other patrol units had arrived. Seeing the two original officers on scene, the other men in the new cars positioned their vehicles on either side of the Michaels house, bracketing off the crime scene.

Within fifteen minutes of the first arrivals, an ambulance showed up, pulling up to the curb about fifty yards down from the house. The attendants had been informed the victim was DOA, and they didn't want to have their vehicle blocking any of the action.

Herndon, though officially its own town, was small enough that it secured both fire and police services from the larger city to the east. This reciprocal arrangement, which some residents routinely complained about, served in this case to speed things up quite a bit, and as word went out over the air as to the decedent's identity, the call went out for every available Herndon unit to move on scene.

When word made its way up the floors of the central division and to the detective squad room, exemplified by the presiding sergeant downstairs calling up as quickly as he could to the office of Lieutenant Pete Jarvis, things really began to happen.

Glancing out the windows of his office, Jarvis saw only one of his detectives in the squad room.

He stood up from his desk, grabbed his suit jacket from its hangar and made his way out.

Richie Lattimer, the newest member of the squad, glanced up.

"Boss?"

"I'm heading out. Off line for a while. Has Hollis checked in yet?"

"Not that I've seen. He had court today."

"I know that." Jarvis worked to keep his voice level. He glanced at his watch. "They should have been done by now. Get hold of him and have him meet me at Roy Michaels's house."

"Boss?" The younger man's brow furrowed. "Roy checked out about an hour ago. Why…"

The kid's voice faltered and his face took on a blanched look.

"Do me a favor, Richie. I need you to stick around for a while tonight. We're going to need someone to relay messages and coordinate things here. Okay?"

Lattimer had transferred into the squad six months before. Prior to that, he'd worked out of the city's south division, so he'd had experience with violence directed specifically against cops.

"Is Roy…?"

"Don't know, kid. You'll stick around for a while?"

"Sure, boss. And I'll catch Hollis right away. Send him out there."

Jarvis clapped the younger man on the shoulder and

headed out of the squad room.

Waiting for the elevator, Jarvis silently cursed himself for not already filing the retirement papers that had been sitting in his desk for the last two months.

Yet he had no way of knowing that, bad as today would turn out, the ensuing weeks would be even worse, not only for himself but for all of the men and women under his command.

CHAPTER THREE

Within an hour, both marked and unmarked police cars congested the street of the crime scene. A patrol car wedged into each intersection kept other vehicles at bay, forcing some of the neighbors arriving home from work to park on the off streets.

An inconvenience for those folks, to be sure, but not nearly as inconvenient as the afternoon had turned out for the dead man.

Lt. Jarvis stood on the porch, surveying the varied activity around him, as Jack Hollis came up the sidewalk from the west, hurrying to meet up with his superior.

"Sorry, Pete," Hollis said as he stepped onto the porch, puffing a bit more than someone of his age should. "The judge was on a tear and wouldn't let us go till he got things straightened out."

"How'd it go?" Jarvis asked.

Hollis shrugged. "The ADA thinks she's got a shot, but the kid sounded awful contrite and truthful on the stand, so darned if I know."

"Your part done now?"

"Far as I know. Unless they need to call me back."

"Good. Because as of now your caseload is gone. This right here is your entire caseload."

Hollis frowned as he stepped aside to let one of the crime techs pass into the house.

"You sure, Pete? I'm in the middle of—"

"You said they wouldn't need you back, right?"

"Probably not, but—"

"Pull whoever you need. We'll reshuffle however we have to, but we've got a dead cop executed on his front lawn. And after what happened last year, what do you think the press will do with this? Let alone the higher ups."

Hollis didn't answer for a moment. Staring at Jarvis, he saw a whole new scattering of wrinkles on the boss's face.

"You realize," Hollis said, "that I was part of that 'business' last year. You sure you want me as the primary on this?"

"No way around it. After Harrison retired, you're one of the most senior people I've got. And I'll need to tell the higher ups that I've got my top person on it."

"Helen's a grade above me."

"Maybe so, but she's not with us anymore."

One of the tech people came out of the house and headed down the drive to snap some pictures. In the distance, past the blocked out intersections, TV news vans had begun to arrive, threading their way through the gathering crowd of neighbors craning their necks to see what had happened.

"I need her, Pete. If you really want this done right, I need her."

The camera guy made a motion with his hand and, two shakes later, a couple of paramedics hustled over and began loading Michaels onto a gurney.

Hollis wondered where Lori was, and started to ask Jarvis when the boss cut him off.

"Forget it, Jack. You know how I feel about her situation, but it's out of our hands. And you think with something this big, one of our own gunned down, they'd let Helen anywhere near it?"

"Dammit, Pete. You know as well as I that—"

"What I know is that I've been trying like hell to get her back for months. No luck. And with the way the media's going to be all over this, even a hint of Helen Lipscomb working it would bring twenty different kinds of hell down on us. Can you imagine how the mayor and chief would react, let alone the city council?"

Hollis stuffed his hands in his pockets and continued staring down the driveway. The paramedics, in this part of the state, experts at handling dead weight, had Roy loaded onto the gurney now and were strapping him down.

"Last year wasn't her fault," Hollis finally said in a tone that acknowledged they'd already had this argument uncounted times.

"I know that, Jack. And you know I know it. But we're not talking reality here, we're talking politics. And as they say, perception is everything."

"Hell," Hollis said, "if they wanted to blame anyone they should have blamed me. I caught the first one, if you remember, and didn't see it for what it was. So why the hell not me?"

A local television reporter, camera girl in tow, tried to sneak his way under the yellow restraining tape on the other side of the Michaels' yard. Two of the uniformed officers, both rookies, hustled over and, with hardly any fuss, ushered the two back on the other side of the tape.

"We're not going to have this argument again, Jack. I know how good of a cop she is, but we both know why things went down like they did. I used up damned near every chit I had in the department. Nothing."

Hollis circulated his head in a clockwise motion, working to get the kinks out of his neck.

"I guess politics is all, huh?" he said.

Jarvis looked at his man for a minute.

"Just do what you need to do," he finally said. "We can't have someone roaming the streets gunning down cops."

"Do what I need to do, just short of making use of all the resources possible."

The tension in the lieutenant's shoulders that had been building during their conversation eased, but only a fraction. He turned and surveyed the entire scene, and Hollis saw some more of the tension evaporate.

"Don't take it all out on me, guy. If you remember, so far she's managed to hold on to her job."

"Sure. Just as long as she can't actually do it."

The two of them headed down the sidewalk toward the lieutenant's car. As they made their way, a small cluster of reporters behind the tape tried to corral them, but the uniforms along the sides cut them off.

"Okay," Jarvis said to him, shaking his head. "There's a chance. They're going to want this cleared up as quickly as possible, and if I give an all hands on deck speech, it may just work."

Hollis nodded, his mind already mapping out the various steps ahead of him.

"Tell them you're shorthanded. Hell, tell them anything. But get her back on the squad."

Jarvis nodded, then moved over to speak to a couple of uniforms.

Sighing, Hollis turned on his heel to head back to the house. He realized, as he crossed the threshold, that he might have been arguing with the boss simply as a way to forestall having to confront Roy's widow.

CHAPTER FOUR

Helen Lipscomb cinched her jacket tighter as she slouched down farther in the seat. The March cold had been seeping into the car for hours as she'd trailed a suspect. For the last half hour, he'd sequestered himself away in his apartment, doing God only knew what.

"Goddamit," Helen muttered, the breath frosting out of her mouth. She would have kept the engine running, along with the heater, but three weeks of surveillance made clear that once he got home, the guy wouldn't stir for hours.

Instructions from the lieutenant, however, were clear.

Keep on him at all times.

Don't let up for a minute.

She'd decided some time back not to include in the reports that she broke protocol every five or six hours to go to the bathroom.

A partner would have helped, and upon assignment to Property Crimes, her third transfer in the last five months, she'd asked for one. But the lieutenant had made it clear that the latest budget from the city had tightened up his manpower allotment.

Then again, as the boss had pointed out, it wasn't like her assignments would be dangerous or anything.

At the moment, she would have killed for some danger, even mild excitement, to compensate for the nights on end sitting in the car, feeling her butt go numb.

Watching Tommy Andrews didn't even remotely count as excitement.

****

"His name's Andrews," Helen's new boss had told her on that first day. "He used to run with some of the Irish street hoods, but for the last six months or so he's been pretty much doing his own thing."

"And what is that?" Helen had asked, hoping that this reassignment was legitimate, even while knowing it wasn't.

"Pawn shops," Lt. Ronson had said.

"Pawn shops?"

"Yes, detective. Tommy here makes a habit of dealing through pawnshops, hocking merchandise that he steals off the street and selling it around."

"So you want me to pick him up?" Helen asked, her heart tightening at the possible answer.

"No," Ronson replied. "You need to observe him for a while, chart his patterns of activity."

Helen smothered the first words that came to mind.

"Patterns of activity? He's a street thief, right? What pattern of activity?"

"That's what we need to know. We need it charted."

Helen stared at the lieutenant for a couple of heartbeats.

"Let me get this right. You want me to shadow this person, without a partner, and keep notes of where he goes and what he does? And I'm to do this for an extended period of time?"

"Correct."

"But don't you want twenty-four hours?"

Ronson waved his hand.

"Not really. We figure that twelve a day, seven days a week will do. Say early evening to early morning."

Helen took in a couple of deep breaths.

"Lieutenant, that's—"

"Don't worry. OT's been approved for this, so at least you'll be raking in the bucks."

Yes, Helen thought. *Raking in the bucks but driving myself to exhaustion, and in the process destroying any sort of social or personal life.*

"For how long?" she asked.

Ronson stared at her, and for a second Helen thought she saw regret, maybe even a bit of guilt, in his eyes.

"Until I say different, detective. That's all."

Dismissed, Helen had gone out to secure a desk, but the only one untenanted at the time sat in a far corner and had a bit of a wobble to it. On top of the desk rested a pile of case files, several inches high, with a Post-It Note stuck to the top file.

"In your spare time," the note had said, "please convert these old cases into computer files."

Helen didn't sigh or let her shoulders slump.

Not so easy to discount the stares of everyone else in the Property Crimes squad room. Even with her back turned, she could feel them looking at her, no doubt most out of compassion but probably a few with some secret glee.

Still, Helen didn't give them even the slightest response. No matter what, she'd vowed back in the beginning, she wouldn't let one iota of complaint or self-pity seep back to either the chief or mayor.

If they were going to get rid of her, they'd have to do better than this.

****

Three weeks later, Helen shifted in her seat, contemplating saying the hell with it and taking the night off. Down the street from the ramshackle apartment building sat a pizza parlor, and though it displayed peeling paint and a grimy window, merely imagining the aromas inside the shop made her stomach tighten.

Half an hour more, she decided. Thirty minutes and she'd call it a night, returning early in the afternoon to begin the whole stake-out all over.

About twenty minutes later, movement flickered in the doorway to Andrews's apartment building, and the man himself came sauntering out, leather jacket zipped and headed up the street.

"Oh for the love of…" Helen muttered.

All this time, and the one night she figured on heading out early he decided to go for a stroll.

Thoughts of sausage and pepperoni pizza fading, Helen got out of her car and began paralleling his movement up the street.

****

It only took half an hour or so before Helen realized she may have lucked out. After meandering back and forth through the inner city streets, Andrews finally seemed to focus in on a particular destination, ending up on a short stretch of 18th Street filled with dollar stores, liquor establishments, smoke shops and small markets.

Oddly, Helen began hoping that Andrews was actually going to pull off a robbery. It would give her a valid excuse to haul the little scumbucket downtown and move on to her next dead end assignment. Even Lieutenant Ronson, or whoever was directing her chastisement from up on the top floor, couldn't fault her for stopping a robbery in progress.

She paused as Andrews entered a mini mart, complete with barred windows across the front. As far as she knew, managing to remain undetected by her quarry. From her pocket, Helen pulled the remote unit she'd brought from her car. Until Andrews made a move, the remote was ready to call for backup.

She debated just walking into the store, but that would alert Andrews to her presence. It still being early evening, numerous people were walking back and forth on the street outside the store. Acting as if on the most normal of errands, Helen approached the market.

Stooping in front of an antiquated newspaper machine, she bent down as if to insert some money. Noticing the price, Helen shook her head and remembered why she hadn't read a newspaper in months.

Or one reason, at least.

The other being the way the local media had taken to trashing her after the entire Amos-Kettering mess.

Helen reached into her pocket, and as she did so glanced up through the barred windows of the store. With that one glance she dropped her pretense and, not taking time to key up her remote and call for backup, moved inside.

This store must have been some other type of business in the past because the layout didn't correspond to most mini marts.

The door actually opened to the back portion, leaving customers to walk forward the entire length of the store before reaching the counter. Because of this, Helen managed to get inside without either Andrews or the clerk he was holding up noticing her.

The store's layout, about twenty feet by thirty and

with three aisles leading to the counter up front, revealed itself in one glance. Helen saw only one customer, a little old lady with a cane in the back corner looking over the assortment of bread and buns.

Helen wondered if the old woman was actually so engrossed in choosing a loaf of bread that she didn't see what was transpiring up front, or if she did and was trying to appear uninvolved.

Up at the counter, which unlike most stores in this part of town didn't have a plastic glass between the clerk and customers, Tommy Andrews had a gun pointed toward the clerk, a young girl who, as she backed up against the shelf full of cigarettes, appeared to be a few months pregnant.

Helen's mind flashed through possible responses. At any moment, someone else could wander in, or Andrews could notice either her or the old lady. On the one hand, she could let him pull the robbery, hope he didn't begin firing and arrest him on his way out the door. Nothing in Andrews's history said anything about overt violence, but that could only mean that he'd never been caught at it before.

She could intervene right away, which would basically come down to her weapon against the robber's. But she didn't want to attract his attention until his gun was pointed somewhere other than at the girl behind the counter.

She decided to get at least halfway up the aisle and attempt to catch him flat-footed as he turned to leave.

"Come on, bitch. Open it up."

It was the first time Helen had heard the man's voice, and the high, almost girlish pitch shocked her. Andrews, twenty-one years old, stood almost six feet tall and had broad shoulders, although his gut had already begun to expand. And his reddish hair, she'd noticed before, was already thinning.

"Open that goddamned thing up!"

"I'm trying," the young clerk quavered. "Please."

From the back of the store, Helen could see the girl's hands shaking, shoulders trembling. If she didn't get it together, Andrews would lose his temper, and who knew what would happen then.

The scenario up front continued as Helen crept forward, service weapon out and up. She wanted to get close enough to control the scope of the scene, but not so close that she'd be right on him.

Then, with the clerk fumbling to open the recalcitrant register, Tommy Andrews jittering with tension and Helen still about twelve feet away, her cell phone buzzed.

Helen silently cursed. She'd been sitting in the car for hours on end without even thinking of her phone. When the possibility of action, of movement, had come along, she'd jumped in without thinking. But she'd made the one mistake of not turning the phone off.

A rookie mistake, and for a flashing moment she wondered if the city leaders had a point concerning her future in the department.

Although soft, in the near silent store the phone's buzz sounded like an alarm, and Andrews began turning, his entire body now teetering in Helen's direction.

His gun out and extended, she knew she'd have no choice but to shoot. No matter what, she couldn't let him line his weapon on her, even for an instant. She lowered to a half crouch, bouncing slightly on her thighs, and raised her own weapon in the standard departmental stance.

As Andrews completed the turn, pistol sweeping a scant distance ahead of his body, Helen began squeezing her trigger.

At the last possible instant, she held her fire as she noticed Andrews had his finger outside of the trigger guard.

Now they stood facing each other, the clerk behind Andrews almost forgotten, both of them understanding that before he could hope to fire, she would have him down.

"Police. Get down," Helen said, keeping her voice as calm and steady as possible.

Andrews stared at her for a second, glanced back at the cashier, now half huddled under her counter, then back to Helen. A slight clang behind her announced that the old lady had left the bread section and rushed out of the store.

Andrews only had one way out of the market, and that was past Helen.

"Okay, lady," he said, dropping the gun and raising his hands. "You've got it."

"Kick the gun away. Then get down."

He complied, sending his pistol skittering, then lowered to his knees.

Helen's cell buzzed again, reminding her of how the briefest splits of seconds can sometimes seem to take hours.

But she ignored it again as she reached behind her back to pull a pair of cuffs off her belt.

"Flatten," she said. For an instant, it looked like Andrews would refuse, then he lowered himself all the way, face down on the floor, and spread-eagled his limbs.

A moment later, she had him cuffed.

"I'll deal with you in a minute," she said as she pulled her phone out of her pocket.

"Hello," she said after checking, but not recognizing, the number.

"Helen," a young man answered. "My name's Richie Lattimer. I just recently transferred to—"

"I know who you are." Despite the merry-go-round of assignments she'd endured for the last several months, Helen had managed to keep track of what had been going on in her old squad.

"Well, Jack Hollis asked me to get ahold of you. He says he wants you to come in for a case."

Puzzled, Helen looked down at the Andrews kid, who'd struggled to a sitting position but hadn't moved from his spot on the floor.

"I'm not assigned to Central anymore, Lattimer."

"I know, but Hollis said he'd cleared it with the lieutenant to call you in."

She paused again. For the last ten months, the powers that be had done everything they could get away with to push her farther and farther to the periphery. Now, here came a call out of the blue inviting her back, in some way or other, to her old job. It almost sounded like a joke, a cruel twisting of the barb in even further, except that such an idea almost defied plausibility.

Then again, what did she possibly have to lose?

"I'm in the middle of an arrest," she finally said. "You think you could call a unit in for me?"

"Sure. Where you at?"

Helen gave him the address of the mini mart, and the pertinent info on the situation. Lattimer put her on hold for a minute, then came back on.

"They're on their way," he said.

"Okay, so where's this place Jack wants me to go to?"

"It's—it's Roy Michaels's house." The kid's voice began to stutter a bit. "Roy was hit a few hours ago."

Helen clenched her jaw, knowing now that this could in no way be a joke or prank. Michaels was older enough than her that the two of them didn't have all that much in common (hadn't had, Helen silently corrected herself), but he was one of the team.

Former team, she corrected herself once more. Since the Green affair, the top floor was making it clear that she had no permanent place in the department to call home.

And not much of a future either.

But obviously, she had more of one than her former colleague.

CHAPTER FIVE

After Jarvis headed out, Hollis had called into the station and spoken with Richie Lattimer in the squad room. He gave the younger detective a set of instructions, then decided he'd wasted enough time and turned to face one of the most distasteful duties he'd ever had to deal with in his career.

Over his years in Homicide, Hollis had interrogated dozens of grieving spouses, usually as quickly as possible while memories and emotions remained fresh. But he'd never had to question the wife or husband of a friend, let alone a work colleague.

Before heading inside the house, Hollis stood on the porch and gazed over the scene. The neighborhood folks were still there, of course, the crowd only having grown in the last half hour or so. The ambulance had taken off with Roy's body, leaving a space that TV news crews had quickly swooped in to occupy.

While the media skipped and hopped all over the place, the bystanders were being fairly civil. That was Herndon for you. A relatively small and peaceful suburb, the folks here just stayed back and observed. If they were in the larger city, the way things had gone around the country the last few years, the cops would be facing a battery of onlookers with their cell phones out, recording everything going down.

Hollis assumed most of the residents, at least those

on the same block, knew Roy had been a cop, and they had probably taken some solace from that, believing their neighborhood just a little bit safer. Now, with the cop shot down in his own driveway, what must they be thinking?

Hollis wished he still smoked because now would be the time for a cigarette. Concurrent with that thought, though, came the realization that he was still avoiding the chore ahead, and since it had to be done, he might as well get it over with.

Hollis took one last glance around the area, placing all the various personnel, where they were and what they were doing, before turning to head into the house.

He'd never visited Roy at home, but the interior, at least what was visible from the living room, looked about as he'd expected. Three easy chairs and black leather couch that could seat four, all placed in a semi-circle in front of a TV mounted on the wall.

A fireplace off to the side, but despite the fact winter was still hanging around the fireplace didn't look as if it had been used for a while. A couple of pictures positioned here and there, nothing outstanding but nothing too cheap looking either.

All in all, a nice, homey room, and Hollis assumed that the rest of the two-story house would look the same. On the force for several years, Michaels didn't rake in the big bucks, but had made a decent salary. Hollis and Michaels had never talked much, so he didn't know about Lori's job, or if she even had one, but did know that they didn't have any children, so they had more disposable income than most police couples.

Entering, Hollis saw Lori sitting in the middle of the leather couch, a woman on either side half hugging her.

One of the two, gray-haired and slightly stooped even sitting down, Hollis assumed to be the neighbor lady who'd been first on the scene, and made a mental note to talk to her alone at some point.

The other woman, appearing about the same age as Lori, he didn't know.

As he walked over to the three, Lori Michaels looked up. The two of them had only met a handful of times, usually when Lori had dropped by the station on an errand, but the acquaintance was enough that Hollis could tell she recognized him, and she no doubt knew what lay ahead.

"Jack, right?" she said, as if unsure of anything on this evening.

"Right. Lori, I know this is the worst time, but we need to talk for a few minutes."

"Of course," she said, settling back into the couch.

A couple of beats passed before Hollis realized she hadn't quite gotten his meaning.

"I'm sorry," he said, "but I mean we need to talk alone."

The older woman stood up and walked away, but the younger one remained sitting, her face flaring.

"Exactly why?" she demanded. "Mrs. Michaels is suffering a shock right now, and she needs her friends—"

"Linda." Lori reached out and patted the woman's arm. "It's okay. I'm sure Roy had his fair share of encounters like this."

As she said her husband's name, Lori stiffened a bit and her face took on a kind of a shine. As the other woman stood up, almost huffing, to walk away, Hollis took the opportunity to study the new widow.

Hollis couldn't pin her age exactly. She looked like she was homing in on late thirties, but he could have been off a handful of years either way. She had lines in her face, but they were slight and marked her as a woman who would no doubt age gracefully as the years went on.

Hollis also noted that she didn't display any of the puffiness or redness that usually indicated sudden grief, except for that shiny, almost greasy quality to her features, and he wondered if she was in a mild form of shock.

Or possibly not all that broken up by Roy's death?

"I'll be in the kitchen if you need me," the other woman said as she walked off.

Lori watched her go for a moment, then turned back to Hollis.

"She means well," she said.

"Friend?" Hollis asked.

Lori shrugged.

"Neighbor from the next block over. We've known each other for a while."

Hollis sat down, careful to keep some distance between them, and took out his notebook.

"I really am sorry, but we've got to do this as quickly as possible."

"I know. Roy told me lots of times how this has to work, so let's go ahead and do it."

Hollis proceeded to question her for nearly ten minutes, backtracking through all of her movements during the day, beginning with when Roy headed off to work and up till the moment she'd stepped outside to see why he hadn't entered the house.

"You didn't hear any shots?' Hollis asked.

"No." She paused, her brows puckering. "Did

anyone else hear any?"

Hollis shrugged, not wanting to provide information one way or the other to a possible witness, no matter who she was.

"I've got people out talking to your neighbors, the ones who were home at the time, but I haven't heard back yet."

Lori nodded.

"At any point today, had you noticed anything wrong with the mailbox?"

"Our mailbox?"

Her tone clearly displayed puzzlement.

"Yeah," Hollis said. "Your mailbox is half broken and canted on its side. We're wondering if it's been like that for a while."

Lori shook her head, giving him a quizzical look, and Hollis began to realize that she was far from a stupid woman.

"You're thinking someone may have done it deliberately?" she asked. "Like in order to catch Roy's attention?"

"It's one possibility, especially as that's where he—where they got him." He looked at his notes again. "You say you went grocery shopping around noon. Did the mailbox look okay then?"

Lori shrugged.

"I really don't notice things like that. I don't remember seeing anything wrong with it, but Roy often said that I was kind of oblivious to stuff."

Her face tightened again, and became shinier. But still no real redness or waterworks.

"You have somewhere you can stay for the night?" Hollis asked her.

She nodded and glanced toward the kitchen. "I'm pretty sure Linda will put me up."

The neighbor who'd kind of bristled at Hollis hadn't returned from the kitchen yet. From around the corner he could hear cabinet doors opening and closing. He gestured to a patrolman off in a corner.

"Go in the kitchen and ask the lady in there to sit down at the table, please," Hollis said. "Explain to her that this is a crime scene, and even though the murder happened outside we don't want anything more disturbed in here than it is."

The officer nodded and headed off in that direction.

Hollis continued questioning Lori for a few minutes longer. In particular about any concerns Roy had had, unusual occurrences around the house or neighborhood, telephone hang-ups or odd messages. As they continued, Lori's face grew tighter, and Hollis could now clearly see her fighting back tears.

Finally, he'd had as much as he could stand.

"I'll let you go now. We need the house secured for a couple of days, so when you leave just pack enough to get you by, and don't take any of Roy's stuff with you. Sorry, but I'll also have to have one of the officers escort you as you pack."

She nodded, her face growing tighter by the second.

"What about..." she gestured in the general direction of the front door.

"Yeah," Hollis said, "we'll take you out the back. The lab people are going to be at it for a while yet, and as dark as it's getting they won't be able to get much done until tomorrow. So we need to keep the whole front part of the yard secured."

Lori sighed and looked down at her thighs, idly

running her fingers up and down them.

"We were having problems, Jack. You might as well know that. But it wasn't too serious, and God knows this isn't how I'd want it to end."

Hollis kept silent. He wanted to offer some kind of comfort, but as an investigator he needed to let the witness say whatever she felt like saying.

However, it seemed as if that short declaration was all the widow had in mind as she immediately retreated back into herself.

"Leave a number with the officers who take you, and we'll call first thing," he finally said. "Let you know how things are going."

"What about the-the—when can I have—"

"We'll put a rush on it," he said, knowing she referred to Roy's corpse. "We plan to wrap this up as soon as possible."

"Just promise me, Jack."

"Huh?"

"Promise you'll get the bastard."

Rule number one when speaking to family members. No promises. Too many variables involved in the job, too many things the cops couldn't control, and too damned many cases that never got solved. No matter what, never make a promise that could come back to haunt you later.

But screw the rules. Roy had been one of theirs.

"We'll get him, Lori. Don't worry about that."

He got up from the couch and headed out to talk to the people working outside. A few words with them, including assigning uniform to escort Lori, and then he had to get back to the station.

Hollis had just made a damned fool promise, but he intended to keep it.

CHAPTER SIX

The elevator dinged, preparatory to opening up on the floor that held the detective squad room. Without thinking, Helen jabbed the button, keeping the doors closed.

She wasn't sure if she really wanted to do this, invitation or no.

It wasn't like she was returning from a vacation, or a long-running illness or anything. She'd only been gone a matter of months. But in that time, who knew what changes had taken place. As she'd told Richie Lattimer, she'd kept abreast of the comings and goings of the squad, but there was more to the atmosphere of a squad room than simple personnel shifts.

Who was partnered with whom? Who was mad at whom, and for what? How many, if any, of the people on the other side of those closed doors blamed her for the increased scrutiny that the department as a whole, and they in particular, had undergone in the last year?

Helen had done her best to keep in touch with certain people. Hollis and Janey Turner for sure, and of course the lieutenant. But the constant shifting of her own assignments and schedule had made it difficult to stay current with people, both in and out of the department.

Including the lawyer she'd begun dating. That particular little affair, one of the few she'd instigated since her divorce so many years back, had kind of petered out on its own.

One more debt she owed to the suits up on the top floor.

Still, it seemed kind of stupid and self-pitying to stand in an empty elevator, especially considering the circumstances, so she jabbed the button again and walked out into the squad room.

It was busier than Helen could remember seeing it in a long time. Nearly twenty detectives in a room that ordinarily only saw six to eight at any given time. Didn't matter what the duty roster said as to days off. Everyone was there, no doubt all receiving the same clipped summons that Helen had. Off in the corner, she saw Janey Turner sitting by herself, staring off to the side, and she remembered that Michaels had been her training partner when she'd first arrived on the squad a little over a year ago.

The movement and activity in the room didn't exactly come to a stop, but several of the assembled people turned as she entered the room. Beyond some general surprise, Helen couldn't read much of anything in their expressions.

She was saved from any embarrassing scene when everyone swiveled around as Lt. Jarvis and Jack Hollis came out of the boss's office, Jack carrying a large number of folders under his arm.

Jarvis didn't look to either side or make eye contact with any of his people. Instead, he headed straight for a large round table in a back corner of the room. Once there, he caught and held Helen's gaze for a second, giving her a slight nod of recognition.

She figured anything more formal would come later.

The table had been on site for so long that no one could remember who had originally brought it in. The detectives used it mainly for a conference area, when several were working on one case and wanted to spread the evidence folders out so they were in eyeshot of everyone.

Sometimes, when dealing only with run of the mill murders, the table went for week or months without any serious use. During other times, especially the summer months when violent crime was guaranteed to intensify, usually geometrically, it received almost daily use, as attested by all the dried coffee-cup rings and nips, chips and scars it contained. In fact, the table must have been around in the room since at least the eighties or early nineties, as evidenced by the numerous cigarette scars that swirled across its surface.

Then, of course, it made a nice surface for the occasional let-the-hair down pizza party or similar celebration.

Jarvis didn't hold anything in his hands. No binders, files or artifacts, and as he and Hollis headed toward the corner everyone followed him. Walking around the end that abutted the corner, the lieutenant turned and surveyed his people.

"Okay," he said, "here's what we've got. At approximately five-thirty this afternoon, Roy arrived home and was greeted by an assailant carrying what seems to be a nine, though we won't know for sure until ballistics comes back."

"Were they waiting to ambush him, or was it some kind of random thing?" asked a middle-aged cop.

"Far as we can tell, it was a deliberate ambush. Which, rough as that is for us emotionally, actually gives us a clear direction to begin investigating. I've designated Jack here as the primary, so as of now he gets to call the shots. Before I turn it over to him, any general questions?"

Janey raised her hand.

"Yes?"

"I'm assuming we're on some sort of press blackout? If anyone calls or contacts us, what do we say?"

Jarvis sighed and rubbed his face.

"I'm almost certain that right now someone down at the city building is being designated as the press junction for this one. Within an hour we'll probably get some sort of specifics as to whom to refer inquiries to. Until then, hell, just don't answer your phones."

A light, though strained, chuckle drifted across the room, and Jarvis stepped aside and motioned to the lead detective.

Hollis walked up to the table and began spreading out his mass of file folders across its surface.

"For now," he said, "we're going to operate on the most basic assumption. That one of Roy's former collars, or someone connected to one, is responsible for this. A revenge thing. He was killed at home, with no attempt to enter the house, as in a burglary, and initial indications are that a plant was set to catch his attention and make him pause before entering the house."

"The mailbox," Janey said.

"Exactly. Because of that, we're going to approach this in the most systematic way possible."

"Wait a minute," the detective from a moment ago spoke up. "He was coming up on his twenty. How many possible collars are we talking about here?"

As Helen watched, Hollis set his shoulders a little more squarely and his eyes clamped down a bit.

"Not as many as you would think," he said. "We're going to assume that any sort of misdemeanor beefs are off the table, simply because what would be the point?"

"Maybe it wasn't an actual case," Lattimer pointed out. " Just something or someone he encountered out on the street. With a true nutso, any sort of clampdown of authority could set them off."

"You've got a point, Richie," Hollis said, "but if we start with that our work grows exponentially. If it comes to that, we'll go through other possibilities, but it's safe to assume that what we need to focus on is felonies only. At least for now."

"And only violent ones," Helen spoke up from where she stood on the other side of the room, immediately regretting that she'd done so.

Now, everyone in the squad had no choice but to turn her way. While most of the faces seemed friendly, she figured almost all of them were wondering just why she'd shown up at this time.

"I guess this is as good a time as any," Jarvis said. "Earlier this evening, I spoke with the top floor. I pointed out that we needed every experienced person we could spare on this, especially considering the anti-police sentiment that's been sprayed across the media the last several months. So they agreed to reassign Helen back here, temporarily, while we sort this mess out."

A handful of her colleagues nodded their heads in agreement. Despite the grimness of the situation, she couldn't help but feel a bit of a glow. It was a long way from actually being accepted again, but at least it was a start.

Even if under the worst of circumstances.

"And she's right," Hollis said. "If it's safe to figure we need to look only at felonious collars, we can narrow it down even more to the violent ones. Someone who'd been sent up for embezzlement, say, wouldn't be likely to take a gun and go after someone."

"It could have been hired out," Janey said.

"Maybe. But before he got here to Homicide, Roy handled all sorts of things, including robberies and drug busts. So we're going to look at those."

"All of them?"

This from Lou Whitmore, a thirtyish black man who happened to have the highest conviction record on the squad. Standing slightly over six feet tall, Whitmore sported a forty-four inch chest and twenty-nine inch waist.

"We're going to look first at most recent arrests. Barring some sort of legal shenanigans, most of his homicide arrests will still be in prison, but there may be some other factor."

"Like a pissed off relative or lover," Whitmore said.

"Exactly. But if we hit nothing there, then we'll just work the parameters back, a year or two at a time, until we hit something."

"Kind of the reverse of first hired, last fired, right?" Ben Santos, a Cuban-American originally from Chicago, asked. Santos usually wore long sleeves and hardly ever rolled them up. Even so, someone standing close would notice the tattoo marks that crept above his collar.

"Exactly."

"Is that it?" Helen asked..

Everyone turned to her, including Jarvis, who had stepped far to the side to let Hollis do his thing.

Considering that she'd just been accepted back in, Helen hadn't meant for her question to sound challenging, but seeing Jack's frown she saw that he'd taken it that way.

"Meaning what?" Hollis asked.

"Are we going to look at his past collars, known associates of them and such, and nothing else? Aren't we kind of overlooking something here?"

A number of the detectives began staring either at the floor or off to the side. Hollis himself frowned, but Helen knew he was too damned good of a cop, and too experienced, not to understand her implication.

"Meaning what?"

"Meaning," Helen said, working to keep her tone measured, " that we shouldn't throw normal procedure out the door just because the victim's one of ours. If Roy wasn't a cop, where would we start looking?"

Now they all looked at her, and she hoped she wasn't about to screw up any modicum of goodwill that she still retained. By the same token, she knew she was right.

More than that, they all knew it as well.

They had to know.

"You mean Lori?" Hollis finally said.

"Ten times out of ten, who do we look at for a murder like this one? And eight times out of ten, who does it turn out to be?"

The spouse or significant other. She hadn't really had to cite the stats. Everyone in the room knew them as well as she did.

But once she came right out and said it, there was nowhere to hide.

"You honestly think Lori had something to do with

this?" Lou Whitmore asked.

"I'm not saying one way or the other. What I am saying is that in any other situation we'd be looking at her first."

"But this isn't any other situation," Janey pointed out. "The idea that Roy's wife could have—"

"Needs to be looked at!" Helen snapped. "Just because we don't want to get uncomfortable doesn't mean we throw out normal procedure."

"Yeah, but look what normal procedure got you last year," someone muttered.

Helen's face burned.

"Hold on a sec," Hollis jumped in. "Let's not start cutting each other down. Fact is, Helen's got a point. If this was any other case, we'd be looking at the spouse right away. At the very least concurrent with any other avenues."

"But we all know Lori, or at least have met her," Janey said.

"Which is all the more reason not to discount her," Hollis said.

He took a step back so he could encompass everyone in the squad room in one glance. He pointed to Janey Turner, Lou Whitmore, and Hal Smith, an ordinary-looking guy of about thirty-five. "I need you three to work with me on going through Roy's collars. Helen, start backtracking Lori. As soon as you get her cleared, you can jump in with us on these cases."

"What about the tech folks?" Lou asked. "How far along are they?"

Hollis turned to the lieutenant for that one.

"They checked in about a quarter hour back. They're securing for the night, but plan to be back on scene crack of dawn. The chief ordered a rush on the results. So if all goes right within a day, two at the most, we'll have everything the techs can give us."

"And the rest of us?" Lattimer asked.

"We still have an entire city to serve," Jarvis pointed out. "Six should be enough for now. But as you all get freed up on other cases, feel free to coordinate with Jack here. So let's get to it."

"One more thing," Helen spoke up. The group movement that had begun ground to a halt.

"What?" Hollis asked.

Helen took a deep breath, knowing that if any more cords would be cut, she was about to start the snipping.

"Where is Lori tonight? Has she been questioned?"

"The boss and I spoke to her earlier. We were leaving more formal questioning until tomorrow."

"It should be tonight," Helen insisted.

Hollis and Jarvis glanced at each other before Hollis turned back to her.

"Okay," Hollis said, "handle it tonight."

"Where is she? Surely not at their house?"

"She's staying with a neighbor."

"And after?"

"What's your point, Helen?"

Now even Jarvis was beginning to glare at her.

"She needs to be watched. I'll go out and talk to her now, but someone needs to be on her for the rest of the night. Even if it's a uniformed unit."

Helen had never really understood the meaning of the term "pin-drop silence" until that moment. No one moved, and she could have guessed that most of those in the room were holding their breath, waiting for some sort of response.

"She's right, Jack," Jarvis said. "If we're going to follow procedure, let's follow procedure. Ideally, we should have brought her in, and that's on me for not ordering it. But she does need to be watched."

"Okay," Hollis said, his frown from a moment before deeper, almost stone like. "I'll speak with the sarge downstairs and set it up."

With that comment, something seemed to have snapped in the room. Everyone moved again, and Helen's muscles began relaxing.

She hadn't messed up her second chance.

Yet.

CHAPTER SEVEN

Common decency would say wait till the next day to talk to the widow.

Procedure said to get to her as quickly as possible.

Obviously, Hollis and Jarvis had covered the initial contact, but had been loath to carry it all the way. They'd both spoken with Lori, the lieutenant to extend the natural condolences and Hollis with the preliminary questions.

But that wasn't enough. There needed to be a full-on interrogation. Ideally conducted in a room here at the station, but if not it should, nevertheless, be an official questioning.

And the best time was right now, tonight. Before information and memories faded.

Or, more cynically, before stories began to be concocted.

"It was kind of creepy," Hollis revealed before Helen headed out of the squad room. "Kind of a stone cold reaction. She just sat there, as far as I could tell she hadn't even been crying, and stared off to the side. She looked a little tense, but none of the gnashing and wailing you'd expect."

"Maybe she's the type who just takes it hard and silent," Helen said.

"Maybe. Or maybe she was just doing her best to hold it together until she had some privacy. If so, when it hits the delayed reaction's gonna be tough."

"Did you get anything out of her at all?" Helen asked.

"Not really."

Hollis handed over his notebook, turned to the pages of the interview, and Helen began skimming through the notes.

"Nothing about Roy's mood the last few days?"

"Nope. Nothing beyond the usual stress and aggravation. Actually, all his open cases were kind of cold and nothing too exciting, so I gather he hadn't been talking about work much."

"Jack," Helen said, "surely you've heard some of the talk? Hell, I've been out of Central for months and I've heard whispers about it."

Hollis hesitated, indecision crossing his face.

"Look," he began.

"When's the last time you saw Roy pick up a check? And don't tell me you haven't noticed his clothing. I hear it's been getting kind of threadbare and soiled for months."

Hollis ducked his head, as if not wanting to admit the truth of what she was saying.

"There could be all kinds of reasons," he said.

****

It was coming on to ten o'clock, with the cloudy March night about as dark as it could possibly get, when she pulled onto the Michaels's block, looking for the home of Linda and John Murland, the neighbors who had taken in the widow Michaels.

As she passed by Roy and Lori's house, Helen slowed down to a crawl.

There were only two vehicles at the moment, one a

marked police car and the other a forensics van. Jarvis had mentioned the tech people were done for the day, but maybe they were just maintaining the scene.

She accelerated past, and a moment later pulled up in the Murland's driveway.

Getting out of her car, Helen admitted to herself that she didn't really believe Lori had anything to do with Roy's death. But the last thing they needed to do, especially after the black eye the entire department got last year, was skimp on procedure.

And just maybe, she mused stepping onto the porch and ringing the bell, she was being so conscientious now because she herself, in no small part, had been the reason for that black eye.

Her finger barely away from the bell when the door opened, a woman who matched Hollis's description of Linda Murland looking out at her.

"Yes?"

"I'm sorry to bother you," Helen said as she flipped open her badge case. "I'm Detective Lipscomb. I was wondering if I could see Lori for a few minutes."

"She's not feeling very well right now, as I'm sure you can understand."

"I do," Helen said, "but it really is important that I talk with her. It will only be a few moments."

"The one detective already questioned her earlier."

"I know, but there's still some follow up. The situation's ongoing."

"Have you caught him yet?" Murland asked.

"Who?"

"The punk who…" Murland hesitated, then shook her head. "I'm sorry," she continued, moving back and opening the door wider. "It's just been kind of stressful around here. I'm sure you can understand."

Helen nodded and stepped into the house, hearing the low buzz of muted conversation and counting, at a quick glance, nearly a dozen people standing or sitting around the living room that opened off the front hall. Not seeing Lori in that mix, she turned back to Mrs. Murland.

The conversation was subdued enough, and the people looked just confused enough, that Helen figured they were various friends, neighbors and acquaintances, wanting to help but not knowing what to do other than provide a semblance of community.

"Where's Lori?"

"Let me get her for you. She's lying down in my room."

She began to move off, but Helen moved in step with her.

"That's okay, Mrs. Murland. If you can just point me the right way, I'll find her."

Murland frowned. She opened her mouth, but instead of saying anything merely indicated the hallway off to the right.

"Second door on the left. Be sure and knock first. I think she was sleeping earlier."

Helen nodded her thanks and moved in the direction indicated. But within three steps she realized the woman was following her. She turned and gave her a blank look in return.

"She's very upset," the woman said. "I'm sure you understand."

Helen shrugged and continued toward the room.

She knocked on the door, then had to knock again before hearing a tremulous "Come in."

Helen entered, Linda Murland still shadowing her,

and saw Roy's widow.

Helen and Roy hadn't really been friends. Co-workers for many years, true. But the extent of their socializing had usually taken the form of several members of the squad getting together for drinks at the end of one of the tougher days. Helen guessed that, in the five years she'd been a detective, she and Roy had possibly had a total of twenty or so personal conversations, and couldn't remember them ever working a case together.

So she barely knew Lori and figured that she'd met her maybe five or six times, usually when she came by the station house to drop something off. Had the two of them encountered each other in the store, or at a movie theater or coffee shop, it probably would have taken Helen a second or two to recognize her.

With such little familiarity, Helen would have no way of knowing how the new widow would react to stress or shock.

And Helen had to agree with Hollis that Lori didn't look all that shook up. Sitting in an old-fashioned rocker, one no doubt intended more for decoration than utility, she gently rocked back and forth. Helen stopped in the doorway.

They'd never had kids. Helen knew at least that much about the couple, which helped explain a figure that, even sitting down, still looked fairly girlish. Although her light blonde hair looked rich and thick enough, Helen had a hunch that in better light a streak or two of gray would show up.

As she stepped across the threshold, Lori Michaels looked up and focused on her.

"Yes?"

"Mrs. Michaels, I'm sorry to bother you. But I need to ask a few questions."

Lori focused on her for a moment, then nodded slightly.

"You're a policewoman, right? You worked with Roy?"

"Yes. Detective Lipscomb. We were in the same squad, but we didn't work together that much."

Helen had almost given her first name, but caught herself in time. In a textbook interrogation, the police only gave their last names, giving them a perceived position of authority over the other person. This emphasis on last names for the cop became crucial whenever you used the suspect's first name, putting them down a peg or two below their interrogator.

And while Lori either possibly knew right off or would remember her first name in time, Helen had made a big deal back at the squad room about doing this investigation the right way, so she needed to stick to procedure as much as possible.

"It's okay, Linda. I'll be all right here."

Helen could hear Mrs. Murland, behind her, sniff a bit before withdrawing down the hallway. After she'd left, Helen came all the way into the bedroom and took a seat on the queen-sized bed.

"How are you doing?"

Lori shrugged and gave a half smile. "I can guess why you're here," she said.

"Oh?"

"Don't worry about it, detective. I was married to a cop long enough, heard all the war stories. I was pretty sure those few questions Mr. Hollis had wouldn't be enough."

"I wouldn't put it that way."

"Do me one favor, Miss Lipscomb. Please don't patronize me. I'm the surviving spouse, and you guys have to consider me. It's somewhere in the official handbook, isn't it?"

Helen smiled and relaxed a bit.

"Something like that," she said. "So you don't mind if we go through this now?"

"Of course I mind. But I can't see how it will be any better tomorrow, when most of those people out there are gone. Or the day after, when I've come back from making arrangements at the mortuary and have to go back to the house. Thank God we never had kids. Makes all this a little easier to handle."

"Okay, then." Helen pulled out a pen and a small, old-fashioned spiral notebook from her jacket. "Honest, I'll make this as painless as possible."

"Don't worry about it. I think I've had enough pain so far today that I'm immune to any more."

As she spoke, Lori raised her legs up onto the seat of the rocker and cinched her arms around her knees.

Helen couldn't help but wonder if the "little girl in distress" pose was accidental or deliberate.

"Roy's shift ended at a quarter to four today, but he didn't get to leave until nearly four thirty. Did he call you, or text, to let you know he'd be running late?"

"No," Lori said. "Usually he wouldn't call unless he was going to be over an hour late. Even then, sometimes, he didn't get the chance and I just had to figure it out. But I'm sure you understand how that goes."

Helen mumbled a quick uh huh, then jotted something on her pad.

"So when was the last time you two actually spoke?"

The rocker began moving again, slightly, back and forth.

"I'm sorry, but exactly how does that matter?"

"Well…" Helen began.

"I mean, someone came running up to our house and shot Roy. What does when I talked to him have to do with anything?"

The chair moved a bit quicker.

"It probably doesn't," Helen said, "but we have to establish a timeline for his entire day. Nail everything down, as it were. That way, when we get to court, we have every possible ramification accounted for."

She paused, wondering if she'd stepped too far over the line into gobbledygook, but Lori leaned back in her rocker, and the chair slowed down its oscillation.

"I was still in bed when he left this morning. I wasn't feeling well last night, something like a touch of flu."

"Did he say anything at all when he left?"

"Only that he wanted to bring Kevin over for lunch Saturday."

"Kevin?"

"His brother. Younger brother. He got pretty much torn up several years ago in Iraq and has to live in a home now. Whenever he's got a free weekend, Roy swings by and picks up little bro and carts him back here."

Helen looked up at the change in timbre of Lori's voice. A bit of tension there. A slight amount of resentment, maybe? No doubt nothing to do with the case, but she filed it away in her mind anyway.

She continued the questioning for another fifteen minutes or so, covering as many aspects of their lives as she could come up with. Maybe it was fatigue, or the stress of the entire experience, but despite the fact that

Helen asked questions about their neighbors, how long they'd lived in the neighborhood, Roy's friends outside of work and a myriad other subjects, Lori didn't ask any more questions as to relevance.

"I know this is delicate," Helen said at one point, "but how were you guys doing financially?"

The woman in the rocker stiffened.

"What do you mean?" she asked.

"I mean, were you getting on okay? Any unexpected expenses or anything like that?"

Lori planted her feet, causing the rocking chair to abruptly halt.

"You worked with Roy, right?"

"Well, not for a—"

"So you probably noticed him looking a little–ragged–lately. We had some extra expenses come up, sure. But nothing that couldn't be set right."

"Did you ever argue about money?"

The widow's expression became more set, sterner than even a minute before.

"I really hope you're not implying what I think you are. Goddammit, my husband was just slaughtered, and you're carrying on about money? So things were tight for a while. It happens. Have you ever been married, detective?"

The book said not to get personal with an interviewee.

"Yes," Helen replied. "But it didn't last long before we realized it wasn't going to work."

"Okay, then. So please do me a favor and don't sit in judgment over how we handled our lives. You know what a policeman's salary comes to. Surely you can imagine that there could be hard times now and then?"

Helen backed off and went on to more innocuous questions. It took a few minutes, but Lori Michaels went back to rocking in that slight, abstracted motion.

Eventually, they got around to earlier that night.

"Why did you step outside?" Helen asked.

"I'd heard his car pull up, but he didn't come in. After a while I stepped outside to see what was keeping him."

Helen thought about that one for a minute.

"Did you hear any shots?"

Lori paused, her forehead crinkling the slightest bit.

"Not that I can remember, and I was right there in the living room, so I'm sure I would have heard something."

Helen nodded. She'd check with any neighbors she could, but if Lori was telling the truth the killer had probably used a silencer. Which could be significant.

She continued the questioning for a while longer, but when she saw the widow's eyes struggling to stay open, she relented.

"Thanks for your help. I'll let you go now. And again, we're all sorry about this."

"Will you get him?" The words were barely a whisper, so low that Helen didn't quite catch them.

She leaned in the other woman's direction.

"Will you get the person who did this?" Lori repeated, her voice a bit stronger this time.

Like Hollis, Helen had been a cop for a number of years, and a detective for the majority of those years. Like him, she absolutely knew how, according to the book, she should answer that question.

But just as Hollis had, she decided to hell with the book.

"Yes," she said, offering a promise she couldn't possibly know she could keep, "we'll get him."

CHAPTER EIGHT

They didn't wait for standard business hours to begin the autopsy. A chain of phone calls went out late that night, resulting in the chief coroner sending in a veteran man, with twenty years and dozens of homicide autopsies under his belt, at four in the morning to begin the post-mortem examination of Roy Michaels.

Hollis got word ahead of time, but he was in the process of assembling the case file. As a result, and knowing that nothing much of a revelatory nature would happen in the first half hour or so, he stayed at his desk till he had his chore completed, then headed out to sit in on the procedure.

The coroner's office was located in a building about four blocks from Central, and considering the early hour traffic, he got there in about three minutes. Actually, in the deserted night he would have preferred walking, but this particular March was tenaciously holding on to its lion status.

After showing his ID for admittance and being directed towards Examination Room Four, he stopped in the anteroom and donned one of the all-encompassing, pale blue coverall suits, complete with booties and skull cap. The spate of television forensics shows over the years had made potential jurors that much more savvy (or so they thought) as to how criminology worked. As a result, defense attorneys had become cagier when it came to finding angles to refute forensic evidence. The end result being that the old days of cops wandering into the middle of autopsies clad in their street clothes and munching on pastrami from the local deli were long gone.

When Hollis entered, he breathed a short sigh of relief. Even with the skullcap and face mask, he recognized Dr. Lynn Marshall. He'd worked with this particular "twenty-year man" before and considered the five-foot nothing redhead as one of the most meticulous medical examiners he'd ever met.

"Good morning, Jack," Dr. Marshall greeted him. "How long have you been up by now?"

"Longer than I can remember," he replied. "I thought I was done when court let out yesterday, and today's supposed to be my day off."

"Best laid plans, huh?"

Hollis nodded and stepped closer to the table.

Hollis knew that detectives, even the primary on a case, weren't really needed at a PM. The doctors knew their business, and anything of any note would be included in their reports. In his much younger days, he'd attended the PM's on his first few cases before realizing that he was both kind of in the way and wasting time that could be better spent elsewhere. So after those first few instances, he'd stayed away, trusting in the professionalism of the coroner's office to give him everything he'd need.

This time was different, though. This one mattered to the entire department, and no one was going to relax until they'd found Michaels' killer. On top of that, the lieutenant had given him enough people to work with that he figured he could spare the couple of hours it would take to see the exam through.

Dr. Marshall looked up, a circular bone saw in her hand and a question in her eyes.

"You sure you want to be here for this? You'll know anything as soon as I do."

"I know, Lynn. But I still think I should observe."

Dr. Marshall shrugged, flipped a switch on the side of the saw, and began cutting Roy Michaels' skull in half.

****

"We're getting the slides processed now," the doctor said about an hour later. "but the basics are simple. Three shots to the back of the head. And you saw the damage caused when they came out the front."

"Type of weapon?"

"You know that's not my field, Jack. But offhand, I'd say your lieutenant's guess was right. I'd almost stake my retirement on a nine mm pistol."

"Which was the kill shot?"

"Hell, take your pick. Each entry wound was practically on top of the other. And whoever it was, was really close to him."

They were relaxing, if that was the term, in her office three floors up from the lab.

"The stippling?" Hollis asked, referring to the tattoo-like skin discoloration around the wounds.

The ME nodded as she poured herself a cup of coffee. She held out the pot to Hollis, who nodded quickly. It was now closing on six in the morning, making it a solid twenty-four hours that he'd been up.

"Primarily," Dr. Marshall said as she poured a second cup and handed it to him. "How could he have gotten that close to Roy without some awareness?"

"There's a stand of trees right along the front edge of his lawn. Only a few feet away from the mailbox. If I had to guess, I'd say the killer huddled behind those and waited."

The ME shuddered and looked down at her cup.

"Awful chancy, if you ask me. How easy would it have been for someone to look out a window and see them waiting?"

Hollis drummed the fingers of his right hand on his thigh.

"And it must have been for some time, too. Roy didn't get home at his usual time last night, which meant the killer would have had to either known he would be late or lain in wait for him."

"Any chance for tracks?"

"We'll know for sure as soon as sun's up, but with the kind of slush that the ground's been the last few days, I doubt it."

A few minutes of silence went by as the two of them contemplated whatever wisdom could be found in their coffee cups.

"How's Roy's wife doing?" Marshall finally asked.

Hollis shrugged. "About as well as could be expected, I guess. Helen went out to question her some more last night."

"Question her? That sounds awful."

Hollis grimaced. "Has to be done, doc. Need to follow the book."

"Maybe so, but…" Marshall let the sentence dribble as she took another drink.

More than the beverage was beginning to warm Hollis. The doctor's work was done, she could be going on to other things, but instead she was sitting there talking things over, whether she knew it or not helping him to process the events of the last several hours.

"Word went around quickly that Helen had been brought back in for this. How's she doing?"

"Too soon to tell," Hollis said. "We've barely had a chance to talk."

"You know, most people in the ME's office think she got a raw deal last year."

Hollis nodded as he stood and finished off his cup.

"Me too, but you know how it goes. Ours is not and all that."

Marshall nodded as she finished off her own drink.

"I'll get you the prelim within the hour," she said, suddenly all business.

"Thanks, doc."

Hollis was at the door, but turned back.

"Thanks for everything," he said.

"Don't mention it, Jack. Just go out and get the bastard."

Giving her a half-hearted salute, he turned and left the office.

CHAPTER NINE

Helen returned to the neighborhood the morning after the murder. Not to see Lori again, but to conduct a canvass, as she'd done dozens of times in her career. The kind of slog work that, even in the high-tech age, had to be done on foot, and one for which there was no substitute. Talking was only part of it. You had to see people's faces, in particular their eyes, to know whether you were getting the truth or not.

After a quick breakfast at a Burger King drive-thru, she made her way to the suburb where, until yesterday afternoon, Roy Michaels had lived.

Today, she would have to hit as many houses as she could, then turn around and come back in the evening to try again.

She pulled her car in under a bare-branched elm and turned off the engine. This kind of thing was probably easier back in the old days, when the majority of women stayed at home. Up until the mid seventies or so, she probably could have been sitting here looking at an entire block filled with housewives no doubt full of information.

All the while, she figured the entire exercise wouldn't amount to much of anything. Despite her protestations in the squad room the night before, more likely than not they'd find the killer among Roy's previous collars, or at least known associates, and get the job done that way.

Still, Helen had argued for going by the book, so she had no one to blame but herself.

Climbing out of the car, she adjusted her lightweight jacket (worn this morning more for wishful thinking than practicality) and headed up the sidewalk to her first stop.

She waved at the crime scene people, already on site and no doubt finishing from the night before, but didn't bother them in their work. Considering the ground around here was slushy and snowy in the morning and frozen at night, she had no idea what they'd be able to accomplish, but if they did manage to come across anything it would be all the better. She made a mental note to check with Hollis and make sure that a team searched and examined the interior of the house.

Standard procedure again. If the spouse was a suspect, as she had to be until definitely crossed off, then they had to search the house. If nothing else, for the murder weapon itself.

Or some evidence of a motive.

****

She began, quite naturally, with the Williams home.

Sean and Lucy Williams were the neighbor couple that lived next door and had been the first to respond to Lori's distress. They'd given a brief statement, though nothing officially recorded, to the first officers on the scene. Then Hollis had done a perfunctory interview with them before heading back to the station for the all-squad meeting.

Before they'd split the night before, he'd copied his notes for Helen.

But even though the elderly couple had already been talked to twice, there had to be a more thorough interview.

Once again, standard procedure.

****

"We were just getting ready to go out to eat," Sean Williams said. He, his wife and Helen were in their living room, the elderly couple sitting together on their couch and Helen facing them in an old-fashioned La-Z-Boy recliner. The green vinyl chair must have been at least thirty years old, but it didn't show a crack anywhere.

"Every Wednesday night we meet up with some friends for dinner," Mr. Williams said. "It was our turn to host."

"And you were getting ready when it happened?" Helen asked.

"Sean was watching the news," Mrs. Williams said, "and I was working in the kitchen."

"Did you hear a shot of any kind?"

Both of them shook their heads.

"First we knew," Sean said, "was when Lori started screaming. At first, I thought it was something Lucy had on the TV in the kitchen. We've got a little set in there, but when I heard her again, I could tell it was coming from outside."

"How long would you say from the time she screamed the second time till you made it out?"

Mr. Williams stopped and thought for a few seconds.

"Less than a minute," he said. "At least till I got to the porch. To get across to their yard took a minute or so all told."

"Did you see Detective Michaels right away?"

"No. First I saw Lori standing there on her porch, shrieking her head off. I'd say I was about halfway across the yard when I noticed Roy's body."

"And where were you, Mrs. Williams?"

"Right behind Sean. He headed off to check Roy out, and I made my way to Lori on the porch."

"So we're talking less than a couple of minutes all told."

The two oldsters looked at each other for a second before turning and simultaneously nodding.

Helen almost grinned. The two of them, sitting side by side on their couch and clasping hands together, looked so much like the perfect picture of an old married couple that they seemed a bit unreal. If things had gone better with her ex-husband, maybe in another thirty years or so she and Thomas would have been this couple.

She tilted her head, left and right, an almost imperceptible motion, to get her thoughts back on track.

"Did either of you hear a shot?" she asked.

This time without looking at each other, they both shook their heads.

"And my hearing's real good," Mr. Williams said, drawing himself up a bit straighter. "Eyes aren't what they used to be, and some of my joints are gone to hell and back, but no problem with my hearing."

"Would you know the sound of a shot if you heard it?" Helen asked, knowing that most civilians had, at best, imprecise notions of what gunfire sounded like.

The old man beamed and clutched his wife's hand even tighter.

"I served in the Marines twenty years, young lady. And Lucy and I both grew up on farms. We for damned sure know what guns sound like, and I'm telling you there wasn't any."

Helen nodded. It was looking even more as if the

assailant had used a silencer.

But for obvious reasons that didn't make a lot of sense.

"Did you see anybody?" she asked.

The old man frowned.

"That young cop last night asked me the same thing. Didn't they tell you?"

Helen smiled.

"It's been a rather hectic several hours, and we're still collating everything, so I'm just going over it all again."

His frown deepened.

"That's what gets me," he said. "It wasn't all that long before I got out there, and I didn't see anybody either running or driving away."

"Mrs. Williams?"

The old lady shook her head and leaned in closer to her husband.

"I only had eyes for poor Lori. Didn't even see Roy at first. In fact, as we rushed over there I wondered where Sean was going."

"Nobody running away? No cars speeding down the street? Nothing?"

Both the oldsters shook their heads, as if wishing they could do more.

****

A few minutes later, as she was leaving the Williams' house, Helen solved at least part of the mystery. She kind of kicked herself for not thinking of it sooner, but for whatever reason that she missed it in the beginning she got it now.

Stepping out on the Williams' porch and intending to move on to the next house, and from there canvass the entire neighborhood, she stopped first and glanced over to Lori and Roy's house.

As a childless couple without any pets, their yards, both front and back, contained no fences.

She stepped right off the Williams' porch and across to the Michaels' home, then from there around the east side of the house and into their backyard, thankful she'd decided to wear tennis shoes instead of flats.

No gates, no fence, not even a decorated walk.

Behind the Michaels' and Williams' homes were a few other houses with, as far as Helen could tell, no fences either. She saw a few trees, which probably served as boundaries between the properties, and that was it.

So okay, a change of plans. Rather than proceeding on down the block as she'd intended, she headed down the driveway to talk to the tech people. Once she got them combing through that back area, she'd continue with her interviews and eventually come around the other side of the block.

She was now convinced that if anyone saw anything, either someone fleeing on foot or a car driving away, it would be on the next street over, but she still had to cover the original interviews first.

CHAPTER TEN

Helen began to see progress with the third house.

The first two had no one home, and she made notations in her book to come back around six or so and try again. Interrupting people at dinner time never put them in the best of moods, but it was usually the best time to catch someone at home.

Nice reasoning, she considered. *If they ever boot me from the force I can get a job as a telemarketer.*

But at the third house, she not only found someone at home, but someone who, for obvious reasons, was more than willing to spend a little time talking to a grownup.

"Sure, I was watching it all yesterday, but I barely saw Lori at all. I thought about going over to offer help, but figured if there was anything specific I could do they'd come over and let me know."

The brown-haired woman in her early thirties, who had introduced herself as Karen Jenkins, bounced a baby on her right hip. When she had first opened the door, Helen had shown her badge and introduced herself, and the young mother had invited her inside right away.

Now, the two of them sat in the living room, Helen in an easy chair and the woman and baby on the couch, and talked.

"Was anyone else home at the time?" Helen asked.

"Just me and Art. Dave, my husband, is out of town

this week."

As she spoke, Karen Jenkins hefted the baby up and down in the air a couple of times.

"How well did you know the Michaels's?"

"Like neighbors, but not really close friends. Dave and I just moved here a little over a year ago."

"What's your husband do?"

"He's a welder. Independent, but a couple of firms use him almost constantly."

"Working on anything in particular now?" Helen asked.

"That new hospital going up in Springfield. As far away as it is, he stays there during the week and just comes home for weekends."

"A baby, and him only around two days a week. Sounds like a handful."

Karen smiled. "Three days. He's good at what he does. Good enough that he only has to work through Thursdays. When he comes home he sleeps for about twelve hours straight, then takes care of Art the rest of the time so I can begin to feel like a human again."

They continued talking for a while, a bit more of the small talk that, while friendly, was actually intentional. Get them at ease, the book said. To where they feel like they're talking with an old friend who just wants to catch up.

Then get around to what you're actually after.

"Did you ever notice any problems with the Michaels's?" Helen asked.

Karen drew back on the couch a little and ruffled what little hair her son had. "Problems?"

"You know. Fights. Unusual movements at night. Time apart. Anything like that?"

Karen stared down at her baby for a minute. "Why are you asking? You think Lori had something to do with this?"

"Not at all. I just need to…"

"I thought it was just some random nut who came by. That's what everyone's saying. Lori was inside when it happened. How could she have done it?"

Off hand, Helen could think of half a dozen ways.

"Mrs. Jenkins, in an investigation like this, we need to develop a complete picture of everything leading up to and right after the incident." Inwardly, Helen grimaced at the idea that it was almost the same explanation she'd given Lori Michaels the night before.

"Kind of dotting the I's and crossing the T's?"

"Exactly."

The young mother began bouncing the baby on her knee, again staring down at the kid instead of looking at Helen, who began to get a tight feeling about where all of this was headed.

After several seconds, Karen lifted her gaze.

"I don't want to get anyone in trouble," she said.

Helen, figuring silence would work best here, merely nodded.

"And like I said, I don't know Lori, or any of the other neighbors around here, all that well."

Helen sat quietly and waited. Whatever was on the woman's mind, she would get to it in her own time.

"But she seems like a nice lady," Karen continued.

Helen, that tight feeling becoming even more constrictive, gave another encouraging nod.

Eyes down once again, Karen lifted little Art up and hugged him tight. For a moment, everything seemed suspended. Three people in this room and hardly any motion or sound, save for a faint cooing from Art.

"But I think she may have been fooling around," Karen said, moisture squeezing from her eyes.

CHAPTER ELEVEN

Sometimes, Janey Turner still felt like a rookie. She'd joined the force the week she turned twenty-one and had been on the detective squad for less than two years. Although in that time she'd made a couple of decent arrests and was already in line to move up a paygrade the next time the city had some extra money, she still felt inexperienced compared to the veterans on the squad.

And lately, though she couldn't see herself admitting this to anyone, she also felt like a bit of a fraud.

Nearly a year ago, Janey had done well enough as the secondary on a couple of cases that the lieutenant finally handed her her first case as a primary. The death of a young black woman, murdered in her home, had seemed at first like a clear cut case of the boyfriend having done it. Especially when Janey unearthed that said boyfriend had had a restraining order issued on him by the victim. It seemed like an easy win for the good guys, and it also seemed like a standalone affair.

Neither of which turned out to be true.

Janey's slam dunk, standalone case actually ended up being a part, though just a part, of the whole Ronald Green mess. By the time they got it all sorted out, they had a whole raft of deaths on their hands, all of which eventually turned out to be the work of a serial killer with a truly bizarre grudge against a group of innocent people.

Janey had taken part in most of that, along with Jack Hollis (one of his cases had turned out to be the first of the serial victims), but for some reason Helen Lipscomb had taken the brunt of both the public and official outrage. The fact that Helen had been instrumental in nailing a serial murderer somehow got overshadowed when compared to the idea that she'd spent a good amount of time pursuing an innocent man.

More than that, the press, and eventually the public, caught hold of the notion that if Helen hadn't expended so much time and energy chasing Green (who, truth be told, hadn't been exactly squeaky clean in the whole mess) she would have tumbled to the serial angle earlier, and possibly saved some lives.

Nonsense, no matter how you looked at it. Any objective examination of the facts showed that several of the victims were dead before Helen even entered the matter, and the connection between the various victims was so tenuous, even down to the lack of similarity between the methods of death, that no one could have possibly guessed the truth.

But once the idea took root, the whole thing turned into a public relations disaster for the department. And since the resolution of the whole thing, Helen had become pretty much a pariah. Considering all the black eyes that police departments around the country had acquired lately, the last thing anyone wanted was some sort of walking, talking embarrassment in their department.

Janey had even heard more than the normal amount of scuttlebutt to the fact that the mayor and city council were putting the pressure on for Helen to be fired.

Ever since, Janey had lived and worked under a

burden of her own guilt. To her mind, she and Hollis were as culpable in the whole thing as Helen, yet somehow they had managed to escape the public glare, while Helen had had to live with it every day for nearly a year now.

In the time since, Janey noticed herself developing something of a trepidancy when it came to her work. On a few occasions, she didn't push a witness as hard as she should have, or ended up clocking out and heading home when she still had a lead or two to wrap up. She was doing her job, she told herself that nearly every day, but wasn't throwing quite as much energy into it as she could.

Because of this, she felt relieved when Hollis assigned Lou Whitmore to help go through Roy Michaels's various cases, those that could have possibly lead to his death. The third detective assigned, Hal Smith, was doing what he could through phone and computer while Lou and she handled the field end of things.

Beginning with Joey London.

Shortly before noon the morning after the Michaels killing, they pulled up in front of a bar situated at the south end of a short strip mall on the city's west side. The strip held a total of six establishments, including an ice-cream shop and a pet store. The business in question, The In & Out, squatted at one end of the mall. It looked from the outside like one of those bars on that TV show where the screaming, nearly-incoherent host tries to "fix" the business in a couple of days, each day screaming louder and louder, till by the end of the hour astute watchers can actually see the spittle flying from his mouth.

"We could be polite and just call it a dump," Lou

said as they sat there, neither one making a move to leave the car.

If they hadn't been able to make out the address numbers over the door, they couldn't have identified the place for sure. The blackened-over windows didn't display a single logo, decoration or emblem that marked it as a drinking establishment. The green walls and red roof, both pale and scabrous from years of neglect, could have belonged to any abandoned squatters' hovel.

All of four cars were parked outside the In & Out, none of them manufactured in the last decade and a half.

"His PO says he's working here?" Lou asked, his voice rising half an octave in skepticism.

"Says he's employed," Janey replied. "The man's exact words were 'I'd shit me a brick if he's actually working.'"

"Which probably means that some distant, jerk-off relative owns the place, or at least manages it, and is giving Joey baby a story to satisfy the PO."

"Be my guess," Janey said. "Who the hell in the respectable world would hire London? You saw his sheet. Roy was only the latest in a long line of us who've bagged that scumbag."

Lou looked at her.

"What?" Janey asked.

"Just odd to hear such a gentle lady use a word like that."

Janey grimaced, not sure if Whitmore was kidding or not.

"He's awaiting trial for assault and rape," she said. "Roy was the arresting officer and, to date, the only witness against him."

"Except for the victim," Whitmore said. "Who

seems to have been so damned intoxicated she barely knew where she was."

"So without Roy, there's not much of a case."

Whitmore shook his head.

"It's still a long way from that to a murder rap. Especially of a cop. Seems to me a guy like this Joey wouldn't take such a chance."

Janey scrolled down her phone's screen, reacquainting herself with the file on London, which she'd downloaded before they'd left the station.

"His last stint upstate was three years, pled down from five. He's only been out about six months."

"So?" Whitmore asked.

"So for all we know going back in is the last thing he wants. Enough that he decided to do a damned fool move and take out the main witness against him."

"I don't see it," Whitmore said. "This dude's been in and out of the joint most of his life. Sure, one more ride wouldn't be pleasant and he'd try to avoid it, but if he has any brains at all he'd go for the lesser sure thing rather than the gold medal of taking out a cop."

"Unless there were some reason why he particularly didn't want to go back this time."

Whitmore shrugged and flung open his car door.

"Why don't we go ask him?"

The In & Out was even dingier and smellier on the inside than the exterior had prepared them for. Which was saying something. As they stood in the doorway, late morning light framing them like a halo, Janey and Whitmore didn't even bother to conceal their copness. They knew the types who inhabited such a squalid piss hole, especially in the middle of the day, would be able to peg them no matter how they tried to hide it, so why bother? Instead, they spent several seconds roaming their gazes over the interior, looking for London.

It didn't take all that long to find him. The bar only held eight people, including the two behind the stick, one of whom, at least from several feet away and in shadow, sure looked like their guy.

Tall, skinny, with a greasy mop of hair plastered around his head, even from their distance they could see the coiled sleeve tats that the file had cautioned them to look for.

And while they checked London out, he stared right back at them. Hard to tell in the uncertain light, but he seemed to be fidgeting back and forth, damned near hopping from one foot to another, as if debating the never ending question of fight or flight. Or at the very least stand your ground and tough it out or flight.

And within about five ticks of the clock, the perennial loser opted for flight.

He darted out from around the bar and ducked through some kind of shadowy corner just off the side. For all Janey and Whitmore knew, he could be either heading straight through a back door or, depending on his state of lucidity, the dead end of a storage room.

Going on the admittedly risky assumption that London knew what he was doing, Whitmore charged head on in the direction the guy had taken, while Janey reversed course and headed back out the door they'd entered.

Their decision, reached without discussion, wasn't so much sexism as practicality. With London gone, seven men, of unknown disposition, still lurked inside. And Whitmore, with his bulk and experience, not to mention the scary street quality of his blackness, had a damned sight better chance than Janey, despite her training.

Although ordinarily kind of modest and quiet voiced, when Whitmore desired he could take on the persona of a gangster supreme.

And since one way or the other one of them had to cover the back possibility…

Janey bolted onto the sidewalk and headed to her right. With the bar sitting at the end of the strip, she assumed that any back exit would be just around the corner, rather than crowding in on one of the other establishments. Janey had run track in both high school and college and kept herself in decent shape in the years since, so she made the back of the building in a few seconds.

In time to catch Joey London spilling out of a steel door positioned next to a dumpster.

Literally flopping out into the sunlight, the kid sprawled on the concrete, scraping his hands and knees on the dirty, trash-strewn gravel that comprised the back lot. When he got his bearings and raised his head up, he found himself gazing into the bore of Janey's service gun.

"Stay right there," she said. "You have any idea where my partner is?"

"Right behind him."

Janey didn't look up at Whitmore's voice. She didn't so much as flick an eye away from her captive.

"You okay?" she asked. "No trouble inside?"

"Naw, kid. I'm fine."

Whitmore now came into her view as he sank to his knees and yanked London's arms behind his back, preparatory to cuffing him.

"But Mister Joey here's got some 'splaining to do."

Up to this point, London, the hardened con, had remained silent. He grimaced a bit as Whitmore cuffed him, but still didn't utter a sound.

No doubt, Janey figured, he intended to keep quiet all the way up to when his court-appointed lawyer told him what to do and say.

And it pretty much worked out that way.

****

"Said anything?" Jack Hollis asked as the three of them stared at London through the mirrored window of the interrogation room.

"Only enough to ask for his lawyer," Whitmore said. "Wants to know what we were doing hassling him and when's his PD getting here."

"Did you tell him you just wanted to ask some questions?"

"I tried," Janey said, "but he just spit out that he wasn't answering anything till he saw his lawyer."

"This guy probably has the PD's office on speed dial," Whitmore interjected, "but I'm not sure about this one, Jack."

"Why so?"

"Well, he would have the motive for killing Roy, possibly. But if you'd gunned down a cop would you go right back the next day to your regular hangout and just wait for us to pick you up?"

Hollis patted his hand against his thigh as he stared through the mirror. London had sprawled himself out, his chair pushed back about a foot from the table and his foot tapping in time to some internal rhythm.

"Done a run through of family and acquaintance?" he asked.

"We asked Smith to do it, seeing as he's working the desk," Janey said. "He told us a few minutes ago that he'd managed to backtrack Joey here for the last thirty-six hours, and he was basically accounted for the whole time."

"Which as we all know," Whitmore said, "accounts for exactly squat."

"Except that he ran," Hollis said.

"Sure, but that may have just been instinct."

"Or it may have been that he did something else, something unrelated to Roy's death, and he thought we were coming for him for that."

The three of them went silent then, looking not at each other but at the punkish youth in the other room, who now looked like he'd fallen asleep.

"The last possibility's the most likely," Hollis finally said. "So he may be set on not talking, but why don't you guys go back in and see if you can get him riled into saying anything before…"

"Too late," Janey said as the door to the other room opened and a young, slightly balding man in a brown suit went in, sat down, and began talking with London.

THE AVENGER–AFTER THE FIRST

He woke up late the morning after the execution. The sun, shining through the balcony windows, had done its usual job, pulling him out of slumber and into the waking world. He couldn't remember the last time he'd actually set an alarm clock, and these days the times when a willing bedmate nudged him awake were painfully rare. Most mornings it was just him and the sun, communing together as they began a new day.

On this morning, though, the sun beamed so brightly that he swiveled his head to the small clock on the nightstand.

Twelve thirty.

Not an unusual time for him to wake, but rather shocked that he'd managed to sleep at all the night before.

It had taken some time. His eyes had barely closed when the "first timers" began.

"The first timers," his pet name for the vicious, blood-soaked dreams that always came after the first one. Faceless people reaching out, blood-red rains falling down, and skeletal hands rising out of the ground to pull him to his grave. All these images, and more, usually came to him after the first one.

And they had come the night before. Eventually, though, the images had tapered off, and somewhere around the early morning he'd finally managed to lapse into slumber.

He often wondered if, at some point, the act of killing would cease to have this effect on him. Indeed, he'd been trained for that very thing. But he'd never managed to reach the top level of his job where he could turn the emotions off entirely. Some men, the truly calloused ones at the top of their game, lived only to follow orders, not letting anything as plebian as emotions or remorse enter the equation.

The Avenger had never quite reached that level, which became evident to the Company when he didn't meekly go along with the official story of the Director's fate. And that morsel of humanity that he'd never let go of, that unwillingness to merely dip his head and follow protocol, had led directly to his estrangement from the only family he'd ever known.

There wasn't any emotional regret for his actions of yesterday. That cop had deserved his fate. True, he was peripheral to the main action, but he'd still involved himself, so in order for The Avenger to clear up this mess once and for all, the cop had to go.

The Avenger swung himself out of bed, stretched his arms overhead and took forty-eight deep breaths. The only exercise he ever required. He'd convinced himself years ago that deep breathing held the key to long life.

After the final breath of the set, the Avenger swung his arms down and strode over to the balcony. Flinging the doors open, he stepped outside.

It was still technically winter, though spring hovered right around the bend, and the cold concrete stung his feet. Even so, he remained motionless, soaking in the cold, bright sun and looking down at the street below— cars and people moving back and forth, scurrying around, as they could only do in the heart of a large city.

He felt safe for the moment. The gun was securely hidden away for later use, his cache of money secure on his person, and his tracks covered so well that the Company couldn't hope to track him down.

On the other hand, they'd sniffed him out more than once, ending up in situations he'd rather forget.

His head shook, almost growling at himself to banish all doubts.

He had a particular job to accomplish in this city. The day before, he'd performed the first step in the sequence, but there was much more to do. He needed to get himself going and begin planning for the next step.

But first, time to break the fast. He walked over to the desk and scanned the room service menu.

Eggs Benedict sounded pretty good, and if anyone in the kitchen squawked at preparing breakfast so late in the day, well, he had more than enough money on hand to silence them.

CHAPTER TWELVE

"Well, it definitely gives us another angle," Lieutenant Jarvis said.

"To say the least," said Hollis.

Helen and Hollis were seated in Jarvis's office. It occurred to Helen that it hadn't taken her long to once again consider Jarvis her boss. Now, as she and Hollis slouched in front of his desk, she took a good look at him.

And didn't like what she saw.

She had no clue as to the lieutenant's real age even though she'd worked under him for years. Somewhere in his late fifties, probably, though with the stress of the job it could be ten years either way. Now, seeing him for the first time in months, she felt a little alarm at his appearance.

He'd always had bags under his eyes, but not as deep, almost the color of bruises. Salt and pepper hair appeared full, but in the harsh office lights it looked brittle, as if it could snap at the slightest motion. And he leaned against the desk with slumped shoulders.

Even a few years back, when his wife had died from heart trouble, Helen couldn't remember him looking so bad. It was long past time for the man to retire, and she couldn't help but wonder why he hadn't already.

In the next instant, as a possible answer occurred to her, she felt a flush of shame.

It was late enough at night that the squad room held

only one detective, a near-retirement guy named Hoskins, working away at his desk. While the night shift nominally held a small number of plainclothes people—crime never sleeping and all that—the handful of men who made up this shift were currently out on various tasks.

All of which left the entire squad room, save for Hoskins toiling away at his desk, feeling somehow crypt-like.

"So how solid was this Jenkins woman?" Jarvis asked.

"Only about halfway," Helen answered. "Said that she saw Lori from time to time leaving during the day and not coming back for hours. The average person would probably just think errands or some such. And with her husband gone away a lot and a new baby, it could be that Jenkins simply needs something exciting in her life, even if by proxy."

"Coming and going doesn't seem like much evidence for an affair," Hollis said.

"True. Except that she often noticed Lori on these trips being 'dolled up.' Her words. And she mentioned seeing the car."

The three of them stared at each other. Helen had no doubt that the two men, one as experienced as her and one much more so, had the same idea she did.

"Lori's a decent appearing woman," Jarvis said.

"Sure. But she's heading into her late thirties. And trust me, boss. Any woman at that age, especially one who's been married forever and a day, needs to know she's still desirable."

"It still sounds thin," Hollis said.

"Right," Helen replied. "Which is why I continued

the canvass, then went back tonight to see if I could catch some folks who'd been gone during the day."

"And?"

Sighing, Helen stretched back in her chair and pushed it a few inches away from the table.

"I came across four women who hadn't been home earlier. Several men, too, but for obvious reasons I was more interested in what the ladies had to say. One wouldn't talk to me, and another said she barely knew Roy and Lori. But the other two had quite a tale to tell."

The two men leaned closer. Off on the other side of the room, Hoskins was placing files in his desk drawer. A uniformed officer came through the main door, walked over to Janey's desk and placed a file on top. Other than that, nothing moved in the squad room. In the near solitude, Helen wondered just how far she could go with her info.

"What kind of tale?" Jarvis asked.

"One of the women pretty much conveyed the same things Karen Jenkins did, but with one twist. About three weeks ago, she was shopping in the mall out on the west side of town and came upon Lori walking along with some guy."

"What kind of guy?"

"That's where it gets a bit tough, boss. According to this witness, the man she saw Lori with impressed her as 'kind of thuggish.' She said he looked something like an old lounge lizard from the eighties, but a lot younger."

"Approximate age?"

"She figured mid twenties or thereabouts."

"More to it?"

"Yeah, she said that Lori didn't see her at first, and the two of them looked fairly intimate."

The squad room door banged open, and two men of the building's cleaning crew entered, pushing their equipment cart in front of them. The janitors headed over to the far end of the room, close to where Hoskins was standing up and putting on his jacket.

"You said two women had info for you?" Hollis prompted.

"Sure thing. The second works at a bank downtown. Usually gone during the day. But a week ago she was home with the flu for a few days. Spent most of her time crashed out on her couch, which just happens to be situated across from the living room window."

"So?" Jarvis asked.

"So for three days that week she saw a yellow sports car, she pretty much figures it for an old Stingray, parked outside of the Michaels' place. The same car that Mrs. Jenkins told me about."

The three of them went silent again while Hollis and Jarvis digested this news. Helen looked off to the side at one of the janitors sweeping under Hoskins's desk. She knew that they did a full cleaning of the squad room twice a week yet, even so, the amount of dust bunnies that came out from under the desk shocked her. She began to understand why in the past her shoes had always been so dusty at the end of the day.

"It's far from conclusive," Jarvis said.

"Yeah," said Hollis, "but I think Helen ought to follow it up, see where it takes her."

"If anywhere," Helen chimed in.

"Right. If anywhere." Hollis turned to Jarvis. "Boss?"

Jarvis didn't answer. Instead, he put his hands flat on the table and pushed himself out of his chair. He walked over to the window on the other side of the room and stared down at the street below.

After a few minutes, his shoulders slumped even more, and he jammed his hands in his pockets.

"No idea yet on the 'thuggish-guy?'" he asked Helen.

"Nothing even close. Just the vaguest of descriptions. But if there is some connection between him and Lori, and there at least seems to be that, we should be able to run him down fairly quick."

"Any likelies at all on Roy's case log?"

"Not yet," Hollis said. "Turner, Whitmore, and Lattimer have been working on it all day. We did have one guy that Janey and Lou had to bring in in cuffs. Made a run for it when they showed up to question him."

"But?" Jarvis prodded, his back still turned to them.

"But turns out the guy just recently got out, had pulled a roofie trick the night before, and he figured that's what they were after him for."

"He copped to a date rape?" Helen asked, her voice rising in surprise.

Hollis grinned.

"Damned straight. As soon as he figured they wanted to question him about Roy's murder, he spilled everything he had. Gave us enough names and times to fill up about three days worth of alibis, including enough information to track down the girl."

"And," Helen said, "I'm assuming that Janey and Lou talked to her?"

"Janey did. Lou had the paper work to finish up. According to her, when the kid realized what a skeeze like this London punk had done to her, she wanted to come down here and kill him herself."

"So the alibi times he gave all checked out?" Jarvis asked.

"So far. Which, as we all know, doesn't mean a thing in and of itself, but my gut tells me this guy's clean."

"Any other possibles on Roy's old cases?"

"Not so far. We've got a ways to go, hopefully have it wrapped in another day or so."

Jarvis finally turned from the window and went back to his desk. "The lab?" he asked as he sat down.

"Hardly anything yet. We know 9mm for sure. Haven't found the casings or slugs yet. They're still working the scene, but we may have several days of waiting."

"Anything else on site?"

"Nothing much in the way of tracks or impressions. Hell, you were out there, boss. With all the snow falling and melting over and over, everyone's yards are basically swirls of mud. They haven't given up yet, but as of this afternoon, nothing so far."

Hollis nodded to Helen.

"Helen got the techs to expand their area to the adjoining backyards."

"Why?"

"No fences," Helen said. "Neither Lori or the two old folks who rushed to her aid heard or saw anyone running or a vehicle leaving. So I figured that maybe whoever it was parked on the opposite street and left via the backyard. None of the adjoining houses have fenced yards, so it would have been easy to get away. Plus, no one hearing a shot inclines me to think whoever it was used a silencer."

The three of them paused at that. So far, they were

soaking in possibilities, and not one dry area other than the possible silencer involved.

"Which also implies," Hollis put in, "that this wasn't a random act. Whoever did this, embittered con or someone else, had Roy's place scoped out and did their homework."

"At the very least, not an ordinary criminal. We may be dealing with someone who has some sort of specialized training."

Hollis frowned and shook his head.

"Talk to the people on the back side of the street?" Jarvis asked.

"Yes, sir," Helen said. "Nobody saw or heard anything, at least not after the commotion started. We figure those few moments in between the killing and when Lori started screaming gave whoever it was time to slip away."

"It was planned."

"Yes, sir. But we pretty much knew that because of the mailbox."

Jarvis sighed and stood back up. He stretched his arms over his head then cracked his knuckles.

"I'm packing it in for the night. I'd suggest you two do the same."

Then he shifted enough to fully focus on Helen.

"If we hit a dead end with the rest of the case file, your line becomes the most likely."

Helen nodded.

"You realize, both of you, that we may end up looking at a cop's wife for his murder."

Both nodded in agreement.

"If–and I'm stressing *if*–it comes to that, it's going to become public real quick."

"What's your point, boss?" Helen asked, though she had pretty much guessed where he was heading.

"You're not exactly the most low profile member of the department these days, Helen."

Of course. No matter what happens, no matter what gets in the way, the damned Green business, like a noose around her neck, may loosen up for a while, but at some point it tightened all over again.

She wondered if Jarvis was considering reassigning her.

"I'll step lightly, boss, at least until there's a reason not to."

He cocked his head, stared at her for a second, then nodded.

"See that you do. Don't give the press or, God forbid, the city council, any more reason to come down on us than they already have."

"We'll be careful," Hollis chimed in.

The lieutenant nodded at them, then headed out of the squad room. After he left, Hollis and Helen turned to each other.

"How long's he been this way?" Helen asked.

"What way?"

"Come on, Jack. He looks like an old man, like he's aged a decade in the last year. What the hell's up with that?'

"It's been kind of rough. Ever since–you know. He called in a lot of chits to keep you on the force."

"I knew he'd covered for me a bit, but..."

"More than covering, Helen. You may not believe it, but I bet you don't have a clue just how much pressure there was to get you out of here."

Helen felt herself flush again, but this time from

anger rather than embarrassment.

"Are you freakin' kidding me, Jack? Who do you think's been shuttled from one end of this city to the other, doing every single dirty job the chief could think of?"

"That's what I'm saying." Now Hollis's tone became a little heated. "The only reason you've been shuttled around like that, the reason they didn't go with the first excuse to kick you out the damned door, is because of Pete."

Helen couldn't look her partner in the eye. Instead, she focused her attention on the doors through which Jarvis had left just a few minutes before.

"Sorry," she said after a moment. "Seems like lately I've been overdoing it on the self pity train. Especially considering."

"With reason." Hollis's temper had gone down a couple of notches. "Dammit, everyone anywhere close to this knows you got a raw deal. And it's only through some fluke that Janey and I weren't roped in as well. But it's time to face it, partner. You're on the top floor's shit list, and we all know that once on, it's almost impossible to get off."

"Granted."

"And Pete's right, you know," Hollis said. "If we go after Lori, it could get messy."

"I know."

"On the other hand, assuming we have to really ramp up on her, that's about as bad as it could get, right?"

Shaking her head, Helen gathered her jacket, signed out on the board by the door, and left Hollis alone. At some point during their discussion the janitors had departed, but as she stopped at the elevator and looked at her partner one more time it seemed to her that the squad room was as dirty and disheveled as ever.

CHAPTER THIRTEEN

Two mornings after Roy Michaels's murder, Janey and Lou were almost at the end of their list. Pushing themselves for the last thirty-six hours, not bothering when shifts officially ended or began, they'd managed to eliminate, one way or another, ten possible suspects that Hollis and the lieutenant had compiled. They were down to the last one, and while Janey knew they could always find other angles of investigation, everyone from the beginning had agreed that a vengeful perpetrator was the most likely candidate.

Except that it hadn't quite worked out that way.

They pulled up outside a bedraggled apartment building on Roarke Street. Janey, blonde and blue-eyed, felt like an alien creature in this part of town. Not that she shirked from entering any area, but it felt good to have Lou alongside her. Though he stood out as a cop, he was at least the right color to make some progress in this neighborhood.

"Good thing I'm along," Lou said.

"Oh?'

"Yeah, with your coloring, you'd probably have to crack some skulls to get any answers. Then you'd have double the paperwork."

Janey grinned, hoping nerves were kept hidden from him.

"Seriously, kid," Lou said, "we'll just stick together

and get through this. We go to the apartment, see if the punk's home, and work it from there."

He left unspoken the main thing bothering Janey. So far, all their leads on Roy's cases had turned up nothing. Either the people in question had moved on, had decent alibis for the timeframe of the murder, or had already been picked up on other crimes. If this one didn't work out, tracking down their colleague's killer was going to get a whole lot harder.

"Let's go," Janey said.

Lou nodded, and both of them exited the vehicle.

****

The person of interest's name was Luis Pinon, convicted of burglary about seven years ago. During his apprehension for that incident, Pinon and Detective Roy Michaels had gotten into what the official report called an "altercation." Pinon, flying on meth at the time of the arrest, had assaulted Michaels with a butcher knife. By the time he was subdued, the suspect had sustained a broken arm, three cracked teeth, and numerous lacerations.

Detective Michaels had come out of the encounter with several injuries of his own, including three that required massive stitches, one on his arm close to the brachial artery.

Pinon had been released two months ago after having served six years of a ten-year sentence.

As Janey and Lou entered the single five-story apartment building, the usual panoply of odors assaulted them. Takeout food, urine, vomit, and the general stench of unwashed bodies commingled into an effluvium that would have sent the average person stumbling out onto the sidewalk. Janey and Lou grimaced but kept on going.

These stenches weren't new to the two professionals.

Two elevator cages rested on the ground floor, but handwritten signs indicated both were out of order.

"Great," Lou groused. "Pinon's up on the fifth floor. You had your exercise yet this week?"

Janey turned and headed for the nearest bank of stairs.

By the third floor, she'd left Lou a turn behind, though she could still hear him grumbling on the stairs below.

She made it to the fifth floor and waited for her partner. He came up a minute or two behind her, wheezing and hacking in a somewhat dramatic fashion. Janey, who knew the guy was in decent shape, figured he was just letting off steam at the frustration of the last few days.

"This reminds me of that dumbass TV show my wife likes so much," he said. "The one with those nerdy guys and the blonde chick? For the life of me, I don't see what Megan sees in that thing."

Janey, who knew the show he meant and counted it as one of her top three favorites, just nodded.

"Apartment 5-C, right?" she asked.

"Five- C. Right there about twenty feet from us. Let's hope to hell we find something usable here. I don't want to go back and tell the boss that we have to start over from scratch."

Janey headed down the hallway, Lou trailing behind her. They'd talked it over in the car, figuring it better to have her approach the door on her own, with Lou just off to the side.

They figured good ole Luis would be more likely to open the door to a pretty young woman than to a big, hulking man.

Janey took her gun out and held it to her side, half hidden by her leg. Lou, his own weapon unholstered, positioned himself about three feet to the side, far out of the range of vision of a peephole.

Janey knocked.

No answer. Pushing herself into the door, she listened as hard as she could but sensed nothing from inside the apartment.

At least, nothing auditory.

"You smell that, partner?" Janey whispered.

Lou hustled over to her side, leaned up against the doorjamb and took a quick whiff. He stepped back, his face tight, and glanced at his partner.

"PC?" Janey asked.

"Enough to satisfy me."

Hoping to find the door unlocked, Janey took hold of the knob and twisted.

No give.

As she stepped out of the way, Lou hoisted his leg and gave the door all he had.

Not as easy as in the movies, even for a guy his size. It took two solid kicks before the panel gave way and the two of them rushed in.

Both held their arms over their faces to keep out the stench.

With the door open, they now heard the distinct buzzing of flies. The apartment was so small that the standard move of each detective breaking to opposite sides, to present less of a target, was pretty much impossible. A simple studio, with a small, dirty kitchenette off to the side and a 70's vintage waterbed resting against the far wall, they could visually sweep the entire place within a second of entering.

Only two windows, on the wall opposite the door, both shut tight against the March cold outside.

But inside, the stuffiness of the room only added to the smell that enveloped the place.

Luis Pinon waited for them on the waterbed.

Janey, younger and not as experienced as Lou, faltered as she approached.

Even Lou blanched at what awaited them on that bed.

As far as they could tell, from a quick eyes-only inspection, someone, or several someones, had beaten Pinon to death.

Crusted blood, most of it probably from a busted nose, smeared across his face. They'd caught him at home, clad only in dingy white boxers, and his chest, abdomen and legs, what they could see past the decaying marks of death, formed one large bruise. Stepping closer, Janey saw that both of his eye sockets appeared broken, one eye yellowed and cloudy in death and turned upward to the ceiling, and the other plopped half out of its socket.

A mass of insects crawled along the body and in the feces, which had leaked out in the moment of death, staining the legs and mattress beneath.

Where the hell the flies had come from, in the middle of winter, Janey didn't want to think about.

"Good Lord," she heard Lou say behind her.

She turned.

"Look," he said, motioning across the floor.

Janey glanced down and saw various yellowed, pebble-looking items scattered on the floor. She stared at the objects for a minute before looking up.

"His teeth?"

Lou nodded, still keeping his sleeve over his nose.

"I say we back out of here," he said, "and wait for the techs to show up."

Janey felt the urge to go over, open a window, and let some of the stench dissipate, but knew better than to contaminate the scene even a little. They edged out of the apartment, not stopping until they made it to the end of the hallway.

"What do you think?" she asked.

The overwhelming stench now further away, their hands fell away from their faces. The odor of rot still clogged her nose, and Janey figured she'd be breathing it for several days.

"Hard to tell. More than likely, someone he managed to piss off came looking for him. I doubt that it has anything to do with Roy, so even though we came on the scene first I'm betting the boss hands it over to someone else."

Janey didn't answer at first, instead stared down the hall toward that apartment.

"How long?" she asked, turning to Lou.

"Days," he said. "At least three or four, maybe a week. Though the ME's will give us a better window, all things being equal."

"Three or four days," Janey repeated, her voice a near whisper.

"That's right, kid." Her partner wiped his brow with the back of his hand. "Unless there's something we don't know about, my best guess is that young master Pinon in there's been dead since before Roy's shooting."

"Damn. That means we're right back to square one."

Without saying another word, Lou pulled his phone out and called in their discovery.

Square one, Janey thought, and she wondered if Helen might just be onto something.

CHAPTER FOURTEEN

LOS ANGELES

Lawrence Sears stood at the picture window that gazed out over the harbor, deliberately keeping his back to the people in the office. It was his power pose, one he'd cultivated over several years, and one that he thought he performed damned well.

He wanted the men in his office to receive the very clear idea of who was in charge.

Although Lawrence pretty much figured that the man he most wanted to impress was actually impressed the least.

"What you're saying is you have no goddamned idea," he said with his back to the room.

"Not exactly, Mr. Sears."

"Oh?"

He turned, pinning his gaze on the middle man in the cluster of three sitting on the sofa against the far wall.

The two on each end looked like typical drones, average height, weight and coloring. The kind of men you'd pass on the street and not even notice. But the third, Trevor Morton, was something altogether different.

Although average-sized, Morton's ramrod posture and bright, clear eyes bespoke confidence. His clothing continued the motif. A simple tan suit and blue shirt, with a muted pastel tie, he wore the clothes in such a way that dictated the impression of costing a couple of thousand dollars.

"My apologies, then," Sears said. "I must have misunderstood. Please tell me where he is."

"Well we don't–we don't exactly know just yet."

"As I said, you have no goddamned…"

"Oh for God's sakes, Lawrence. Let the man talk."

Sears turned to the fifth person in the room. Older, though with smooth skin and good posture, sitting behind his desk as if it belonged to her.

He didn't like it when she came in and took over his office, but considering their relative positions he couldn't do much about it.

"I'm trying to, Lois, but he's not saying anything."

Lois smiled at him, then turned back to the men on the couch.

"You were saying?"

Morton continued. "What I mean is that we've got several possible leads, but as you know the kid's rather good at—"

"Andrew!" Lawrence Sears interjected.

"Sir?"

"His name is Andrew, not 'the kid.'"

Lois puffed in disdain. "Go on, Mr. Morton. And try to excuse Mr. Sears. He's been under some stress lately."

As she spoke, the woman sent Sears a brief glare.

"As I was saying, Andrew is rather good at covering his tracks. This makes, what, the fifth time he's taken off like this?"

"Fourth," Sears said, "but who's counting."

"Mr. Morton, what do you know for sure?"

"Well, ma'am, we're pretty certain he didn't fly out

on any commercial airlines. And, of course, he didn't use the jet."

"He tried that with Chicago," Sears remarked, "which made us put in some stiff security around the hangars."

"Yes, sir. And his car is still in his slot at the condo. Though, of course, it wouldn't have been difficult for him to purchase a new vehicle."

"How many times have I said this?" Lawrence asked the older woman. "We need to cut off his money. We should have closed his checking account long ago, and, for God's sake, why does he still hold credit cards?"

"Because," Lois replied, "as I've told you so many times, his doctors say he needs to be treated as much like an adult as possible. And hamstringing him financially won't help him progress. They all say so."

Lawrence did his best to keep his face calm, but couldn't keep himself from clenching and unclenching his fists.

"Those doctors,"—and even he could hear the sneer in his tone—"don't have to keep cleaning up after him. All they have to do is take their salaries and tell you what you want to hear."

Lois's lips curled as her eyes narrowed to slits.

"Any lines of inquiry at all, Mr. Morton?"

The two men sitting to either side of Morton shifted their gazes downward and did their best to look like part of the furniture of the room.

"Well," Morton said, "there are some new files we found on his laptop."

"Oh, dear Lord." Now Lawrence Sears didn't even try to keep the disgust from showing in his expression. "Is he back to that again?"

He turned to the woman. "Did you know?" he asked her.

Lois stood and smoothed her dress. "How many this time?" she asked.

Morton looked to the man sitting at his right. "How many files did you catalogue?"

His subordinate, shorter than him and wearing a brown suit, cleared his throat. "Eight. At least that we can be sure of. He's gotten better at covering his tracks, so it took us a while to go through them, but we have eight good possibles."

"Wait a minute, here. Are you saying he took off and left his laptop behind?"

"No, sir. We've been making spot checks of his activity."

Lawrence whirled toward his desk again, his eyes narrowed. "Goddammit, Lois. If he goes off again and…"

"Find him, gentlemen." The woman cut him off. "Find Andrew and bring him back."

Without another word she walked out from behind the desk and left the office, four men staring after her.

CHAPTER FIFTEEN

"So where exactly are we going?" Janey Turner asked.

It was the next day, and she and Helen had checked a car out of the station garage and headed out.

It was Saturday, but nearly everyone, unable to rest until they'd found their colleague's killer, had showed up before seven.

"Checking out a lead," Helen said.

"A better one?"

"Huh?"

"Well, I'm assuming you've heard about what Lou and I found yesterday? We've busted our rears going over Roy's old cases, and came up with nothing but a date rape bust and a week-old body."

"Yeah, I heard about that. Are you guys going to have to work the case?"

"No," Janey replied, "they gave it to someone from South station. It was in their area anyway."

Helen didn't answer for a minute, instead focusing on negotiating the downtown traffic. Weekend or no, the streets were packed. Although the temps were still low, with snow and slush everywhere to be found, people no doubt could sense Spring right around the corner.

"So," Janey prompted. "Is this a new lead or something?"

"Not a new one," Helen answered.

The younger cop stared at her for a minute.

"Lori," Janey said, not as a question.

"Turns out there's a strong indication that she was fooling around on Roy, to the point where the guy may have been coming over to her house for hours on end."

"That's pretty blatant."

Helen shrugged.

"Maybe, maybe not. If you consider a detective's hours, once he was out of the house in the morning she could have rightly assumed he wouldn't be home for hours. It's not like we get to take breaks in the middle of the day."

"Sure, but even so..."

"Like I said in the squad the other day, if Roy was an accountant or a shoe salesman, we would have looked at the wife right off. But since he was a cop, and our friend, the main thrust of the investigation started off the other way."

"Yeah," Janey grumbled, "and so far we've come up blank. I've got a feeling if this thing doesn't turn soon someone's going to take it out of Jack's hide."

"I can't quite see the boss doing that."

"I wasn't talking about the boss," Janey said. "Yesterday, trying to get the stink of that body out of my nose, I stopped at the Cuff and had a few beers with a couple of uniforms. Lou and I have been out of the shop so much the last few days that we've hardly seen anybody."

"Yeah?"

"Well, no surprise, according to these guys a couple of the suits have been parading in and out almost non-stop. The chief, a couple of councilmen. Word is they've been hanging around Pete's office and putting the screws to both him and Jack."

"Jack didn't say anything about that," Helen said.

"Probably doesn't want to worry any of us more than we already are."

Helen didn't respond, and for the next several minutes they rode in silence.

They'd made it out of the city proper and were on the bypass heading toward Herndon before she finally spoke up.

"Which means we've got to come up with something, at least some sort of possibility. Something to help the guys out."

"If somebody doesn't turn over something soon," Janey said, "they're probably going to kick this to a special unit, maybe even the staties, and we'll be out in the cold."

Another several minutes of silent driving, then they hit the slower speed limits of the suburb.

"You ever meet her?" Helen asked.

"Lori? No. Saw the pictures Roy kept on his desk, but that's it."

"We're dealing with a woman in her late thirties. Still fairly attractive, but that damned clock's ticking away. No kids, and the husband, as we've already noted, has a job with godawful hours."

"You're saying it's reasonable to assume she fooled around?"

"Of course. You know we all need it as much as the men do."

The last words came out clipped, harsher than she'd intended, and Helen could feel Janey staring at her.

"You all right?" Janey asked.

Helen nodded. "Sorry. It's been a rough couple of

days."

Janey continued staring at her friend.

"I haven't heard you talk about Rick lately. Everything okay there?"

Helen didn't say anything, but gripped the steering wheel tighter.

Janey nodded.

"So what exactly are we up to?"

****

The Michaels's neighborhood was just as quiet this morning as it had been the last few days. Three cars were parked in front of Lori and Roy's house, two of which Helen recognized from the night of the murder. She figured the third car also belonged to family or friend.

The tech folks were nowhere to be found, but their yellow tape still circled the lower half of the driveway. At the moment, neither the home, nor the entire neighborhood, held any sign of activity.

They pulled up alongside the curb about fifty feet down from the Michaels's home.

Craning her neck, Helen spotted more circles of crime scene tape, three in all and held aloft by steel rods driven into the ground, decorating various parts of the adjacent yards she'd noticed the other day.

"Did you check with the techs?" Janey asked.

"Yep. They finished up yesterday with the driveway and front yard. They're basically done with those back yards as well, but Thornson said he had a bit of work left out there."

"Wonder where he is?"

Helen shrugged.

"So did she move back in?"

"That's what Thornson said. He had no real reason

to keep her out, since the house itself isn't a crime scene, at least so far."

Janey shivered. "Isn't that kind of cold? To move back into the house so soon?"

Helen gave another shrug. "She's got family in the area. I assume they're with her."

"Still," Janey said, "I wouldn't want to do it. I think I'd stay with friends until I could get the place sold."

The two of them sat for a minute in the parked car.

"This is going to be tough," Janey finally said.

"I know, but we've got to do it."

"The memorial's tomorrow. Couldn't we at least wait until after that?"

Helen, beginning to feel like the proverbial broken record, shook her head.

"If she wasn't Roy's wife, we wouldn't. You know the book. Initial questioning of spouse, follow up investigation, then requestioning as soon as possible. That's how it's done."

Janey stared at her for a second, and Helen turned sideways.

"What?"

"You don't have to take it all on yourself."

Helen frowned and shook her head. "Meaning what?"

"You know you don't have to prove anything. What happened last year could have happened to any of us."

Sighing, Helen could feel her shoulder muscles tensing up. "I had this conversation the other night with Jack. I really don't feel like having it again."

"You went by the book last year. Did everything right. You know you did. The review board afterwards, the one that reported to the mayor, didn't find a single thing you should have done differently than you did."

"Doesn't matter what they found." Helen could hear the bitterness in her voice. "I hounded an innocent man, and in the meantime several more people got killed."

"Don't forget, one of those victims was mine. And I went after the boyfriend, same as you went after the straying husband. And I was wrong too."

"Yeah, but your suspect was a bad dude all around, so the people upstairs didn't see it as nearly as egregious an error as mine."

"My point is you're doing it again."

"What?"

"You're going by procedure again, Helen. You went after Green last year because he was, according to the stats, the most likely suspect. Now, you're gunning for Roy's widow. Going for the spouse is nine times out of ten the right move, but are you sure it is this time?"

Helen flung the door open and got out.

"I'm not gunning for anybody," she said as she leaned back in the car. "I'm doing the job the best way I know. You coming or not?"

Janey clamped her lips together and got out her side of the car. Together, the two of them headed up the walk.

****

A woman answered the door. Not Lori, and not the Murland woman from the other night. This one looked to be somewhere in her forties, possibly a well-kept fifty.

Helen wondered if she were another friend, or maybe a much older sister.

"Can I help you?" She was letting her blonde hair show its gray, and she showed the faintest signs of pudginess.

Helen held up her badge and nodded to Janey.

"Detectives Lipscomb and Turner. We know this is a bad time, but we'd like a few minutes with Mrs. Michaels."

The blonde woman, still rooted in the doorway, stared at Helen.

"You were here the other night," she said. "I was in Linda's dining room when you showed up."

Helen nodded. She didn't remember the woman, but that night her focus had been entirely on Lori.

"Didn't you ask all your questions then?"

Helen bristled a bit, but considering the circumstances let it pass.

"It's an ongoing investigation," she replied, "and as new things come up they need to be checked out. And you are…?"

"Susan Wasserman. I'm Lori's aunt."

Helen nodded and, figuring the woman wouldn't invite them in without a nudge, began giving out her cop stare, taking a quick moment to glance at the woman's left hand.

"We'd really like to talk to Lori for a few minutes, Mrs. Wasserman."

"I'm sorry, but she isn't home. She and Betty, Roy's mother, are down at the funeral home, taking care of a few last minute things. The service is tomorrow, you know."

Helen nodded, then glanced back at the driveway and street.

"Do you have any idea when they'll be back?"

"No," the woman said, "but I'll be sure to let her know you came by."

The door shut on them.

"Gee," Janey said, "you think maybe Lori bitched about being questioned?"

CHAPTER SIXTEEN

Helen and Janey were sitting patiently in the car when Helen received a call from Sgt. Thorson back at the lab. "The bad news," he said, "the backyards didn't give us much in the way of anything usable."

"Nothing?"

"There were some vague footprints in the mud under some trees," he said, "and we did a quick questioning of the residents in those two houses. Did you talk to them yet?"

"I did. But only about what they did or didn't see or hear."

"Okay," Thorson continued. "So there's the single lady who lives in one, and in the other a divorced dad with two kids, a boy and a girl. The boy had been tromping through the yard the last few days, but he's only seven so we could eliminate his possible tracks. The dad said he hadn't been out at all. We did find some smudges that look to be from about a men's 10 M, but nothing identifying at all."

"Dammit," Helen said, "what about the woman. Anything from her?"

"Said she hasn't been out in the yard in over a week. The night of Roy's murder she only got as far as her back porch to see what the commotion was, then got spooked and headed back inside."

"That's what she told me as well, but at the time I

hadn't thought to ask her about any visitors who may have been in her yard."

"Yeah, well, according to her, zip on that end of things."

"So you have a possible size ten or so print?"

"Actually, a couple that may fit the bill. But like I said, nothing distinguishing in terms of marks or imprints. Nothing really worth preserving. And I wouldn't want to stake my pension on it."

Thorson had just rung off when Janey nudged Helen's elbow.

A maroon Ford was pulling up to the curb on the far side of the driveway. Helen wondered why, with the techs obviously done processing the scene, the yellow tape hadn't yet been taken down. She'd mention it to Hollis.

Two women got out of the Ford and began walking up to the house. Helen and Janey exchanged glances.

"Roy's mom," Janey said.

Helen nodded. Even without the aunt's mentioning it earlier, she would have guessed that the older woman was one of the couple's parents.

"No mention of Lori's mother," she said to Janey.

"Or father. Are her parents even alive?"

Helen shrugged.

As the two women got to the front porch, Lori Michaels turned and looked directly at the two detectives.

"Well, I guess that's it," Helen said as she opened her car door.

The two women stood waiting for them on the porch. The older one, a slim, well-kept woman in her early sixties, looked confused at their approach.

Lori just glared.

"Yes?" she asked as Helen and Janey got within about ten feet of them.

"Sorry to bother you again, Lori," Helen said, "but we have a few more questions."

The glare sharpened. Helen had hoped that using the first name, as a means of assuming dominance, would set the widow back a bit. She felt a bit cruddy employing standard techniques on a cop's wife, but figured she could live with it if it got them closer to the truth.

"Questions?" Roy's mother, frowning in her puzzlement, asked.

"Yes, ma'am. We need to talk to your daughter-in-law for a minute."

"I just came from the funeral home, detective. We'd planned on making all the arrangements. But it seems nobody thought to tell me that his body hasn't been released yet."

"Well, we are in the middle of an active investigation."

The widow sighed and slumped against the door.

"Whatever it is, Detective Lipscomb, can't it wait? I really need to—"

"Sorry. But like I said, we're in the middle of the investigation and—"

"Lori?" the older woman's voice quavered just the slightest. "What's going on here?"

"Nothing, Betty They just need to talk to me for a minute. Come on in, ladies."

As the four of them moved inside, Helen and Janey received another glare, this one from Lori's aunt, standing in the middle of the living room. Regardless, at Lori's insistence the two other women moved off into the kitchen, leaving her and the two cops alone.

"So when can I bury him?" Lori asked as she slumped into a brown leather recliner.

Helen and Janey took opposite sides of a sofa that faced the chair.

"I'm not sure," Helen said. "That's not really why we're here. You'd have to check with Jack Hollis. He's the primary on the case and—"

"Goddamn, the bureaucratic run-around never stops, does it?"

"I'm sorry," Helen said. She wondered at the harsh change in attitude from the day before, but had a hunch what had caused it. "But I'm guessing you know how this works."

A small glint appeared in the other woman's eyes.

"Of course I do. I heard enough of it over the years. But if you count the lieutenant and Hollis, this makes the fourth time that I've been questioned."

"Well, then you know—"

"'Course two of those," Lori interrupted, "took place with my husband's body lying out in the driveway. So tell me, detective, do those count as interrogations or not?"

Helen leaned forward a bit, fixing the other woman with her gaze.

"Some new information has come out," she said.

Lori Michaels's mouth set, her jaw clenching.

"I can guess all about your new information," she said. "I watched you yesterday parading up and down the street, talking to anyone you could. I can only imagine what you may have been told."

Helen sent the merest of glances in Janey's direction, so slight she hoped the widow wouldn't notice.

"Lori," Janey began, "you know we have to do things a certain way."

Lori gave a jerky nod, eyes squinting for a splint second. "So what are your questions?" she asked, looking directly at Helen.

Helen took a deep breath. *Here goes*, she thought.

"Do you know anyone who drives a yellow Stingray?"

CHAPTER SEVENTEEN

"Straight up, Pete. It's not looking good."

Hollis stood in the boss's doorway as he delivered the news.

Lt. Jarvis looked up from reviewing the duty schedule for the next month and ushered his detective in.

Hollis stepped inside, hand on the doorknob and lifted his eyebrows. When Jarvis nodded, he shut the door and took a seat.

"Define not good," Jarvis said.

"Like I told you already, we came up zip on Roy's case files. Just as we finished those, Lou got called away to court, but he says he should be back in by Tuesday. Helen and Janey are working the Lori angle, which makes me uncomfortable as hell, but it has to be done."

"What about Smith?"

"I've got him going back through unsolveds of random stranger shootings. Amazingly, we seem to have had a drop in those the last six months or so, so he should have it wrapped in another day or so. So far, he hasn't found anything promising that connects with Roy's case."

"The lab?"

Hollis sighed and stretched his legs out. "Nothing much in the way of tracks. Nothing at all anywhere around the body, but they did find some partials in one of the adjoining yards."

"His possible escape route?"

"Right. Which tells us this wasn't some random street hop, not that you'd expect it in a neighborhood like that. Though I guess anything's possible. Cartridges were standard nines. The guy policed his brass, and at such close range there was a fair amount of damage to the cartridges themselves. If we ever get a suspect gun we can possibly match them up, but they couldn't really tell us much beyond the caliber."

Jarvis tapped his fingers on his desk for a minute.

"Lori?" he said.

Hollis squirmed a bit. "When they got through with the case files, I shifted Janey over to helping Helen nail that angle. Helen's pretty sure she was fooling around on Roy. She and Janey went back out today and reinterviewed her."

"How'd that go?"

"About how you'd expect. Until Helen asked her about a guy who drives a yellow Stingray. According to Helen, for a minute there she thought Lori was going to throw them out of the house."

"But?"

"But she gave some song and dance about recently hiring a personal trainer."

"A personal trainer? Who makes house calls?"

"Yeah," Hollis said. "Doesn't quite jive with an unemployed housewife and a cop's salary."

Jarvis thumped his hand on the desk once before rising and moving over to the window.

Hollis knew that the window only looked out onto the back parking lot, but he figured Jarvis was seeing more than streetlights and asphalt.

"What about GSR?"

"Huh?"

"On Lori. We need to bring her in and do a test."

"It's been several days, Pete. Even under normal washing, most traces will probably be gone."

"From her hands," Jarvis pointed out.

Hollis didn't need long to follow the lieutenant's train of thought.

"You're thinking of her clothing?"

"Right."

"She had on some kind of maroon sweater that night, right?"

"That's what I remember," Jarvis said.

"It doesn't feel right. For all we know she managed to change clothes before we showed up. And it probably won't go down too well with everyone out there."

Hollis jerked his head to the nearly-empty squad room. Unlike the uniform division, Saturday nights usually only had a skeleton force of detectives.

"But she wouldn't have had time before the neighbors ran over to her, and she wasn't ever alone after that."

"And like Helen says, we've got to do this one by the book. Especially this one."

Hollis didn't have a reply to that. This case, so far, was eating every remaining bit of effort not to see Lori as their main suspect.

"Helen knows her job," Jarvis said after a moment.

"She does."

"You know how much heat I've had to deflect off her, right?"

Hollis figured Jarvis was talking to himself more than anything, so he kept quiet and let the man ruminate.

But the lieutenant didn't continue. Instead he stood

quietly, staring out into the night.

Finally, he shook his head and turned around.

"Last year, I had to cash in nearly every favor I had to keep her on the force. Though the way they've treated her since, maybe it would have been better for me to just back off and let them cut her loose."

"Whether you think so or not," Hollis said, "that should be her call, right?"

"But she shouldn't have even had to consider it. Anyone in this department who says they wouldn't have pursued Green just as heavily would be a liar."

Something flickered through Hollis's mind at that. Some stray fragment of realization. He tried to snatch the fragment, but it was gone before he could catch it.

"The point is, we've already had our black eye. And the brass doesn't want us to have another one."

Hollis nodded.

"And we for damned sure can't have our own detectives being gunned down outside their own homes. Especially after all the police animosity across the country lately."

"How bad's the pressure, Pete?"

Jarvis flickered a smile.

"Pretty bad, but I've had worse. But if we don't nail this down pretty quickly, they'll start looking for a scapegoat again."

He turned and snagged his coat off a hook on the wall behind his desk.

"I assume you're going to Roy's memorial tomorrow morning," Jarvis asked.

"Far as I know, the whole squad's going to turn out. That's something else Helen mentioned in her report. Lori's anxious to get Roy's body for an actual burial."

"What'd she tell her?"

"That she didn't know when the coroner would be done."

Jarvis nodded.

"Everyone needs to be back by one in the afternoon. Doesn't matter if it's Sunday. The service is at ten, so that shouldn't be a problem. Then it's time to start drawing outside the lines on this one. We've got to nail him, Jack. Whoever or wherever he, or she, is, we've got to nail them."

"We'll do it, Pete."

"Let's start with asking Lori to allow us to test both her and the clothes she was wearing that night. And possibly her other clothes as well."

"Probably won't be anything on her by this point."

"Maybe, maybe not. We've got a better shot with the clothing. But be ready for her to refuse. And if you have to, get a warrant. Have Lattimer write it up."

The two men faced each other a second without saying anything more, then Jarvis headed out of his office. Hollis watched his superior thread his way through the desks and cubicles that made up the squad room and wondered if he could ever see himself accepting a promotion to command rank.

At the moment, the idea just didn't seem worth it.

Hollis headed back to his desk to grab his own coat. It was nearing eleven o'clock, and he still had a couple of things to do downstairs before a full day coming up tomorrow.

But the day would end up a whole lot fuller than he could have possibly anticipated.

CHAPTER EIGHTEEN

Helen's phone buzzed shortly after four that morning. Trying mentally to swat the annoyance away, by the third ring even her sleep-fogged mind realized that it was her home phone, not her cell, summoning her. She managed to surge out of her restless slumber and grab the phone before the fifth ring.

"'Lo," she mumbled, blinking in the darkness in an attempt to activate her brain.

"Helen."

She recognized the voice, but not the tone. Years of working on the same squad, more often than not as partners, and she'd never heard the guy's voice sound as strained, as hurt, as it did now.

"Jack? What's up?"

"Sorry to wake you, but I need you here. Right now."

Helen sat up a little straighter.

"Where are you? The station? Did we get a break?"

"No," he said, and again his voice carried that odd, wounded feeling. "Not a break. And not at the station. You need to get here right now."

"Jack," she said, her own tone beginning to show annoyance. "What are you talking about? Where are you?"

"I'm at Pete's."

"Pete's?"

"Lieutenant Jarvis. We're at his house. Helen, somebody got him."

"Got him?"

At her core, Helen knew what he meant, but needed to hear it explicitly before she could believe it.

"Someone killed him. Gunned him down right outside his house. They got the boss."

CHAPTER NINETEEN

Helen had never been to the lieutenant's home, but with a quarter mile to go she didn't even bother with her GPS. The cascade of red and blue lights swirling across the scene served as a hundred beacons.

After Hollis had hung up, she'd taken a couple of minutes to sit on the side of her bed. Hollis's call had felt like a punch to the gut, leaving her shaking and shivering in the dark and silence of her room.

She'd had the brief self-pitying notion that once upon a time, though not for a while, she would have had someone on the other side of the bed to hold her, stroke her back and help her get it together.

Then had come a surge of nausea at the idea of sitting there feeling sorry for herself with her boss and fellow cop lying dead. That realization finally got her up, on her feet and headed to the closet to get dressed. If she wasn't dreaming or hallucinating, if Hollis had actually called her with the news of Jarvis's murder, damned if she would sit there weeping while there was work to do.

****

With so many official vehicles of all kinds staggered around the neighborhood, she had to park three blocks down and hoof it the rest of the way.

More cops, paramedics and people from the DA's office than she could count were clustered every which way across the front yard, though most of them avoided the porch. When Helen craned her head in that direction, she saw why.

Jarvis's body lay crumpled in the middle of his porch. Lights flashing every which way allowed Helen, even from a distance, to make out the head wound and the splash of blood and brain matter that decorated the corner wall.

She looked around to see if anyone else from the squad had arrived yet, but couldn't see any, though she did spot a couple of detectives from the West station, whose jurisdiction Jarvis's house fell under.

"Helen."

Hearing Hollis's voice behind her, Helen turned.

"What the hell," she said when he came abreast of her.

Hollis took her elbow and led her off to the side. When they'd made it to a patch of ground under a barren elm tree, he faced her.

"Got to be careful," he said. "The chief's here, and he's ready to let loose on anyone. Roy was bad enough, but now we've got a dead command officer."

"Will they let us investigate?"

"I doubt it. Even before I got here there was talk going around about a special task force. I get the hunch that even West division is going to be frozen out. They'll probably pat us on the head and let us go about our normal cases, including Roy's, but as for looking into Pete here…"

Hollis shuddered, and Helen reached out, placing a hand on his arm.

"Who's in charge right now?" she asked.

Hollis pointed toward the chief, huddling with several of his staff just to the side of the porch. A photographer was taking pictures of the entire area, with most of the attention going to Jarvis's corpse. Off to the side, several tech people were waiting their chance to come in after the photographer and do their thing.

"Any ideas?" Helen asked.

"Naw. When I first got here, I couldn't figure why the boss's car wasn't in the garage. But when I did a walk around, waiting for the brass to show up, I noticed all the ground back there is torn up, like they're doing some construction or something. So I'm guessing for convenience's sake he just pulled up in the driveway and came up to the front door, and whoever was waiting popped him."

Instead of replying, Helen took two steps back and did a survey of the front part of the house. Then she moved even further back and looked over the surrounding area, what she could see of it in the gloom of near dawn.

"How'd you get the call?" she asked. "Wouldn't it have gone straight to West?"

"It did. But the dispatcher recognized the address and called into the station. I happened to still be there when the night desk got the call."

"Did you get a look at the wounds?" she asked.

Hollis nodded. "But not enough of one to be able to tell much. We'll have to wait for the coroner's people to get in and do their thing."

"Best guess?"

"Couple of gunshots to the head, for sure. Definitely more than one shot."

"Caliber?" she asked, sure that Hollis had already made the same jump as she had.

He shrugged. "Could have been a nine. We'll have

to wait for the report."

Even as he said the words, the photographer backed up, did a sideways nod of his head, and moved off. The tech people sidled up to the porch, moving as gingerly as they could in an attempt to preserve as much of the scene as possible.

Having seen them at their work countless times, Helen and Hollis turned away and looked out to the street.

Helen felt her cheeks tighten, and tears began to well in her eyes.

"What?" Hollis asked.

Helen cleared her throat.

"Remember a few years back? How hard he took it when Miranda passed?"

Hollis nodded, his own face starting to look a little strained.

"At least, thank God, she didn't live to see this," he said.

Helen shook her head, as if throwing off an irritant.

"What about the kids? You know if anyone's got ahold of them yet?"

"Aw, Christ," Hollis said. "I hadn't even thought of that. They're going to hear this on the news in no time."

"Any idea where they are?" Helen asked.

"Hell, no. I think Krissy's still in grad school, but no idea where. As for Ken…"

"First chance you get," Helen said, "make a call to the chief's office. Surely someone up in HR has the info. But we've got to make those calls quick."

Hollis nodded, his face, outlined by the blinking strobes around him, looking almost skull-like.

"There's something else we have to consider,"

Helen said. "I know it's crossed your mind."

Hollis frowned and hunched in a bit at the shoulders.

"It's not going to be our case, Helen. So whatever we may think—"

"It may be more our case than we may want to accept. Come on, Jack. You're too good of a cop not to face it."

At the sound of a clearing throat behind them, the two turned to face Police Chief Allan Howard.

Helen hadn't been this close to the man since the day, over nine months before, when she'd been called into his office for the official reaming out over her handling of the Green debacle. At the time, she'd been the lowest-ranked person in the room, and judging by the faces of most of them, she'd been lucky to get out of there with her badge, let alone keeping her rank.

Standing outside the boss's house in the cold, Helen couldn't help but recall that Jarvis had stood by her side that day, doing his best to advocate on her behalf. When they'd finally left the chief's office, Jarvis had waited till they were in the elevator. Then this staid, professional man, who in nearly half a decade of working for him Helen had never heard utter even the mildest profanity, even in those times when the squad room seemed to be falling down around them, turned and gave her a broad wink.

"Fuck 'em," was all he'd said.

But it had been enough.

Now, the chief sent a nasty, hard glance her way before turning and speaking directly to Hollis.

He didn't even look Helen's way again, though she stood only a foot or so removed from Hollis.

"Detective Hollis," he said, "I want you to get the

word out to everyone on your squad. They're to assemble at Central by seven this morning. We'll do some realigning then and get things started."

"Sir," Hollis said, "some of us are working two or three cases, including Roy's case, and at least two I know of haven't seen their families in something like forty-eight hours."

"Can't be helped, detective. Get them all down there by seven. We're going to have to discuss how to reapportion resources."

"Meaning?" Hollis asked.

The chief raised an eyebrow, and even in the early morning murk, Helen thought she saw his face turn a little red.

"Meaning just what I said, detective. If you haven't noticed, your squad commander just got butchered outside of his home. It's time for someone to step in and take control of this thing."

Without another word he turned to walk away, but only made it about three yards before turning around.

"One other thing." He gestured to the outer perimeter, now beginning to fill with television vans. "Spread the word that no one, and I mean no goddamned one, is to talk to the media. If they do, I'll nail their asses to City Hall."

This time, when he walked away he didn't look back.

"Just great," Hollis said. "Now they're going to send someone in to tell us what a horrible job we've been doing. Tell me there's some kind of silver lining in all this."

"Actually, Jack, it may be even worse than it seems."

Hollis blanched. "Worse? Jesus, Helen, how the hell could this get any worse?"

"Take a good look around. And don't tell me you didn't pick it up earlier."

Hollis's shoulders hunched. "I don't know what—"

"Sure you do. Surely you see how familiar this looks."

Hollis relaxed a bit, as if accepting the inevitable.

"Yeah," he said, "but I didn't want to come right out and say it."

"We've got to, though. We've got to let the chief, or whoever he puts in charge of the squad, know."

"And just how does that conversation go? How do we let them know that we think someone's gunning for cops, that we've got another serial killer, the second in less than two years?"

CHAPTER TWENTY

Helen headed back to her car. She could do nothing at the crime scene, and if anything, would just be in the way.

A feeling she'd gotten all too familiar with over the last several months, one that she didn't feel like experiencing this night.

Or rather morning, since there weren't that many hours till dawn, and the required meeting down at the station house.

Reaching her car, Helen merely unlocked it and sat motionless inside. She naturally should be headed home, but for what reason? She wouldn't be able to get back to sleep, and had nothing to do until the meeting in a few hours.

The tension of the last few days, the unexpected call from Hollis and, more than anything, the sight of the boss's body slumped on his porch, had her nerves so frayed and exhausted that she could barely keep her head up.

At any moment, and probably soon, she would simply crash and burn.

But not, she silently vowed, until they'd gotten this mess resolved. She needed to shed this pathetic blanket of stress and move forward to resolve Roy and Pete's murders.

Her cell phone buzzed from her jacket pocket.

At this hour, it could only be something more about the case.

And it was, but not in the way she'd expected.

"Hello?"

"Helen, hey. It's Tim Johnson. You got a minute?"

Helen groaned. Johnson, a reporter for the local paper, had been an off and on acquaintance for years. But ever since her downturn with the department, Helen had done her best to avoid any of the local media people, no matter how innocuous the occasion.

"Tim, this isn't a good time. I'm at—"

"I know," Johnson cut her off. "I'm there too. About halfway down the street from your car, opposite side."

Helen glanced down the street, and as she did so a pair of headlights several houses down flicked on and off.

"So?" she said.

"So I think we need to talk. Say Murphy's in about twenty minutes?"

"Tim," she said, slow and deliberate, "I can't tell you anything. The chief gave us a definite muzzle."

"So don't talk, just listen. How about it?"

Almost randomly, a slow burn developed in Helen's gut. Irrational, she knew, but it angered her that her caller automatically assumed she had nothing better to do with the rest of the night than spend it in his company at a seedy, all-night place.

But she managed to tamp the anger down, mainly with the understanding that he was, in fact, correct.

"Well," Johnson asked. "What about it?"

The chief had given his orders, no ambiguity at all in what he wanted.

Once again, the scene in the elevator with her and

Jarvis nine months before flashed before her.

"Fuck 'em," the boss had said, and she could almost hear him saying it now.

"Murphy's," she said. "One drink. Twenty minutes."

CHAPTER TWENTY-ONE

LOS ANGELES

Lawrence Sears pulled his car into an empty slot in the apartment complex and killed the engine. He spent a few minutes staring up at a window on the third floor of the nearest building. It had been dark for several hours, and he'd only left the office about twenty minutes earlier.

Since the old man died, the nights kept getting longer and longer.

A slight burning in his stomach reminded Lawrence that he hadn't eaten anything since lunch. When it came to hunger, where most people would experience an empty sensation or growling, Lawrence felt burning. No doubt a sign of something, maybe an incipient ulcer. He really should have it checked out. After all, he had access to the best doctors. Might as well use them.

Except that he kept putting it off. Partly out of simple male obstinance and partly because of not daring to take the chance of being incapacitated.

The idea of just how much things would fall to hell if the condition really were something serious kept him up nights as well.

Despite what Morton had said, and Lois's seeming faith in the security man, Lawrence wanted to see for himself, to make sure that Andrew really had taken off again.

Goddammit, why couldn't Andrew come to his senses?

Lawrence opened the door and climbed out of the car. Getting into the apartment wouldn't be a problem, but he wasn't all that sure he wanted to face what awaited inside.

The building only had the three floors, so with no elevators he headed up the stairs, praying he wouldn't meet anyone coming or going. Although not a public figure, even so, he didn't want any possible link between himself and this building.

He'd originally considered having Morton send one of his goons to check it out, but had decided against it. Andrew was his responsibility, come what may, even if some people, most notably Lois, claimed that for the last several years Lawrence hadn't done a very good job of managing that responsibility.

Exiting the stairwell, Apartment #28 lay about halfway down the hallway. Lawrence had never been inside before, let alone in the building, but he had checked out the complex's web site ahead of time, giving him a detailed understanding of the floor plan.

Standing in front of the door he paused, much as down in the car, and reached into his pocket to finger the key.

It was a single key, never before used and not even on a ring, and as he ran his fingers up and down the length of it, Lawrence worked to get his courage up. But it wasn't until a door opened at the end of the hall that he quickly pulled the key out, inserted it into the lock, and sighed with relief as the door swung open.

Just as someone walked out of the other apartment, he slid inside and out of sight.

Flipping on the nearest light switch, he turned to survey Andrew's home.

Even before turning on the light he sensed that no one was there. Aside from the gentle background hum of the refrigerator, the place held a silence that felt absolute.

Lawrence had half expected a dog to come yapping up to him. Andrew had always been a sucker for dogs, in his youth often bringing half a dozen strays home a year. The fact that there was no animal in the place, and no sign of any pet, made Lawrence pause and wonder if, this time, the kid was so far gone that he couldn't be brought back.

The apartment took the form of a loft, its ceiling reaching about twice as high as a normal apartment ceiling and, while not that wide, the room did stretch a considerable distance in length.

Minimal furniture: a black leather couch, matching recliner and dining room table with only one chair alongside. No TV and no sign of any radio or music player. No computer, though Morton had mentioned that they'd been examining Andrew's laptop, so that made sense.

The tall windows had no drapes or sashes, but walking up to them Lawrence noticed the windows looked out over an empty office building.

No prying neighbors who could peek in.

In the far corner rested a trestle-style bed that held a mattress, but no sheet set or cover.

The whole place, so Spartan and minimalistic, made Lawrence catch his breath as he couldn't deny the truth any longer.

The apartment felt too empty, too desolate. Andrew wasn't just laying low, avoiding his usual haunts.

He was gone.

Once again.

CHAPTER TWENTY-TWO

Murphy's, an all-night place that operated just outside of city jurisdiction, was relatively quiet at this time of the early a.m. Walking in, Helen didn't have any trouble spotting Johnson, a gangly six-footer with a smattering of freckles across his prematurely bald scalp.

"I'm not supposed to be talking to you," she said, sliding into the booth opposite him.

Johnson looked up from a plate of huevos rancheros liberally sprinkled with jalapenos and grinned. "Since when?"

"Since the chief threatened to nail anyone to City Hall who talked to the press."

"He actually said that. Nail them to the Hall?"

"Actually, he said 'nail their asses' but I decided to clean it up for you. I probably shouldn't have worried. How the hell can you eat all those peppers this early in the day?"

"It's late night for me. We just put the paper to bed about an hour ago, right about the time the call came in about Jarvis. Sorry about that, by the way."

Helen nodded.

Along with the food, he had a tall glass that held some sort of multi-colored cocktail. She remembered that Johnson liked to drink the kind of extreme, sickly-sweet drinks that most people had never heard of. Any girl would kill for the secret of how he kept his weight down.

"I didn't think you had to work these kinds of hours anymore. Don't reporters get out of there before the paper starts running?"

Johnson grinned again and scooped up a forkful of eggs and rice.

"You're right," he said, in between chews, "most of the time. But I've been working on a few stories that are kind of hot, and I just happened to be there this late."

Helen didn't entirely believe him, but Johnson had never really deceived her before, even though he did sometimes play it kind of close.

"So what is it you want, Tim?"

The reporter chewed his food carefully, then slurped his drink.

"You guys've got problems, Helen."

A waitress headed their way. Johnson looked at Helen, who shook her head, and he waved the girl off.

"We've got problems? You talk like that's news."

Johnson nodded and drank some more.

"Michaels was bad enough. That had to hit you guys hard. And God knows there's been enough anti-police stuff cranked up around the country in the last year or so. But a plainclothes detective? Not even on duty, but killed outside his home? Pretty damned rough."

"What's your point, Tim? I was jerked out of bed at two in the morning, and I'd really like to get back there. So can we just cut the crap and get to it?"

Johnson grinned and scooped up more food.

"You're not going back home, and we both know it. Jarvis turns it around completely. We're not talking someone ticked off at a particular cop. Now you've possibly got another serial on your hands, and by noon tomorrow the entire town's going to know it."

He sat back as if he'd just turned over a royal flush.

"I'm not going to confirm or deny anything," Helen said, "at least not at this point. But if you called me, there must be something you want."

"Actually, it's not like you think, Lipscomb. We've done each other a turn or two over the years, but I realize that neither of us trusts the other very much."

"So what's the point, Tim? Why am I here?"

"Because I think I may have a lead for you to pursue."

Helen leaned forward and steepled her hands on the table. "Let's assume for a minute that I'm on the lieutenant's case."

"And Michaels," Johnson put in. "Assuming they're connected."

"Not necessarily, but let's go ahead and play it that way. What's your lead?"

"Understand this is just a total brainstorm. Literally came to me in a freakin' second when I heard about Jarvis. Bolt from the blue type of thing."

"Okay."

"It doesn't seem likely to me that you've got some random psycho here. It's too planned, too much information being used."

Helen nodded.

"Again, this came to me in a rush, and maybe I don't have all the boxes checked, but seems to me you're dealing with someone intelligent, someone who knows how to go about things in a methodical, orderly, almost researched approach."

Helen felt a faint tremble at the base of her spine.

"Still with me?" Johnson grinned, making Helen

wonder just how much he was enjoying this. "Then I'd say the other trait you're looking for is someone with a grudge against your department, in particular against the detective squad of the Central division."

That initial tremor intensified.

"What are you saying, Tim?"

He grinned again, but without much mirth.

"What's the latest you hear out of Ronald Green?" he asked.

CHAPTER TWENTY-THREE

Helen walked into the squad room shortly before seven. Jack had managed to spread the word, seeing as how everyone, in various stages of wakefulness, had assembled.

Helen looked around, didn't see Hollis, and moved over to the coffee machine. She poured herself a cup, then sat behind a desk that had been temporarily assigned to her.

Janey Turner ambled over and sat in the rickety chair next to Helen's desk.

"Pretty bad?" Janey asked.

Helen nodded, not quite trusting herself to be able to speak about the morning's events. She'd thought of calling Hollis about her meeting with Johnson, but decided it better to fill him in in person.

Provided she had the opportunity to do so.

"How long did you work under the boss?"

"Five years," Helen said, working to keep the catch out of her throat.

"Jack didn't say much when he called. Just that everyone had to be here. Any idea what's going on?"

"Nothing for sure," Helen said. "And last I knew Jack doesn't either. Not for sure. But I'd say the first thing is going to be a new commander."

Hollis wandered in at that point, a boxful of files in his arms. Even though their department was as computerized as any other in the country, cops, even those of the millennial generation, could not quite break themselves from the habit of actually having paper files in front of them to handle. Helen didn't know for sure, but she was willing to bet that these days police departments were the top customers for companies producing old-fashioned typewriters.

Hollis walked into Jarvis's office and placed the files on his desk then came back out and walked over to join Helen and Janey. Without speaking, the others began drifting over to join the group.

"Downstairs?" Janey asked.

Hollis nodded.

"I'll tell you now, it doesn't look good. Judging by the people collecting down there I'd gather…"

Before he could finish, the elevator doors opened up and three men walked into the squad room.

Helen recognized all three of them, including one she'd seen from a distance but never spoken with.

Chief Howard glanced at the crowd gathering around Helen's desk, then moved over to the center of the room.

"If I could have your attention, please."

Helen considered it an inane request. As soon as the three had entered, everyone's attention had turned their way. It struck her as a trivial little power play. Instead of joining the detectives, he wanted all of them to come to him.

Which they did, because what else are you going to do when the head man himself stands there waiting?

Behind, and a bit to the side of Chief Howard, was the mayor, Louis Dingal, a slight, accountant-looking type with thinning hair. Not a true politico, Dingal had been an administrative aide to the previous mayor, who'd suffered a heart attack about four months before. The city council had voted him in as interim until a new election could be set up.

And then there was the third man.

"First," said Chief Howard, "I want to extend condolences to all of you. This department took a hell of a hit this morning."

"And the other day," someone muttered in the background.

Howard nodded, his face impassive.

"Yes. Believe me, we're not forgetting about Detective Michaels. But this is obviously an unusual time, and we need to get on top of it. So, after some discussion with Mayor Dingal, I'm appointing a temporary person to take over Lt. Jarvis's command."

Howard stepped to the side and ushered the third man forward.

Fairly young, not over forty, with a full mane of black hair and wearing an obviously-tailored suit, the man stepped up alongside of the chief.

"I'm sure he's familiar, but just in case, this is Captain Frank Kendal. Capt. Kendal is currently head of the Special Operations office, and he's agreed to take over the Central squad, temporarily, during this crisis."

Helen forced herself to breathe. Despite its militaristic name, Special Ops was a brainchild of the former mayor, an attempt to "define and refine" the department's image with the community. In other words, basically a PR operation, it worked as an adjunct to the mayor's office. In the sixteen months since its inception, SO had set up a series of "community interfaces," "retroactive public alignments," and "special tactical engagements" with the various populations of the city.

Special Ops had been set up just about the time of a highly-publicized, and nationally-criticized, police shooting in one of the adjacent towns. At the time, most regular cops had bristled, seeing it as another check on them doing their job in the best way possible. And while in the first month or so, SO had made a lot of noise and garnered a great deal of media attention, not always of the best kind, it had eventually settled down and, for the most part, become unseen and unheard.

Except for one particular instance.

Certain voices within the Special Ops office had, some months back, begun pushing for a more aggressive investigation of Helen's conduct during the Ron Green business.

And now the head of that office was her immediate supervisor, at least for the moment.

Kendal looked them over.

"Like the chief said, this is going to be rough for a while. You'll have a permanent commander eventually, but for now we have to keep things going as smoothly as possible."

"I'm not going to micro manage either Capt. Kendal or the rest of you," Chief Howard said, "but we might as well face what's coming at us head on. Obviously, the investigation into Lt. Jarvis's death has barely begun, and ordinarily I wouldn't speculate until we have hard facts, but the captain, the mayor, and I have talked this over, and we believe it's best for all of you to hear the worst."

Helen glanced at Hollis, wondering if he'd spoken to the brass about their hunch.

"While the evidence is obviously still coming in,"

Howard continued, "there are indications that Jarvis was killed with a nine mm weapon. We'll know more in a couple of hours. Obviously, I put a rush on the autopsy and ballistics, but you all can no doubt see where this may be heading."

"Someone in this city is gunning for cops," Lou Whitmore said.

"That's a distinct possibility, detective. But even worse, so far it looks like they're coming after just plainclothes. As soon as we get lab results back on the lieutenant, we'll know more."

"Which could take days," Lou said.

"Obviously," said the chief, "considering the sensitive nature of this the lab's giving it top priority."

"Any plainclothes?" Richie Lattimer spoke up from the background.

"Excuse me?"

"Are they hunting detectives, or just from this station? Considering there's three main divisions in the city, we've got to look at the fact that both killings were from our crew."

"That's possible," Kendal broke in, "but the most important thing right now is to know whether or not there's a match on the bullets. If there is, then we'll move on from there."

"Even if no match," Hollis said, " they could be the same person and different guns. There's a definite pattern with both Roy and the lieutenant. If someone is gunning for us, do we continue the investigation or send it over to the state or county?"

"That's under discussion at the moment," the mayor spoke up for the first time. "Chief Howard and I have put in a call to the state attorney general. We haven't heard back yet, so we'll just have to cross that bridge when we get there."

"Probably for all of you the hardest part," Kendal said, "is that we need you to go about your jobs as normally as possible. Obviously, we want you to take extra precautions, but we can't just suspend cases indefinitely."

Helen looked around at the squad. Before her exile, she'd worked with some of these people a short time, others for years. The thought that any of them, or even herself, could potentially be a target gave her a queasy feeling.

"We'll be drawing up new duty rosters and rotations," their new supervisor continued, "and until we see just how much of a part we'll play in this matter, the chief's agreed to bring in some extra people from both West and East divisions, just to ease the load a bit."

"Are we going to have room for all of them here?"

Helen grinned at Janey's remark, but Kendal ignored it.

"I'll be meeting with each of you briefly, going over your current loads and deciding on any reassigning. For now, go on about your work, and we'll have the new rosters up by noon."

The chief and mayor turned toward the squad room door when Lattimer raised his hand.

"Yes?" Kendal asked, causing the two other officials to turn back.

"Roy's memorial is this morning."

For a moment no one spoke, and the remark seemed to hang in the air.

The chief began to move forward when Kendal spoke up.

146

"I understand. What time is it?"

"Ten," Helen spoke up, wondering why the man didn't automatically know that.

For a second Howard gazed at her, as if unsure of her presence there.

"Then all I ask," Kendal said, "is that you return as quickly as possible. We've all been to a few of these and know they can become an occasion to unwind and let down. But we don't have time for that."

He now made a point of sweeping the room and meeting everyone's gaze directly.

"None of us do. And please, when you're outside of this station be as careful and proactive as you can be. We don't want to lose anyone else."

With that, the meeting broke up. The chief and mayor headed out, and Kendal made his way to Jarvis's office. Helen was trying to think of a way to get Hollis alone and fill him in on her talk with Johnson, when Kendal stopped in the doorway and looked back at the assembled troops, who still stood clustered together.

"Get to it, folks," he said, his voice a bit sterner than a moment before. "And, Detective Hollis? Could I see you for a moment inside?"

CHAPTER TWENTY-FOUR

Hollis exited the office about ten minutes after he went in, and Helen took the first chance she had to get to him.

"Here," she said, standing over his desk and handing him one of two coffee cups she held. "You've had a long night."

Hollis took the coffee. "Not the first one lately."

Helen glanced both ways, saw no one within earshot, then plopped down in the metal-frame chair next to his desk.

"And it may not be over," she said.

"What?" Hollis asked, grimacing.

Helen jerked her head toward the squad room door, then got up and left.

Her partner followed, taking his coffee with him.

****

"Christ, Helen. What the hell were you thinking?"

The two of them were ensconced in a stairwell corner on the second floor of the station. One with, at this hour, no foot traffic either up or down.

"Calm down, Jack."

"Bullshit, calm down. Didn't you hear the chief just, hell, a couple of hours ago, tell us to steer clear of the press?"

"Johnson called me."

Hollis glared at her.

"What the hell difference does that make?"

"No difference." Now Helen worked to put an extra amount of steel into her tone. "What I'm saying is that he's already come up with a theory of the case."

"So what? What's he going to do, write something up with no proof?"

"Jack, what did you and Kendal talk about just now?"

Hollis slumped down onto one of the stair risers and leaned against the wall. He hadn't had a chance to shave yet, and his hair was mussed and rumpled from the day before.

"Well?" she prodded.

Hollis sighed. "First, no shell casings. The guy policed his brass."

"We figured about that with Roy," Helen said.

Hollis nodded. "But it took a while to determine in all that slush. But this was on Pete's porch. Nice and dry. And no brass. Like the chief said, the wounds looked like nines. But not for sure, yet."

"What else?"

"They managed to get ahold of Krissy, so that's taken care of. And like Kendal said, the chief pushed for a hurry-up autop. Results on that should be in pretty quick."

Helen nodded.

"Anything else?"

"Techs are still at it, of course. He never had a chance to enter his house, so that narrows the official scene down quite a bit. But they haven't reported anything in yet."

"What about motivations?" Helen asked.

"That's where we had a bit of a disagreement.

Kendal wants us, or whoever takes over in a day or two, to go through everything we have on both Roy and Pete."

"Huh? What for?"

Hollis looked away for a moment, then turned back to her.

"He wants to see if there's some connection between them, other than the obvious."

Helen took a few seconds to process that. As she did so, a uniformed officer, a young Hispanic woman, came down from the third floor. At first, she looked a bit confused to see them sitting there, but merely nodded a greeting and went on down. Helen waited until the metal door to the lower floor had clanged shut behind the officer.

"What does he mean by some connection? You mean like a case they ran together back when?"

"That's one possibility. But he also wants us to look into whether the two of them had some kind of–he called it an arrangement."

Now it was Helen's turn to slump against the stair rail, realizing that the brass suspected her lieutenant of possibly being corrupt.

"So?" Hollis said. "Your turn. What's Johnson's big idea?"

"Almost as crazy as what you just said. He thinks we ought to look at Ronald Green."

"Shit," Hollis said.

And that, Helen thought, pretty much summed up the whole situation.

THE AVENGER–AFTER THE SECOND

He woke up, as before, around noon the day after his second kill. No nightmares this time (they always stopped after the first encounter) and with a roaring appetite. He'd expected to sleep later, seeing as how his latest exploit had taken place during the late hours of the night, but the internal alarm clock that had regulated his movements for all these years had him springing out of bed at the standard time.

With, he noted, a raging hard on.

It had been quite a while, over a year in fact, since he'd experienced this particular sensation upon awakening. Too young to have any natural deficiencies in that department, he'd worried about it for a while, and had in fact considered going to see a doctor. But after careful consideration decided not to.

Even if he'd consulted one of the doctors approved by the Company, too much chance of some kind of publicity getting out.

The Avenger knew that his name would attract attention, and even trusted doctors would be tempted to let information leak to the media. So any medical problem, as long as it didn't become debilitating, he simply swept under the rug.

If nothing else, a known physical ailment would give the Company one more reason to lock him away.

But this particular malady, at least if this morning

151

were any indication, had passed.

He wondered, as he stepped into the shower stall and turned the knob nearly all the way to the left, if his actions of the last several months had not brought about some metamorphosis, a change in his very makeup, that would soon elevate him to a higher level.

The water slammed down, stinging him with its near-boiling barbs. Lifting his face to the spray, he succumbed to the overwhelming onslaught of the shower.

A higher level? Something beyond ordinary humanity? It sounded insane, or would if he broached it to anyone. And yet…

If such were the case, he figured while slathering soap over his frame, then the next several days, as he took out the rest of his targets, would really be something to see.

Because, one way or another, all of them, all those responsible for so much pain and turmoil in the lives of others, were going down.

Eventually, even his hardened tissue could take no more, and The Avenger shut off the spray, stepped out of the stall and began toweling himself off.

The towel, as was often the case in higher-end hotels (and why deprive himself by staying in anything less?) was plush and bouncy. So he had to rake it extra hard across his form in order to work up the stinging, scraping sensation he desired.

When finished, between the heat of the shower and the regimen with the towel, his skin tingled, almost screeched, allowing him to feel more alive than he had for some time.

Walking naked into another room in the suite, the

Avenger sat on a black leather couch, reached out and booted up his second laptop, one the Company didn't know about.

Opening up the folder for this city, he began scanning the files.

Time to decide who would be next. Although his targets were plentiful, their numbers had quite naturally begun to diminish.

After some minutes, he'd narrowed his options down to three, their profiles lined up side by side on his screen. He flicked his gaze back and forth over the three, absorbing all the information he'd managed to acquire in the few short days he'd been on scene.

Finally, his attention fixated on the profile on the far right. With a few key strokes, he relegated the other two back to the folder and enlarged the remaining file to fill the screen.

Yes, the Avenger thought, settling back on the soft, brushed leather, luxuriating in the feel of the animal hide on his own naked skin.

That's the one.

For sure.

The mere thought began engorging his flesh all over again.

Target number three would be really good.

CHAPTER TWENTY-FIVE

Everyone returned to the station around noon. Although wearing standard work clothes, rather than more formal dress wear, all had black armbands stretched around their right biceps. Most of them usually wore clothing closer to dress casual, with on any given day an assortment of sports clothes, knit shirts, jeans and slacks parading around the squad room. Like most female detectives, Helen and Janey rarely wore skirts, slacks and low slung shoes being much more practical for physical activity when required.

And while before the ceremony nearly all would have preferred going home to change into dressier outfits, the necessities of the day didn't allow for such luxuries.

Even if, as they all knew, the time they had left on the investigations probably numbered mere hours.

Despite Capt. Kendal's taking over the squad, most of them assumed there'd be some sort of shakeup before the end of the day.

Still, they determined to make as much progress as they could before they had to hand the matter over to interlopers.

But the worst news awaited them as they returned to work.

Shortly after noon, with most of the detectives back at their desks, Kendal opened his office door and stepped out into the common area.

Helen jumped a bit when his door opened. Back when she'd been a permanent member of the squad, Jarvis had, for the most part, always kept his door open, in order to allow a slightly freer flow of information. He would often close it if someone needed to speak in private, but other than that it had been rare to see the boss's door shut. She automatically assumed Kendal had stepped out. Instead, he'd been inside all the time.

Helen's stomach did a slight turn as she realized that, even if she were allowed to remain, working in the squad would never quite be the same again.

"Everyone?" Kendal called out as he strode to the middle of the common area, about equidistant between Hollis's and Lou's desks. "We've got some news."

He held a sheet of notepaper in his hand, though in the next few seconds Helen wondered why. Surely he could have remembered the information easily.

"Chief Howard pushed ballistics, as he promised, not that they needed a lot of pushing, and we got the results on the bullets that killed Lt. Jarvis."

Kendal drew a deep breath, gripping the paper somewhat tighter than necessary from Helen's viewpoint.

"It turns out the same weapon, more than likely an H&K, was used to kill both Michaels and the lieutenant."

Helen's stomach flipped again, and she realized she'd been holding her breath.

"That means we've got a serial killer, again," Richie Lattimer said.

"Not necessarily," Lou piped up. "The feds define serial as at least three kills. We've only got two so far."

"And you think whoever it is will stop at two?"

Helen heard a catch in Richie's voice. One of the younger ones, and somewhere down the line Helen would mope a bit at the fact that she considered herself a veteran, Richie was a flashy kid, proud that he'd made detective and usually flaunting it a bit. But in the last few days they'd been handed a couple of doses of reality, and she figured the kid was growing up damned fast.

"There's actually two main possibilities here," Kendal interjected, "and yes, some sort of serial attacker is definitely one of them. But there's another, more likely possibility, at least at the moment."

Kendal nodded to Jack Hollis, and everyone turned his way.

Helen listened to Hollis with half of her attention, but the other half was cycling rapidly, her meeting earlier that morning with Tim Johnson serving as the foundation.

"With two plainclothes dead," Hollis started off, his voice tight, "we have to naturally consider some sort of revenge-minded serial killer. But as the captain said, at the moment that seems a bit remote. Such a suggestion would imply that the perpetrator is targeting not just cops, and not just detectives, but detectives out of only one of the three divisions in this city. That seems a bit of a stretch."

Unless, Helen mused, Johnson was right, and Ronald Green was somehow involved, taking out various members of the squad that had helped ruin his life.

Helen shook her head, forcing herself to pay attention.

"What's more likely," Hollis continued, "is that someone was after both Roy and Pete specifically. That there's some connection between them, and we need to find out what it is."

"Did they ever work any cases together? Or was Pete already boss when Roy came on?" Janey asked.

"There's a bit of overlap," Hollis said, "which will help. Not here, but there was about a six-month period when they were both assigned to the East division, so there may be something there. But we've been spending the last several days running down Roy's old cases, and nothing's come of it. So it feels like an awful long shot. But the captain and I have been talking, and there's another angle we need to seriously consider."

"We've heard about that one," Hal Smith spoke up. Hal, a fairly average-looking guy of about thirty-five, was one of the quiet ones who hardly ever put in a comment.

But they were all, Helen reflected, probably acting a little out of character today.

"We've heard it," Hal repeated, "but we aren't really going to go there, are we, Jack?"

Kendal seemed to have faded out of the picture, even though he stood only a few feet away, as everyone looked to Hollis.

"We have to go there, Hal. I don't like it any more than you, but we have to consider all the possibles. And one of the possibles, uncomfortable as it is to believe, is that Roy and Jack may have some connection, either now or in the past, that's not exactly on the up and up."

It was a nice little euphemism, Helen thought, but it didn't take the sting out of his words.

"How long," Helen asked, "before this gets taken over from us?"

Now they all turned to Kendal.

"I haven't heard any more from the chief in that regard," the captain said, "but I think it's safe to guess that we're on a short string. I have heard about an emergency meeting of the town council this afternoon, and we may know more after that.

"Hollis here was the primary for the Michaels case, and since the two are linked, I'm keeping him as the primary for both. At least, of course, until we hear different."

Looking around the squad room, Helen saw a few perfunctory nods, quite a few slumping shoulders, and not a single happy look among the lot.

CHAPTER TWENTY-SIX

The confessors began appearing later that day. They hadn't shown up after Michaels's death. But a police lieutenant murdered at his home received major exposure on the news, not just locally but nationally. Add in the various pieces of bad publicity that police around the country had received in the last several months, plus the fact that Jarvis had been in charge of the detectives who had pursued the notorious Ronald Green case, and you had a combination that ensured maximum exposure.

And along with that came the confessors.

In a way, Hal Smith considered as he sat at his desk and began interviewing the man who had showed up at the station a few minutes before, it would have been worse in the past. These days, a lot of confessing was done via social media of various sorts, so at least initially the investigators didn't have to sit and listen to long-winded, bizarre explanations for the crime in question. On the other hand, the ease of using social media geometrically increased the number of confessions that appeared.

But here one sat right in front of his desk, and while Hal was naturally skeptical of anyone who simply walked into a police station confessing to a crime, he had to admit that the man facing him didn't really look like the stereotype.

No unwashed hair, splotchy complexion from living in mom's basement, or bloated gut hanging over a worn pair of Dockers.

Dude even had all of his teeth.

"Name," Hal said while jotting down notes on a legal pad.

"Anthony Cent."

"Age?"

"Forty-two."

Hal paused. The man, around five ten and with a full head of blond hair, looked thirty-five at most. He wore blue jeans, tee shirt, and a black leather blazer and had either just recently shaved or was naturally light-bearded. Middle of the afternoon and no trace of stubble.

"Forty-two?"

"That's right." Neither smiling nor frowning.

Hal thought the fellow looked kind of bored by the whole thing. "Are you married, Mr. Cent?"

"I was. But my wife and I separated a few years ago. The divorce was finalized last month."

Hal drew a heavy line under the word "divorce," intending to come back to it later.

"What do you do for a living?"

For the first time, some animation appeared in the man's face. His eyebrows crooked upward and a faint grin appeared.

"Are you sure you want to know that, detective?"

Hal worked to keep his expression neutral.

"It's part of the standard question set," he said. "Is there something wrong with telling me?"

"No, it's just that it may not be the safest thing for you to know what I do for a living."

Hal leaned back in his chair and did a quick scan of

the squad room. With everyone having half a dozen jobs to do and the promised help from West not yet having shown up, at the moment the squad room was almost empty. In a far corner, a civilian employee worked with a computer, and Hal could see the captain's profile in the window of his closed office.

Other than that, he was alone with Mr. Cent.

"That wasn't a threat, was it, Mr. Cent?"

The confessor smiled and placed his hands palms down on his thighs.

"Not at all," the pleasant young man said. "Actually, it was me looking out for you. The knowledge could be dangerous just to possess."

Hal was now convinced he had a false confessor sitting across from him. Ordinarily, they were fairly harmless. Usually just lonely people looking for a little excitement. They never came out for ordinary crimes, but when something unique came along, a case that caught headlines and had a bit of spice to it, look out.

"Well," he said, wanting to keep the man talking, "I guess I'll just have to take that chance, won't I? How about telling me your occupation?"

The young man looked all around, no doubt seeing the same empty squad room as Hal saw, before leaning forward.

"I'm a spy," he said.

Although it almost hurt to do so, Hal kept his face straight.

"A spy?" he said.

"That's right."

"I'm guessing you wouldn't tell me the name of the agency you work for?"

The young man looked around again before turning

back to Hal.

"I don't think that would be wise, no."

"Okay, so how about telling me exactly why you're here?'

"It's about those two officers. The ones who were killed recently?"

"Yes, what about them?"

"I think I know who did it."

Hal took a deep breath. From this point on, he had to go cautiously.

"How so?"

"Well, it seems to me that they were killed by someone like me."

"Like you?"

"Yeah, another spy."

Okay, possibly one for the books. Usually, confessors offered themselves up as the perpetrator, expecting to bask for a few minutes in fleeting fame. But this guy was going at things a bit differently.

The problem was that, although Hal believed he had a false one here, the book said you had to take them all the way through the steps.

Just in case they turned out to be the real thing.

For the next twenty minutes, Hal did just that. Cent would never say anything that implicated himself directly, but he did provide a detailed explanation of how a trained spy would have gone about stalking the two victims, getting to know their habits, and eventually surprising them at their homes.

Hal took dutiful notes, waiting for something, some slight indicator, that would definitely mark this as a falsie. And about thirty minutes in, he got it.

"Of course," Cent said, "you probably figured out

that something was off because of the gold."

"Gold?" Hal asked.

"Yes. Once you saw the gold you had to know you were up against someone special."

Hal leaned back, taking a moment to process that last statement.

"What gold are you talking about?" he asked.

Cent stared at him, frowning. "Are you involved directly in the case?" he asked.

"Yes."

The confessor now looked worried and darted his gaze back and forth.

"Detective Smith, you may be in real danger. They're keeping you out of the loop. That must be because they don't trust you."

"I'm sorry, Mr. Cent, but what—"

"The gold bullets. The killer used gold bullets. Just like in that old James Bond movie."

Sighing, Hal closed his notebook and stood.

Yep, definitely a falsie.

All that was left now was to escort the man downstairs to be processed.

And maybe ask the captain for some more manpower.

Hal had the feeling this was only the first of many to come.

CHAPTER TWENTY-SEVEN

Tim Johnson logged off his computer and switched off the light over his desk. Barely four o'clock in the afternoon, but the fact that he'd only had about three hours of sleep between meeting with Lipscomb and coming back to work the Jarvis murder made him feel like something the cat had not only drug in, but chewed up then drug back out again.

In the rain.

Right in the path of a rabid pit bull.

No doubt about it old boy, he silently mused, *you're starting to soften up. Been at the game too long and too hard.*

He knew that it happened to all reporters, especially the old-fashioned shoe leather type. Somewhere down the line you'd come upon enough bodies, have enough doors slammed in your face, and have to listen to too many fake politicians spew too much nonsense.

At some point, it had to get to you. And Tim remembered the advice of Jack Grigson, an old hand with one foot already out the door when Tim had first been hired at the *Tribune*.

"You'll know it when you get there, kid. When you have a simple eight-hour day, rare in this biz, that leaves you exhausted and breathing hard. When your favorite food suddenly tastes like shit and your favorite drink at your favorite bar tastes like piss. When your work

164

clothes feel like shackles, kid, that's when it's time to either move out or move up."

As an energetic twenty-three year old, Tim had blown Grigson off, considering him just a bitter, beat-up old man. But today, barely able to keep his head up, he was beginning to understand what the old guy had been trying to tell him.

Standing up, he reached down to the back of his chair and snagged his jacket. It was still on the tail end of winter and pretty damned frigid outside. But Tim had only worn a light maroon windbreaker to work. He rarely wore heavy coats, as you never knew when you'd have to suddenly take off after someone who didn't want to talk to you.

Joe Gardner, the editor of the Metro section, had talked about retiring at the end of the summer, and Tim wondered if he should apply for the post.

Zipping up his jacket, he looked up and saw Tracey Walters, a recent transplant from one of the *Trib*'s sister publications out west, heading his way.

"Tim, got a minute?" she called out.

Tim sighed and strained to keep his shoulders from slumping. So dead tired that he was seriously thinking about just curling up in the janitor's closet rather than attempt the drive home, he'd never felt less like talking to one of the junior staff.

But before he could think of a reasonable excuse to dodge her, the kid stood in front of him. All five feet eight and shoulder-length honey blonde hair.

"What is it, Trace? And make it quick please 'cause I'm about out on my feet."

"Gardner put you on the Jarvis murder, right? Along with Mike?"

"Yeah. The first one, Michaels, was Mike's, but now that it's expanding Joe wants to make sure we've got all the bases covered. Why? You want in on it?"

Tim consciously put a bit of edge into his tone. A slight warning to the new kid–don't try to climb the ladder over me.

"No, not like that." Tracey shook her head, her hands actually shaking in front of him. "But tell me this. Is it true that there was a nine millimeter used in both murders?"

"That's what I hear, but nothing confirmed so far. They haven't officially released the PM yet on Jarvis, but I got a call from a guy who says that's so. So what?"

Tracey nodded, almost as if confirming something to herself.

"Checked your e-mail lately?" she asked.

"No. And I'm sorry to be rude, kid, but I'm on my way out of here and really don't want to think about work for a while. So whatever's bugging you, why don't we take it up—"

"Check your e-mail, Tim. Seriously. Like right now. I just sent you something that I think's going to wake you back up again."

CHAPTER TWENTY-EIGHT

Through unspoken understanding, most of them congregated that night at Larkin's, a restaurant/bar that resided downtown, about three blocks from the central station.

Not all showed up. After all, there were three round-the-clock shifts and other cases still to be worked, but enough of them managed to get away from either work or family commitments that they took up most of the back part of the bar area.

It was a half and half gathering. They were partially there because they hadn't yet had time to properly send off either Roy or the boss, and partially to figure out their next move.

And that second objective held the most peril.

They had a new commander, at least temporarily, but none of them really knew what to think about it.

"Way I see it," someone said from down the table, "the big question is do we stay on it or not. Is that Kendal's call?"

"Naw," Whitmore said. "A decision like that, when you think about it, is really even above the chief. It would be the city council, or maybe the Attorney General, who would decide one way or the other."

"The troopers?" Richie Lattimer asked.

"Ordinarily, it would probably go to the county, but since the city and county are kind of one and the same, well…"

"But would it make sense?" Helen spoke up. Everyone turned to her, ignoring their drinks for the moment. Helen could feel the oddity of her situation like a palpable force. On the one hand, she'd worked with most of these people for varying degrees of time. On the other, she was one of the main reasons they'd taken so much heat from the public over the last several months.

"How do you mean?" Lou asked, throwing her a lifeline.

"Would it make sense for the state police to come in? We're not talking some sort of corruption probe, or a scandal of some kind. When you get right down to it, despite the specifics, this is still a murder case. So where's the justification to turn it over to someone else?"

For a moment, no one answered. Most seemed to be trying to find an answer to her question somewhere in their glasses.

Finally, Second-Grade Detective Manny Thomas, who had transferred over from East a few months back, spoke up. "Do you think Hollis and the cap may be onto something? That there was something going on between Roy and Jarvis?"

If Helen's question of a moment before had been met with silence, Thomas must have felt in the moments after he spoke as if the floor had opened up beneath him. Half of the people at the table turned away from him, while the rest shot glares his way.

Helen, knowing full well how even momentary ostracization felt like, jumped in. "Whether we believe it or not, Jack and Kendal had a point. It has to be looked into. If not, it could come back to bite us down the line."

"You don't really believe that," Janey said.

"Look at it this way. Let's say we catch the person, who killed the two of them for whatever reason. What happens when he, or she, gets to trial, and a defense attorney brings up that a theory was floated but not followed up on? Can you imagine the circus that would follow?"

Nobody had a response to that, and for the next several moments there was silence around the table. Then, a few at a time, people began talking to the person across from them, or next to them, and the conversations followed all the mundane themes of everyday life.

Helen noticed that, for the next few hours that they all stayed together, no one spoke to either her or Thomas.

CHAPTER TWENTY-NINE

Two days later, Tuesday afternoon, Hollis and Helen pulled up about a block away from Rusty's, a bar on the outskirts of town.

Even from that distance, the biker bar vibe nearly slammed them in the face.

"You really think this is worth it?" Helen asked.

"Can't hurt," Hollis replied. "We spent all that time combing over Pete and Roy's work records, and Randy Timson is all that really stood out."

"Kendal kind of talked like this is a long shot."

"Yeah, but the captain isn't the primary, I am. At least for now."

"And this is the best we've come up with?"

"Almost," Hollis said.

The two of them got out of the car and began heading in the direction of Rusty's.

"Only two bikes parked outside," Helen said. "Probably almost empty this time of day."

"That's the idea. Lets us talk to the guy with less chance of interference."

"Bars seem to be where we're going for all our suspects in this thing."

"What can I say? It's where the bad guys are hanging out."

Helen shrugged and followed her partner inside.

****

170

It took several seconds of blinking to get her eyes even partially adjusted to the interior of the place. Standing just inside, she saw Hollis having the same problem. Once they could see, she made out pretty much what she'd figured.

A corrugated tin roof; numerous pages from various porno calendars taped along the walls; a grungy green and white tiled floor; and three fiftyish biker burnout types situated around the place, two in booths and one at the bar.

The man behind the stick looked about as she'd expected. Pushing sixty, at least judging by the amount of gray in his beard and remaining wisps of hair, his huge belly contrasted with the large beefy arms exposed by a sleeveless tee-shirt.

"Recognize him?" Hollis asked.

"Barely. But I think I only saw him once or twice before he retired."

"Same here. Let's go reacquaint ourselves."

When they'd first entered, none of the three customers staggered around the place had bothered to look up, but the man behind the bar hadn't stopped staring at them. Helen had little doubt that he'd pegged them as cops right away, even if he didn't recognize either of them, but so far he'd kept his composure.

She hoped he'd continue to do so.

"Hi there, Randy," Hollis said as they approached. Neither one of them had bothered to flash their badges.

The tough-looking old man stared at them for a minute, then gave the slightest of nods.

"Jack Hollis," he said, "and I'm not sure I remember who you are."

"Lipscomb. Helen Lipscomb."

"Oh, yeah." Timson scratched his head for a moment. "You two were both still in uniform when I left the force. I'm surprised you're still around after that monumental fuckup last year."

Helen shrugged. "Could still happen," she said. "Or maybe the suits figure that some fuckups are worse than others."

The bartender grinned at that, then reached down and, pulling out a rag, began wiping the bar top.

"So what can I do for you two?"

"You heard about Pete Jarvis?" Hollis asked.

"Don't have any ears on the force anymore," the burly guy said, "but I still catch the news now and then. Yeah, I heard about Pete."

"What about Roy Michaels?" Helen asked.

Slapping the towel down, Timson propped himself with both hands on the bar and stared them down.

"Of course I heard about him. What's this about, guys? Why are you coming around here asking me this?"

"Well," Hollis began.

"Look around," Timson interrupted. "What you see isn't much, but it's all mine. No thanks to the suits."

His voice had risen toward the end, and a younger, fitter version of him came from a back room somewhere. The guy slouched at the bar had finally raised his head.

Helen lowered her right hand toward the bottom edge of her wool blazer.

"Randy," Hollis said, "we've just got a couple of questions."

Helen noticed Hollis's hand had also lowered toward his hip.

"Let me answer your questions for you, Jack. Without you even asking them. I haven't seen or talked to Pete Jarvis for nearly ten years, Roy Michaels almost as much. The last time Pete and I jacked it was, you could say, acrimonious."

"This would have been around the time of the hearing, right?"

"Actually, about ten minutes before it began. Just long enough for me to tell Pete what a son of a bitch I thought he was."

"The hearing went pretty quick, didn't it?" Helen asked.

"Started at ten and over by noon. About long enough for both Pete and Roy to give their spiel, present their 'evidence' and before you could blink I was an ex cop with no means of support."

Helen looked around again at the dingy surroundings, illuminated only by a couple of 60 watt bulbs placed here and there.

"Looks like you came out the other end," she said.

"Like I said, detective, it ain't much, but it's mine."

"Did you hold any antagonism toward Michaels and Jarvis? After all, you had a pretty sweet deal going until they broke it up on you."

The younger guy who'd come out from the back moved a little forward, and Helen brushed her hand against her hip.

"Let me tell you something, *detective*," Timson continued. "I was mad as hell at those two for a while, but if I'd wanted to do anything about it, I would have done it then. If for no other reason than enough other people got swept up in it that I could have easily spread the blame. Or the credit, depending on your point of view. But when it came down to it, you could say it was my fault for misjudging Roy."

"How so?" Helen asked.

Timson shrugged his massive, though undefined, shoulders.

"I thought he would take me up on an offer to join in. It was quick, easy money. The last thing I figured was that he'd go to a straight ass like Jarvis and tell the whole thing."

"So you had revenge on your mind?" Hollis asked.

"Sure. For all of about ten minutes. But when I got to thinking about it, those two suckers did me a favor. You'll find out yourself some day, Jack. At something like an hour away from all the departmental bullshit, you'll wonder why you ever put up with it."

Then he turned slightly and stared directly at Helen.

"Actually, after all that stuff last year, you'll probably see what it's like quicker than Hollis here."

"And I'm guessing," Hollis said, "that you managed to get out with enough to buy this place?"

Timson grinned. "Something like that. I had the cash, and I'm not saying it came from anything as nefarious as pilfering the department's evidence locker. So let's just say I left one life behind for another."

"Yeah," Helen said, "you seem to be doing real well here."

He grinned again, larger this time, and Helen could feel the tension lessening in the establishment.

"Hell, Lipscomb. This is the wrong time of the day. Drop in around happy hour and see how we're doing."

Helen and Hollis glanced at each other, and both of them relaxed their hands and lowered them down to their sides.

"We may just take you up on that, Randy," Hollis said. "But do us a favor and be available if we have any more questions."

"Always glad to help my former comrades, Jack. You two take care now."

The two cops turned to head out the door, but as they swung it open Randy called out again.

"Oh, Lipscomb, by the way."

Helen turned back to look at the aging, disgraced ex-cop.

"My dirt may have been intentional, while yours was luck of the draw. But take it from an old hand at this sort of thing, they're going to drive you out as surely as they did me."

"You think?" Helen said, realizing the inadequateness of the response.

"I know, detective. You're an open wound, whether you know it or not. And sooner or later the department stitches up all its open wounds. Say the word and I'll keep a waitressing job open for you."

Grimacing, not trusting herself to speak, Helen turned and walked out, Hollis following behind her.

CHAPTER THIRTY

"You know he was just working you, right?" Hollis asked.

About halfway back to the station, they'd pulled up at a red light. He looked over at Lipscomb, who'd been staring out the window the entire time. It took about four seconds after his statement before she turned his way.

"What?"

"Timson," Hollis said. "That crap about being an open wound. He was just trying to work you."

"Of course. But that doesn't mean he wasn't right."

The light turned green, and Hollis turned his attention back to his driving, at the same time searching for the right thing to say.

"You've probably weathered the worst of it," he said. "If they'd really wanted to get rid of you..." His voice trailed off, realizing how inane his words sounded.

"More than one way to cuff a perp, Jack." For an instant, a grin flitted across her expression. "You know as well as I do that getting rid of me would be too public, but that doesn't mean there isn't some notation marked somewhere in someone's office that this is as far as I get on the force."

Hollis wanted to disagree but knew better. More than likely, she was right.

"And on top of that," Helen continued, "and please don't think this is selfishness on my part, but Jarvis was my main defender on the force. Now we have Kendal in charge, at least for now, and after him, who knows?"

"Maybe I'll get lucky," Hollis said, "and they'll promote me up about three ranks at once."

Helen shook her head and returned to staring out the window.

Looking forward, Hollis could see they'd come within sight of the station house, but with traffic thickening up it would take a few more minutes to get there.

"So what do you think of our boy Randy?" he asked.

"Same thing you do," Helen said without turning. "He was telling the truth."

"You think?"

"I'm not saying he didn't have motive, but it would have been some time in the past. Not now."

"Unless there's some sort of precipitating event," Hollis said, "something we don't know about that suddenly made sense to him to do it now."

Helen's eyes narrowed, which Hollis knew to be her "thinking" expression. As he flicked on his signal and began a right turn into the parking garage adjacent to the station, she shook her head.

"Don't buy it, Jack. Too much of a long shot."

Hollis shrugged and negotiated his way up a ramp. Though the city owned the garage, only the two top floors were for official use, which meant that any time they entered or exited it took several minutes. On top of that, both the ascending and descending ramps were so corkscrewed that even someone trained in pursuit driving had to focus all his concentration on safely getting from one level to the next.

Their car was tagged for slot thirty-eight, on the

topmost floor. When they made it safely into the space, Hollis shut the car off and turned to his partner.

"One day at a time, kid. Sooner or later, things will get better."

"Maybe," Helen replied. "But what if that day's a long ways off?"

Hollis shrugged.

"Right about now, I don't see how things could get much worse."

Five minutes later, when they departed the elevator and walked into the squad room, they saw that things had gotten a whole lot worse indeed.

CHAPTER THIRTY-ONE

At the moment, ten or so people were present. When Helen and Hollis walked in, all of them looked up, glanced toward Kendal's closed door, then bent back down to their work. As Helen walked past Janey Turner's desk, the younger woman caught Helen's eye and shook her head.

Helen and Hollis exchanged glances, but they didn't have to spend much time deciphering the room's vibes. They'd made it barely halfway to their desks when Kendal's door slammed open.

Chief Howard stood in the doorway, hands thrust deep in his pockets and face flushed.

"Detective Lipscomb, would you join us please?"

As Helen stepped forward, Hollis moved alongside of her, but Howard held up a hand, his face getting redder by the minute.

"Just her. This doesn't concern you."

Helen looked sideways at her partner and brushed his arm with her hand.

"It's okay, Jack. I'll catch you later."

Hollis frowned, more at her than the chief, then slumped his shoulders and took a step back.

Helen moved forward, and when she got to the door Howard stepped back and ushered her in. As the door closed behind her, she didn't know why the chief was so pissed, but could make a fairly good guess.

****

When the door closed behind them, Kendal went and sat behind Jarvis's desk while Chief Howard took a position against the window, motioning Helen to one of the two chairs in front of the desk.

It occurred to Helen that any other time she would have considered Frank Kendal a fairly attractive man, one she wouldn't mind seeing socially. For now, though, she saw only an usurper in the boss's office.

Illogical, to be sure, seeing as how Jarvis had died days before and hadn't been her supervising officer for months. Even so, for years she'd seen the man in this office every day, and she had trouble getting past the fact of seeing someone else behind that desk.

At the moment, though, Kendal sat stiffly in his chair, no doubt waiting for Howard to begin.

Which the man did without hesitation.

"Detective, do you know a man named Tim Johnson?"

Helen placed her palms flat on her thighs and willed herself to breathe normally.

"Of course," she said. "He's a reporter over at the *Trib*. Been there a long time."

"How well do you know him?"

"Excuse me?"

"Lipscomb," Kendal cut in, "just answer the question."

"I've dealt with him a time or two, like I have most of the front page folks. We're not bosom buddies or anything. Why?"

Kendal looked down at his desk while Howard huffed and puffed a couple of times.

"He called the OPI today. Actually tried to get to

talk to me. Said that he'd been doing some work on the Michaels and Jarvis cases. So tell me, detective. Would his 'some work' include talking with you?"

Helen's brain moved faster than it had in some time. Her encounter with Johnson the other morning had ended about as inconclusively as possible. More than that, she doubted the reporter would have burned her so haphazardly on such a weak foundation. She couldn't really see the upside in his doing so.

"He was at the lieutenant's house the night of the murder," she said. "At least, I'm pretty sure I saw him there in the crowd. But I don't know when was the last time I spoke with him."

Howard moved away from the window a couple of feet, standing closer to her.

"Johnson says he's working on a story that will strongly imply Professor Ronald Green has something to do with the two murders. So tell me, Lipscomb, where would he get such an idea?"

"I'm sure I don't know," Helen replied. "But he sure as hell didn't get it from me. I know your opinion of me is rather low lately, chief. But do you really think I'm that dense?"

Howard and Kendal exchanged glances, and the chief moved back a bit.

"So tell us about Ronald Green," Kendal said.

Helen took in a breath. "Sir?"

"Ronald Green. What can you tell us about him?"

Helen blinked. "I'm sorry, Captain. I don't under—"

"Quit stalling, detective. And fill us in. Now."

Any faintly attractive qualities Helen may have seen in the man blew away like smoke, and now she saw just another bureaucrat who wouldn't let past mistakes go.

"Well, for one thing, he's not a professor anymore. As I'm sure you know, as a result of our investigation last year he lost his job at the university."

"Yes," Howard said. "And from what I understand there was some talk early on about him suing the department for loss of income, slander, and God knows what else. But you wouldn't know anything about that. Right, detective?"

Helen took in a slow, steady breath. "As far as I know, he never instituted a suit."

"True, but I still haven't heard the latest you know about him."

"He moved out of state, Ohio, to take a new teaching job."

"At a high school, right?"

"Yes," Helen paused again.

"So?"

"I'm sorry, captain, but I'm not sure what you want. The last time I spoke with Mr. Green was last summer, a couple of days before he left town. He told me about the new job, asked how Jack was recovering from his injuries, and that was about it."

"And that's the last you've heard from him?"

"Yes."

At this point, Howard spoke up again.

"You can see how this will look to the public. The death of two men in the same department is a little too specific to be some random act."

"Of course," Helen said.

"And then along comes Johnson, a reporter who's been around for a while, and I have to say that his reasoning may be sound.

"Someone out to get detectives," the chief continued. "And if this is what's happening, we're not talking a random psycho. We're talking someone who has done their homework. Someone who not only knew both men were police but managed to find their home addresses. Someone who has some specific antagonism, not against the department but certain people in the department."

"And someone intelligent enough to ferret out information," Helen said as she noted that Howard was using almost the same lines as Johnson had at their meeting.

"Correct. So when we look at it that way, the man's idea isn't so farfetched."

"But he's not publishing yet?"

Howard and Kendal exchanged glances again.

"That's what he says, but he may change his mind at any time."

The room seemed to push in on Helen, causing a prickling feeling on her skin.

"Mr. Green's in Ohio," she said.

"So you say. But it just so happens that this department, and in particular certain of the detectives within it, practically ruined the man's life."

"He had something of a hand in that as well," Helen said. "Looking at the victim's former lover, especially considering he was a married man and their affair didn't end well, is something anybody would have done."

"At this point we're not criticizing procedure, detective," the chief said. "Neither yours nor anyone else's in the squad. At this point. I'm just pointing out that the man would be justified in feeling extremely embittered toward this department."

Helen could almost hear her heart beating.

"So are you agreeing that he may be a suspect in Roy and the boss's murders?"

"For now."

"But that doesn't make any sense," Helen said. "If Green was really out to get the people who ruined him, wouldn't he start with me? Or at least Jack? Jarvis I can possibly see, but Michaels didn't have anything to do with the Amos-Kettering case."

"Maybe he's just striking out at convenience," Kendal interposed. "Looking for any target at all, as long as it's close to this house."

It was a point, but one that Helen couldn't quite envision as valid.

"Weren't you investigating Michaels's widow, at least initially?" Howard stepped back into the conversation.

"Yes. But now, with the lieutenant's death, we figure that's a dead end."

"You mentioned standard procedure a moment ago. And the standard procedure in the Michaels case was looking at people who may have had a grudge. Now with two of our own down, we need to expand the possible definition of 'grudge.'"

Helen clasped the chair's arms.

"That's what Jack Hollis is doing," she protested.

"Maybe so, but considering that he was also involved in the Green affair, he may have a blind spot in this regard, similar to you."

"Chief, I don't want to be out of line, but have you considered what Green may think, or do, if he finds we're investigating him again? You were right before. The city's damned lucky that he didn't take us to the cleaners in court, but I doubt he'd let us go a second time."

Howard nodded, and for a moment his eyes took on a faraway look.

"You may be right," he said, "but even so, it's a definite lead to look into."

Feeling suddenly weary, Helen looked directly at the chief.

"Detective Hollis is still the primary on this, at least for now. Are you overriding him and assigning me to this?"

"Of course not. If it were to become public that we're looking at Green again, having you be the public face of that effort would be—"

"An embarrassment?" Helen prodded.

"At the least. At the best it would be seen as harassment."

"So you brought me in here to…?"

"To see what you know about him. And to clarify that you are in no manner at all to contact Mr. Green and alert him to a possible investigation."

"Sir, my relationship with the man—"

"I know what you *say*, detective," Howard's voice had now taken on a more threatening timbre. "Now I'm telling you how things are going to be. If and when this department begins inquiries into Mr. Green's involvement in these deaths, you are to in no way help or warn him off. All that Johnson would need is to catch wind of that, and everything would be blown to hell. So you stay out of it. Is that clear?"

Helen nodded.

Howard made a kind of dismissive gesture toward her, while Kendal, oddly enough, shot her a somewhat sympathetic, kind of hang-dog look.

But as she turned to leave the office, Helen knew one thing for damned sure.

Regardless of anything, she had to make contact with Green, and let him know what kind of hell was possibly coming his way.

Despite the chief's orders, Helen would, goddammit, *not* be responsible for ruining that man's life again.

CHAPTER THIRTY-TWO

Leaving the captain's office, Helen went to her desk, plotting out the best way to contact Green. A straightforward phone call would do the trick, but if possible, she didn't want any trail leading back to her. If she had to, if there were no way but to lay out clues for them to catch her at it, she would. At the moment, the idea of an IA investigation, let alone losing her shield due to insubordination, didn't really feel like that big of a deal.

Sitting down at her desk, she shook her head, as if to flick a stray wisp of hair out of her eyes. She had to stop leading with emotion. She was so angry at the chief that losing her job would almost seem a blessing, but she knew that, given another day, or even another hour, she would come to her senses. She had to think, not feel, her way through this.

Which still left the question of contacting Green.

Any sort of electronic medium could be traced, and jetting off to Ohio in the middle of a double-murder investigation didn't seem very practical either. Not to mention that, again, there'd be a record for Howard's stooges to find.

If only I had a personal life, she thought, *this would be a lot simpler.*

With a family, even a niece or nephew, she'd have an excuse to take off, throw a couple of sick days together, and be on her way. But right now, in the middle of a crisis, she'd need some kind of solid reason to ask for a couple of days off, the time it would take to drive to Ohio.

A loud thump caused her to glance toward the middle interrogation room.

Along the west wall of the squad room stood six doors. Three of them led to interrogation rooms, while the door to the right of each led to an adjacent observation room. Two of the interrogation room doors stood open, standard procedure when not in use.

At the moment, the squad room was almost empty, and no one else had reacted to the thumping noise. Getting up from her desk, Helen headed to the middle room, but when she grasped the doorknob it wouldn't turn.

Definitely not standard procedure. These rooms were never to be locked. Despite the best of training and protocols, every now and then a suspect managed to sneak in a weapon, usually a knife or other type of edged weapon. The interrogation room doors being locked could prevent officers receiving help at a crucial moment.

Helen reached out and rapped on the door.

"Go away." She recognized Richie Lattimer's voice from inside the room.

"Detective Lattimer," she said, "It's Lipscomb. Open up, please."

A long moment slipped by before the knob turned and the door opened.

But only far enough for Lattimer to look out.

"I'm in the middle of a sit down, Helen. I'll be done with the room in a bit. If you'd just—"

"Let me in, Richie."

The younger detective's eyes shifted to the side.

"*Now*," Helen said.

In the end, the kid really didn't have much choice. Helen held a rank above him in the department. Sighing, Lattimer swung the door all the way open and ushered her in.

"Oh crap," she said as soon as she walked inside.

A young Hispanic male, looking no more than eighteen or so, cowered in the corner of the room. Lattimer was in the room alone, not necessarily a violation of procedure, provided at least one person sat in the adjoining mirror room, which Helen guessed presently stood empty.

She couldn't see any obvious bruises or injuries on the kid, and a chair, overturned against the wall, had probably been the source of the thumping sound she'd heard.

"What's going on, Richie?"

Lattimer tried to pull himself to his full height, but ended up slumping his shoulders.

"I'm conducting an interview," he said.

"By yourself? With no one in the mirror room?"

So far, the kid in the corner hadn't said anything. On the smallish side, wearing faded and ripped jeans and with his black hair spiked up every which way, his eyes darted back and forth in a thin, fox-shaped face.

Helen kept one eye on him. Although he looked harmless as all get out, you never knew.

"I've got this," Lattimer said, and Helen could almost hear his voice cracking with nerves.

"What's the case, Richie?"

"Nothing, Lipscomb. Don't worry. I've got this."

"Richie?"

The younger detective sighed again and slouched his shoulders even more. The Hispanic kid in the corner started to make a move out of it, but Helen glared him back into place.

"His name's Balleno."

"Balleno?"

Helen had never heard such a name, either real or street.

"Yeah," Lattimer said. "I think it means 'whale man' or something like that. Anyway, it's not his real name. Not by a stretch."

"So what's the case?" Helen repeated, her voice a bit louder.

Lattimer turned her way, but not enough to take his eyes off the kid.

"Got a tip from a CI," he said. "Turns out Balleno here's been going around his neighborhood, bragging about how he offed a couple of cops."

Helen was pretty sure the kid hadn't actually used the word "offed," but that wasn't the salient point right now.

"What else?" she asked.

"Huh?"

"I said what else. Just a tip isn't enough to pick someone up on."

Now Lattimer turned back away from her.

"I didn't arrest him," he protested, "just brought him in for a little talk."

Helen glanced at the prisoner, taking note of how badly his limbs shook. The kid's eyes shot back and forth across the room.

"Keep cool," she told him before grabbing

Lattimer's arm and hustling him out of the room. Slamming the door behind them, she backed the younger cop up against the wall.

"Did you Mirandize him?" she asked.

Lattimer pulled himself up to his full height, kind of difficult with Helen leaning into him.

"Look," he said, "it's just—"

"Did you Mirandize him?"

"I was about to when you charged in. If you'd just let me—"

"Like hell," Helen snapped. "What are you thinking?"

The younger detective's face took on a reddish hue.

"I was thinking this was the guy who killed our two people. Or at least, there's a good chance of it."

A couple of other people had wandered into the squad room by this point, and in her peripheral vision Helen could see them glancing her way.

"You actually think a loser like that could have taken out the boss and Roy?"

"I think I was about to find out when you busted in." Lattimer seemed to be getting his second wind, and he actually put his hands on Helen's shoulders and shoved her back. "You don't have any monopoly on experience around here, Lipscomb. And you also don't hold the lease on anger and frustration. So why not back off and let me do my job?"

"Then do it," she snapped back, "but do it right. Before you start knocking around some punk kid off the streets, double-check your info."

"Meaning what?"

Helen exhaled. "Meaning, you don't just take a CI's word for something. First you check, and then you double-check. For instance, any way your CI and our friend there in the room have some connection? Whale in there looks like a gangbanger, though kind of a green one, to me. Is your CI in one of the gangs?"

Lattimer's eyes darted back and forth, and once again he seemed to deflate a bit.

"Yeah," Helen continued, "and I'm guessing they're in different gangs, right?"

"Uhm," Lattimer had begun to pale.

"What's up?" Lou Whitmore had just come across the squad room.

"Richie has someone in the interview room. And he'd like you to sit in on it. Isn't that right?"

As the younger cop nodded his head, Lou gave Helen a long, searching look.

"That's it?"

Helen nodded.

"So why can't you sit in with him?"

"I've got an appointment I have to keep. But Richie may or may not have a live one here, and no one's as good as you at intimidating people without laying a hand on them."

She was speaking to Lou, but with the last words she glanced in Lattimer's direction.

Lattimer nodded.

"Yeah, Lou. Far as that goes, it's a long shot, so it should only take a few minutes to shake the truth out of this guy. Mind sitting in with me?'

Lou glanced at Helen again, then back to Lattimer.

"Sure, kid. I'll sit in. Probably be easier to get answers with two of us instead of one."

CHAPTER THIRTY-THREE

Los Angeles

Lawrence Sears was late arriving at the house. A sudden crisis in the office, which turned out to be not quite as serious as he'd first thought, had taken up more time than he'd planned. If he were honest with himself, he didn't really want to confront what awaited him at the house.

But some things can only be delayed, never deferred, and so late in the afternoon on Tuesday he wound his way up the crushed-shell drive and up to the porticos that flanked the front entrance.

To Lawrence, the damned place had always looked completely out of kilter. A Southern Gothic mansion set in the midst of California. Considering that the last several owners had been born and bred on the West Coast, how the heck anyone had claimed a connection with antebellum days was beyond him.

He always came out here grudgingly, mainly because Lois seemed to enjoy his discomfort once he was inside. She liked to flaunt to people the things she considered important in life, and she clearly saw the house as a symbol of those important things.

Namely, money, power and obligation.

****

Entering the main family room, Lawrence noticed

that Lois hadn't yet arrived. He cocked an eyebrow at Trevor Morton, the only person in the room.

"She not here?"

"Actually," Morton replied, "Mrs. Sears has come and gone."

"Without getting your report?"

Morton squirmed a bit. "She did receive it. But she wanted me to fill you in and have you decide the next course of action."

From someone else, this would have seemed like a vote of confidence in his ability to handle things. But instead, Sears, knowing Lois as he did, figured the old woman may be hoping that Lawrence would mangle the Andrew mess, allowing her to cut Lawrence out of her life for good.

"So I guess I have to go over it all again?"

Lawrence noted the distinct tone of disdain in Morton's voice and thought of rebuking the man. But he tamped it down.

"If you wouldn't mind."

He headed toward a wet bar tucked away in a corner of the room. With a swiftness that came from much practice, he mixed himself a brandy and soda. He glanced at the other man for a moment, raising his glass, but Morton only shook his head.

Lawrence shrugged and sat in the brown leather chair.

"So report," he said after taking a swallow of his drink.

Morton coughed, then came over and sat on an ottoman across from Lawrence.

"It's taken us a while, sir, but we think we've managed to narrow the field a bit."

"You've pegged Andrew down to a particular location?"

Coloring slightly, Morton shook his head.

"No, sir. Not yet. But we're getting there."

"Define 'getting there', Mr. Morton."

"Well,"—the man stared down at his tablet and began paging through files—"we've been keeping as close an eye as we can on local news coming out of all the major cities, along with the national networks. And we've noticed some–occurrences–that would seem to fit his profile."

Lawrence grimaced as he took another drink. That word–profile–sounded so criminal, so debased.

Unfortunately, it also sounded accurate.

"So where have these occurrences taken place? San Francisco? Denver?" Andrew had visited those two cities in the past. There had been another, the most recent one, and after that final occurrence, a panel of doctors had again assured Lawrence and the other directors that Andrew was well on his way to recovery.

It had taken an ungodly amount of time and money to hush up all of those messes, and only a matter of months later, here they were again.

"No, sir," Morton said. "But the good news is that we believe we've narrowed the geographic area."

"Okay."

"All three possibles," Morton said, "are in the Midwest. And all three are metro areas with a decent-sized core population and a much larger surrounding area."

"He always goes for larger cities. Easier to hide that way."

"Yes, sir. But it helps us that two of them are within

the same state. There's a few outliers that could rank, but my people and I are fairly confident the subject is hiding within one of the three areas."

Lawrence sighed and put down his drink. He hated when Morton began talking in clinical terms.

"Do you have printouts? I'd much rather look at those than your—"

"Right here, sir."

From his briefcase, Morton pulled out three separate file folders, each less than a quarter of an inch thick.

"You'll find the specifics in there. The incidents that caught our attention, progress the various agencies involved are making, and up-to-date media reports."

Lawrence pulled the first folder his way and began leafing through it.

"I assume you have people on site, or close to it, for each of these?"

"On their way. Two operatives dispatched to each area. As soon as I get anything concrete I'll head out myself and—"

"No," Lawrence said, a new resolve forming within him.

"Sir?"

"When you get a confirmation, if you get one, of his presence, inform me before you do anything."

"Of course. You and Mrs. Sears will be the first."

"You're not hearing me, Morton." Lawrence turned his toughest gaze, the one he used on unruly managers, in the man's direction.

"Not my stepmother. *Me*."

Snapping the folder shut, he threw it in Morton's direction.

"You and me, Morton. We're going to end the problem of my little brother once and for all."

CHAPTER THIRTY-FOUR

Early evening, verging on eight o'clock, and the squad room still quiet. One would think that with so much going on the place would be swarming, but such is not the way with detective work. When things are quiet is when they can be found at base. But today, even with the extra help allotted to them, there was so much to do that home plate felt almost ghostlike.

Helen and Hollis had just returned from a quick jaunt down the corner to grab some burgers and fries. When they returned, the first thing they did, almost on instinct, was glance toward Kendal's office.

Kendal had his door closed, but the blinds were up. The captain, hunched over some sort of paperwork, didn't even glance up as they walked by.

"What do you think he's doing in there?" Helen asked.

"Search me, but I doubt whatever it is it's for much longer."

They sat down at their desks, both grimacing at the matching piles of paperwork that had accumulated over the last few days. Ballistic reports, convict records, and witness statements threatened to overwhelm them.

"Hard to keep up with our work," Helen said.

Hollis nodded and began unbending and bending a paper clip.

"Can't be long now."

"What?" Helen looked up at her partner.

"Before they take us off of it. Kind of surprised it hasn't happened yet."

Helen nodded.

"We did our best," he said, "but so far nothing."

"Who do you figure?" she asked. "Troopers or the AG's office?"

"My guess would be the state Bureau. Only thing I don't get is why it hasn't happened yet."

"Maybe they're just…"

Before she could finish, Lou Whitmore came in through the side door and slipped over to their desks. He stole a quick glance in the captain's direction.

"Take a look at this, Jack," he said, flipping a file folder down on Hollis's desk. "Looks like that punk Richie picked up may have given us an actual lead."

Hollis picked up the folder as Helen leaned over his shoulder, leafed through it, then looked up at Whitmore.

"I remember hearing about this. It was just after Pete made lieutenant, right?"

"Right. About three months after he got promoted."

"So he shouldn't have been out in the field?"

"Right," Whitmore said, "but the precinct was short staffed that day, and Roy's partner at the time was at the hospital with a sick kid. So Pete joined with Roy and, well, it's all there."

Helen got up from her desk and came over to pick up the file. She began skimming through it, but only got past the first page before looking up.

"A bank robbery?" she said.

"Yep," Whitmore said. "One handled by Roy and Pete."

"I don't get it. Wouldn't we have screened this one

out when we were looking at Roy's past collars. What's new here?"

"We were focusing on the perpetrators," Hollis said. "But in this case, the bank had to be stormed. One of the robbers gave up and was hustled out, but the other was killed when he fired on Roy."

Helen frowned.

"I must be extra dense today, Lou, but I still don't get your point. This file says that Roy killed one robber and they captured the other, but he's been in prison ever since. And how's that relate to the kid Richie was sweating?"

"Keep reading," Whitmore said.

Helen did so, and on the third page she saw what had caught Lou's attention. She looked up to see Whitmore nodding his head.

"Allen Drew. Twenty-seven at the time of his arrest for bank robbery, was sentenced to thirty years in prison."

"Which he could have cut down to fifteen or so with good behavior."

"Except he didn't. And he was still locked up as of last month."

Helen shook her head, trying to grasp the significance of what Lou had found.

"But he wasn't released last month," she said.

"Not at all," Whitmore replied. "He got on the wrong side of some gangbangers five weeks ago, and they found him shanked in the shower. Word is the same posse that Lattimer's suspect belonged to."

"Relatives?" Hollis asked.

"One. A kid brother. He's on record as visiting Drew at least once a month the entire time he's been in.

Supposedly never gave up hope that Drew would eventually be released."

The three of them stared at each other, the early evening noise outside the squad room fading into a vast distance.

"And that," Helen said for the three of them, "is what we could call a motive."

THE AVENGER

He had a choice to make.

Two down, and most people would consider that success. But the Avenger's lust had only been abated, not quenched. True satisfaction would not really be reached until all of them, anyone even remotely connected, had paid with their lives.

On the other hand, two was a good number, and he had the Company to consider.

But he'd already picked out number three, and his blood was up, in more ways than one.

Clicking the remote, he killed the TV and stood up, pacing the room. So far, he'd seen no signs of the Company, which didn't mean they weren't out there. They'd trained him well, beyond giving him all the financial and physical resources necessary to survive, but there was nothing that said they couldn't do the same for another.

When he thought back over the long and grueling training he'd undergone, the days and weeks of deprivation, confined to a small area and forced to survive on scraps of meat, not to mention the constant, never ending physical punishments designed to toughen both his body and spirit, the Avenger knew that few others could withstand such a program.

But at least a handful of others could, and since he'd departed from the organization, taking their skills, training and money, and struck out on his own, he lived every minute with the expectation of a knock on the door, heralding a new member tasked with bringing him back into the fold.

It had happened before, and he knew they would never let up searching for him.

His skin crawling, the Avenger stopped pacing, threw himself face down on the carpet and proceeded to do a hundred pushups. By the time he'd finished, gasping and sweat stained, he felt calmer, able to think more clearly.

Two was a good number, and anyone would feel proud at having pulled off such a feat. However, more would be better, and if their deeds had been ordinary malfeasance, he may have stopped here. But his targets had done worse, much worse, and the Avenger knew, rationalizations aside, that he couldn't stop.

So, a shower first to wash off the residue of his exertions. Next, a large meal, one fit for a champion.

Then, after a good night's sleep, it would be time to scope out the next target.

Until they tracked him down, he would continue the hunt.

The only question being, which of several possible targets to pick next.

CHAPTER THIRTY-FIVE

When she arrived the next morning, Janey found Hollis, Helen and Lou waiting for her.

"Let's go," Hollis said, "we've got our boy already staked."

As they headed toward the department's parking garage, Helen peered sideways at Janey.

"You've got bags under your eyes, but the eyes themselves are bright and clear. Late night?"

Janey grinned, feeling a bit of blush creeping up her neck.

"Late night combined with an early morning," she whispered. "Been awhile since I've had one of those."

"This the guy you met last month, the electrician?"

"Uhmm hmm."

By this time they'd made it up to the motor pool on the top floor of the garage, and three of them stood by while Hollis checked out one of the newer, SUV type vehicles the department had recently purchased.

Hollis stayed in the driver's seat while Helen slid in next to him, Lou taking the seat behind her.

Climbing into the remaining seat, Janey glanced over at Lou.

"This the guy you messaged me about last night? The con's little brother?"

"The dead con's, yeah," Lou said, "and what the hell, kid? Why didn't you return my call?"

"Sorry," she said offhandedly. "I was busy last night."

"Anyway," Lou continued, "so far this is the last connection we could find exclusive to Roy and Pete. So it's off to talk to kid bro."

"But if you tracked him down yesterday, why wait till now? What if he's bolted?"

"Couple of guys been watching him for the last twelve hours or so," Hollis said from the driver's seat. "He's not going anywhere."

"We arresting him?" Janey asked.

Lou chuckled.

"Not enough on him yet to even come close to that. If we'd gone for a warrant, judge wouldn't have laughed us out of court. He'd have had a couple of bailiffs throw us out."

"We're just going to talk to him," Hollis said. "Short, simple questions. Let him know we're on to him."

"How sure are you guys of this?"

Lou shrugged.

"Not hundred percent, but it's the most likely lead so far."

****

Their destination, a donut shop off Ninth Street, sat only a few blocks from Central, so they got there within a few minutes.

Parked at two different spots along the block were two patrol cars, each holding two uniforms, who got out when they saw the SUV approach.

"Lot of manpower just to question someone," Janey observed.

"No reason to take chances," Hollis said. "If this is

our guy, we don't want to leave him any sort of hole."

"The captain approve all this?" Janey asked.

She meant it as a casual query but noticed Hollis's shoulders tightening.

"Guys?"

Helen turned her way.

"We didn't run it by the boss yet."

"Why not?" Over the last year and a half, Janey had done her best to turn into a hardened, seasoned detective. But right now, she was beginning to feel like an unsure rookie on her first day of patrol.

"Why not?" she repeated when no one answered her.

"The captain's going overtime trying to juggle all this," Hollis finally said. "And since it's a shot in the dark, pardon the pun, we figured why burden him until we have a better idea if there's anything to it."

None of them had yet moved to leave the car, and Janey leaned back firmly into her seat.

"In other words, you don't trust him to back us up?"

Another protracted silence followed her question.

"Let's just say," Hollis finally said, "that we want all of our bases covered before we take it to him. And if this turns out to be another dead end, nobody loses."

Janey wasn't sure if that was the best approach to take, but considering the other three in the car, both individually and together, had far more years of experience than her, she decided to let it go.

"So our boy's one of the bakers there," Lou said, "and considering that his shift starts around two in the morning, he should be about wrapped for the day by now."

"At least close enough to being done that he should have time to talk to us," Helen said.

"Good enough," Hollis said as he opened his door and slid out of the car, the others following right behind him.

They went around back of the shop, after joining up with the four uniforms, and pounded on the gray steel door. It took a second knock before the door flew open, a skinny kid of about eighteen standing there.

"Thomas Drew," Hollis said, holding up his badge. "He here?"

The kid stood there gaping for a moment or two, his brain no doubt unable to process the sight of eight cops standing before him. He opened and closed his mouth a couple of times, nothing but hissing air coming out, before someone from behind shouldered him out of the way, and now the detectives faced a thirtyish woman, tired blonde hair done up in a pigtail covered by a hair net.

The woman turned down the sleeves of her blue, bleach-coated work shirt.

"What's going on?" she asked, and even without the shiny plastic tag on her breast her manner and bearing practically shouted "manager."

"We need to see Thomas Drew, please."

The woman puffed in exasperation.

"He's working. Can't this wait a while? We're in the middle of rush right now."

Janey frowned. Most people would be intimidated as all get out by a passel of cops at their back door. This woman was acting more annoyed than frightened or worried.

"'Fraid it can't," Hollis told her. "We need to talk to him now."

The woman shook her head, that part of her pigtail

not covered by the net swinging back and forth.

"Whatever, just make it quick, would you?"

She moved away from the door, leaving the four detectives to glance at each other.

"Odd reaction," Lou said.

"Not really," Helen said. "You notice the long sleeves rolled all the way down? Feel the heat coming out of this back part of the store? What you bet she's hiding something under those sleeves?"

Before anyone could answer, the door swung open again and a young, average-looking guy stood there.

"Thomas Drew?" Hollis asked.

"Yes, sir." This one had the quavering voice and rolling eyes they'd expected.

Hollis flashed his shield again.

The kid trembled even more. For a moment there, Janey felt he may fall down in his panic.

"We'd like to ask you a few questions, Thomas," Hollis said.

"Tom."

"Excuse me?"

"My name's Tom, sir."

"Fine," Hollis replied. "Would you mind stepping outside, Tom?"

As the kid left the illusory shelter of the doorway and stepped out in front of them, Janey took a good look at their suspect. Looking Thomas–Tom–Drew over, she couldn't quite imagine him having what it took to ambush and gun down two experienced police veterans.

Michaels, maybe. In some sort of heat-of-moment type thing. Janey knew that almost anyone could pull off a violent feat once. It just took the right circumstances and motivation. But most people couldn't make it past that first time. Those who could go back to the well repeatedly were fairly rare. Most people who could do so developed the capability through training of some sort, whether officially or on the streets. Very few could pull it off just by inherent nature.

But Tom Drew didn't look like either of those.

As Hollis and Whitmore began questioning the suspect, Janey drew back a couple of steps. She and Helen were competent, but the two guys looked physically more imposing, thus more likely to rattle the kid.

If there was anything inside him to be rattled out.

They took Drew through the normal paces: how long he'd been at his job, how he felt about it, how he'd handled his brother being killed in prison. Then, they got more specific with their questions, and Drew began shifting back and forth, almost hopping from foot to foot.

Something seemed off to Janey, but she wasn't sure what.

In her peripheral vision, she saw the uniformed cops behind them slouching, as if growing bored with the whole thing. She didn't blame them, but they were far enough back they may not have picked up on Drew's jitteriness.

She saw Helen tense up, then looked back to Hollis and Lou and the kid.

"Waitaminnit," Drew said. "Are you talking about those two cops that got shot? What's that to do with me?"

"Knock it off, kid," Whitmore barked, his tone deeper and more resonant than normal. Janey had seen him pull that trick a time or two before. "You know who those two detectives were, and you know their connection to your brother. So quit acting stupid."

"Easy does it, Lou," Hollis said, sliding into his role. No matter how many times they showed the trick on TV shows, it almost always worked in real life. "Tom," he said, turning back to their suspect, "all we want is to…"

Something flickered in Janey's vision, and she turned to look toward the corner of the building.

Drew's boss had rounded the corner, holding an automatic pistol in both hands.

"Gun!" Janey shouted as she swept her own weapon out of its holster. Around her, the rest of them reacted, pulling their own weapons and splitting in different directions while simultaneously flattening toward the ground.

Hollis had grabbed hold of Tom Drew and was pulling him to the ground as well.

The donut woman had stopped, frozen in place and with her weapon half raised. Janey assumed that the uniforms as well had arrayed themselves, but she didn't dare take her eyes off the woman to check.

"Take it easy," Hollis said behind her. "Nobody wants this to get bad here."

"Tom didn't do nothin'," the woman said, the slightest quaver in her tone. "You're hasslin' him 'cause of his brother when he didn't do anything."

A drop of sweat trickled off Janey's forehead and landed in her eye. She blinked furiously, not caring about the sting but wanting to clear the slight cloudiness.

"We're just talking to him," Hollis said.

"I heard you talking. You think he killed someone. But he didn't."

"Probably not," Hollis said, still playing the good cop he'd begun during the questioning. "But we have to check him out. That's all we're doing, checking him out.

When we determine he's cool, then we're gone."

"Like fuck!" the woman shouted. "There's eight of you. Eight cops just to talk to someone? You planned on gunning him down. Didn't you?"

Janey grimaced, silently cursing the spate of police problems across the country over the last year or so. It had gone beyond a racial thing. Now, it seemed like so many people were against the cops simply as a reflex action, regardless of the situation.

At the same time, remembering Helen's comments about the lady's long sleeves, she figured the woman had some sort of past association with the force.

As the palaver continued, Hollis's tone remained calm, reassuring. Positioned in front of him, Janey couldn't look back to see his position, but she'd noted him pulling the Drew kid down with him, and wondered just how uncomfortable his poise was becoming.

"You let him go," the woman said. "Let Tommy go."

"Can't do that," Hollis said, "especially not at the point of a gun. You put your weapon down, and all of us can sit down and talk."

Janey couldn't help but marvel that with eight of them, four detectives and four uniforms, so far everyone had had the restraint and patience not to do something rash.

"If I lower," the donut woman said, "you're going to shoot. That's what you're here for, right? Think Tommy killed those two friends of yours and now you're going to even the score. Right?"

"Ma'am," Hollis said, "we can't let this go on all day. I don't know about you, but my hand's starting to fatigue a bit here. If we get nine of us with tired gunhands, no telling what's going to happen."

"It's okay, Lucy," Drew suddenly said. "Put it down. They weren't going to hurt me. Just put it down."

Janey, not knowing how the woman would react to the new element, sucked in a slow, steady breath. Like Hollis, provided he'd been speaking the truth, her hand was starting to cramp around her weapon. She drew a careful bead on the woman's right shoulder, the arm holding the gun.

She hadn't been trained that way. They drilled into you not to try for any fancy shots, just aim for the mass and hope for the best. But Janey figured if she had to she could nail the shoulder, hopefully dropping the gun without endangering her target's life.

"Lucy," Hollis again. God, the guy sounded so mellow. They should put him on hostage negotiation. "Listen to Tommy. Just put it down, then we'll lower ours, and we can all walk away from this."

"He didn't kill those cops," Lucy said. "No matter what you think, Tommy there wouldn't hurt anybody."

"If he didn't, he didn't. Just put it down and let us all walk away from here."

Janey's hand cramped up even more, so much that it felt as if any second it would spasm on its own, sending a bullet into the blonde woman's shoulder. Although her mind told her this had only been going on for a few seconds, her body felt as if she'd been couched in this position for hours. Another droplet of sweat floated into her vision, causing things to blur a bit.

Oh God, she thought, please don't pick this instant to start the shooting.

Then, blinking the moisture away, she saw the donut lady lowering her gun, shoulders slumping as her fingers unclenched, and the weapon fell to the pavement. Even so, Janey didn't move, didn't so much as twitch, until two of the uniforms entered her field of vision, one of them grabbing the gun from the ground while the other pinioned the woman's arms behind her, forcing her to her knees.

Only then did Janey, the tension flowing out of her, come to her own knees, then stand all the way up.

The freeze frame had snapped shut, and everything and everybody was moving at normal speed again.

"What the hell was that all about?" she asked no one in particular.

CHAPTER THIRTY-SIX

The two men looked fairly ordinary, if somewhat well off. Casual clothes, even at the end of a brisk winter. One wore Levi's and a camel-hair overcoat, while the other had on black wool slacks and a dark gray leather jacket that came to mid-thigh. One blond and the other dark brown. Mr. Levi's stood a little over six feet tall, and his partner topped out at five nine.

Had they not been wearing the heavy coats, a casual observer may have noticed that they both possessed the same basic body type. Wide shoulders, muscular chests and trim, almost narrow waists. The clothing also covered up well-muscled legs. Someone with the proper training and background would have deduced that the two men had gone through a particular sort of physical regimen.

But with the coats on, they attracted no notice at all.

They were sitting at the bar in an upscale restaurant that occupied part of the ground floor of a downtown hotel. Although a nice hotel, bordering on luxurious, the two weren't registered there. Rather, they had wandered in off the street in the middle of the afternoon, no doubt taking a few minutes out of their busy workday to chug down a few beers in a relaxed setting.

A passerby, if they noticed the two men at all, would probably figure they were playing hooky from work.

However, that casual observer would be wrong.

The two were currently hard at work.

Damned near sweating, in fact.

"We should be split," the blond one said.

"We discussed this," his partner, in the leather jacket, replied. "We checked eight ways from Sunday, and we know he's up in his room. Or at least somewhere here in the hotel. We spotted him going in the night before last, and he hasn't been out since."

"Must be one hell of a room service tab," Blond replied.

"You kidding? You think he cares about tabs? As much as he has access to?"

"Yeah, but don't you think they've been cutting off his funds, especially as he keeps getting away? I wouldn't be surprised if he's down to his last few bucks."

The leather-jacketed man sighed. While the two of them looked about the same age, early thirties or thereabouts, Leather Jacket was actually more than ten years older than his partner. Close examination would have revealed the faint telltale signs of cosmetic surgery around the nose and eyes. Surgery done the old-fashioned way, in a hospital by a skilled doctor. Not a day job done in a spa.

Along with their difference in ages, Leather Man had a solid two decades' worth of experience under his belt, so he was calling the shots.

"Don't count on only a few bucks," he said. "Our boy may be nutty as hell, but he's not stupid. Wouldn't surprise me too much if he managed to get all sorts of dough squirreled away in various places where the company can't find it. He could easily have enough to go on for several months, if not years."

"Okay," replied Blond, shifting a bit in his thick

coat, "but that doesn't really change anything as far as we're concerned. We know where he is, we've got him pinned down. So let's finish the job and get the hell out of here."

As he spoke, the blond man reached into his coat pocket and pulled out his cell phone, but even as he punched the first button his partner reached over and snatched it out of his grip.

The blond lifted his hands, fingers tightening while curling slightly at the tips, and raised half off his stool. Even through his coat, his shoulders visibly tightened.

Then he glanced both ways before easing himself back down.

"What the hell?" he asked the man in the leather coat.

"You're not thinking right, kid. I know you're a pup and all, but we really need to consider our futures."

The blond man frowned.

"Meaning what?"

"Meaning that we call it in, tell Morton we have the kid spotted. Morton comes out, takes him back home like usual, and if we're lucky we get a pat on the head from the old lady."

"Plus continuing to receive our salaries. Which, I might add, are pretty damned good."

Leather Jacket nodded.

"No argument there. But what if, I'm just saying, what if, we go up there and brace the man. Get him to give up his secrets, so to speak."

The younger man paled a bit. Before answering, he took a quick swig of his beer.

"You do realize," he said, his voice a bit hoarse, "exactly what that guy up there has done?"

Leather Jacket snorted.

"Of course, I know. Don't forget who's been with this outfit longer. But when Morton paired us up, I asked for a copy of your file."

The blond man's shoulders tensed again, though he remained seated.

"I thought those were personal."

Another snort.

"Grow up, kid. I don't let them partner me with anybody without first seeing the files. And after looking them over, I have a pretty damned good idea of what you're capable of."

"Even so—"

"And look at it this way. All those other people, they were just targets waiting to happen. They weren't expecting anything, and probably never even knew what hit them. But the two of us together are the recipients of some of the highest caliber training the U.S. government has to offer. And you don't think we can take one guy?"

The blond man returned to his beer, and this time instead of swigging he took a long, protracted drink. When he finally put his mug back on the table, its amount had decreased by almost half.

"Give up his secrets," he said. "By that I'm guessing you mean where he has any money stashed."

Leather Jacket leaned back on his stool, a wide grin stretching across his face.

"That's exactly what I mean, bud. Think of it. We get the kid to tell us where his money is, keep him down for a few days till we get hold of it, and then turn him over to the boss. What's he going to do? Complain that we stole his money? Money the boss doesn't even want him to have?"

Blond thought it over for a few minutes, at the same time finishing off his beer. When the bartender looked his way, Blond shook his head.

"Two problems I see with that," he finally said, "depending on where his money's stashed."

"Such as?"

"If he has it physically accessible, it could be anywhere in the country. Hell, in the world. And if his funds are all electronic, do you or I have the knowhow to access them?"

Leather Jacket shrugged his shoulders.

"In the end, does it matter? Even if we come up snake eyes on this, we've still bagged him, which will get us in good with the boss. And any complaining about us he does will be chucked up to his nuttiness."

Blond thought about that while he swirled his empty mug back and forth on the bar top.

"We've got the room number," he finally said.

Leather Jacket nodded.

"And we know he hasn't moved for at least a day or so," Blond continued.

Leather stayed silent, waiting for the kid to make up his own mind.

Finally, his young partner looked up.

"Then what the hell are we waiting on?" he asked.

Leather Jacket grinned and clapped him on the shoulder.

"Good move, partner. So let's go make some money."

CHAPTER THIRTY-SEVEN

The elevator opened onto the thirtieth floor. The two stepped out and, without a word, turned right and headed toward the end of the hall. As they did so, the one in the black jacket moved to walk along the left side of the hallway, while his partner stayed along the right side.

They'd split without even thinking, thus presenting two different targets instead of one.

Mid-afternoon, the hall sat empty. A hotel this expensive usually catered to either business people or those rich enough they didn't have to work. The former type were no doubt out working their deals, quite possibly in bars similar to the one the two men had just left. Those who didn't have to worry about where their next paycheck was coming from were probably sleeping in, preparatory to another night out on the town.

The hallway was so quiet the two men could hear the sound of their steps in the carpet.

Within a few seconds of departing the elevator, they arrived outside room 3030.

Although both concealed weapons under their coats, neither had yet drawn them. The slight, barely-noticeable cameras they'd spotted as they left the elevator cage were one reason, coupled with the certain knowledge that they could, when necessary, draw their weapons almost faster than one could see.

Leather Jacket moved to the right of the door while

Blond reached out and rapped on the panel.

After a few seconds, he knocked again, slightly louder this time, but the second knock also received no answer.

The blond man glanced to his partner, who shifted his head to the side. The blond one then swiveled his upper body and placed his ear against the door.

He closed his eyes, mashed his ear closer and waited.

After a few more seconds, he stepped back from the door and shook his head at his partner.

The door was locked, of course, with the slot for the key card seemingly the only way to open it up. But these men were trained, carrying certain tools on them, and in less than a minute they were swinging the door open on an empty room.

As they moved inside they split in separate directions, still presenting two targets. Both men looked at each other with raised brows, but they still didn't say anything.

Like most hotel rooms, this one occupied basically a single chamber. Unlike many, a recessed pit in the middle, outfitted with black leather furniture, made the room feel more like an apartment or house. Floor-to-ceiling windows showed the afternoon sun, and over the tops of several downtown buildings an observer could make out the image of the Mississippi River in the distance.

Off to the side was a small kitchenette, complete with full-size refrigerator and stove. Plus a side hallway, down which probably lay the bedroom area, with what looked like a closet door about halfway between the outer room and bedroom.

Still, though, no sound. In the quiet, the men could almost hear the susurration of their circulation. They turned in unison and began heading down the short hallway, bypassing the kitchenette, which clearly held no one.

And with a few short steps they were at the bedroom, its door hanging open.

Leather Jacket held up his hand to his partner, and made a slight motion to the side. Blond Hair nodded and held back.

The two men continued to stay apart, constantly providing two targets instead of one.

Leather Jacket entered the bedroom, glanced around, then motioned Blond inside. The space was empty, the bed neatly made and a small laptop resting on the nightstand.

A slight scraping behind them caused them to turn.

Their quarry stood in the doorway, and past him they could see the closet door now ajar. He held a Beretta in his hand, raised and trained on Leather Jacket.

The gun had a noise suppressor attached to its snout.

"Bad move, boys. Sorry. But I'm not ready to go back just yet."

Both men stood motionless.

"It's time to come home, guy," Leather Jacket said.

The man in front of them cocked his head to the side.

"I know you," he motioned to Leather, then gestured toward his companion. "But him I don't know."

"He's new with the company. I'd introduce him if you'd just lower that weapon."

The gunman laughed.

"I really don't think that would be a good idea, do you? I'm sure you men were told to bring me in alive, but who knows what would happen in the event I lowered my guard here."

He now turned to the younger of the two partners.

"I can only imagine why you guys are sneaking around in here. I would think all you had to do was call back home, tell them where I am, then sit back to collect a nice reward. Right?"

The blond man simply stood there, not saying anything.

The man holding the Beretta nodded, as if confirming something to himself.

"But I'm guessing that your partner here convinced you there was more to gain by taking me yourselves, maybe upping the old retirement funds a bit, eh?"

Leather Jacket and Blond glanced at each other, trying by eye signals to come up with some sort of plan.

"Yeah, that's what I thought," the man in the doorway said as he squeezed the trigger and a loud whuff came out of the Beretta.

The man in the leather jacket staggered, pitching halfway back the length of the bedroom. Two more whuffs, each slightly louder than the first, caused a total of three blood spots to appear on his chest and rapidly soak his shirt. With a groan and a loud, nasty creaking, he fell to the floor, his lower body twisted half under him.

The man in the doorway smiled ruefully at his remaining guest.

"That's the only problem with silencers," he said. "Despite what all the thriller writers tell you, even the best ones only work for a handful of times before the innards get torn up, and you're left with nothing but noise."

He smiled again, and the blond-haired man tensed up.

"But at least," the man in the doorway said, "you know. Middle of the day. Won't be that many people around right about now."

And he pulled the trigger again.

Then one more time just to be sure.

CHAPTER THIRTY-EIGHT

By mid afternoon, they had the answers to most of their questions.

They hadn't been able to leave the scene for some time.

In the old days, the big guns had only shown up if an officer had actually discharged their weapon. Lately, with the spate of bad press departments around the country had been receiving, policy stated that even a cop clearing a weapon from a holster required the presence of both a command officer and a detachment from IA. The command presence, as they'd expected, assumed the form of Captain Kendal. IA was represented by three terse, unsmiling detectives.

Although the detectives of Central Squad didn't see all that much daylight between IA and Kendal's Special Operations unit.

On first arriving, the IA folks had assumed their usual emotionless demeanor. Then, upon seeing Helen on the scene, those normal poker faces became almost etched in stone.

Helen tensed, expecting to take the brunt of their questioning, but instead they divided their time equally between all eight of the officers involved.

Nearly an hour of questioning commenced, with Thomas Drew and Lucy, whose last name they now knew was Hanson, separated in the rear seats of two different vehicles. Handcuffed and with a guard over them, they presented no immediate threat as Hollis and his team worked to iron out the higher-ups' understanding of the situation.

It helped that no weapon had actually discharged, but they still had a ream of processing to go through. Eventually, with Kendal becoming a bit red faced and raising his voice, they were all released to transport their two prisoners back to the station.

Then came separate interrogations, Hollis and Helen dealing with Lucy in one room while Lou and Janey talked to Tom Drew.

****

"So the woman's an addict?" Kendal asked Helen and Hollis.

It was late afternoon by now, and the two of them had entered the captain's office to update him. When they walked in, they saw him standing at the window, looking out over the city, and he hadn't yet turned to face them.

"Yes, sir," Hollis said. "Turns out she's been in and out of treatment centers for about ten years now. Currently, though, seems to be clean."

"And she works in that bakery?"

"Actually runs it. At least, she's the morning manager. Been on the job for about two years now."

"Why'd she go out on such a limb for a guy who worked for her? They got some sort of connection going on?"

Helen and Hollis glanced at each other.

"We're still working on that one, sir. But it seems like Drew's really a hard luck type of guy. A younger, softer version of his brother."

"What the hell?" Kendal said, still without turning. "You saying she was mother henning the boy?"

Helen nodded, then realized that Kendal couldn't see her motion.

"That's what it looks like. We did some digging, and it seems that ever since his brother's death Drew's gone even more downhill than ever. And it turns out that he's been talking a lot about getting even."

Helen could see Kendal stiffen for a moment before finally turning to face them.

"Getting even?"

"That's what we got out of her, sir," Hollis said.

Helen felt the atmosphere in the office thicken. Late day light was coming through the slatted window blinds, yet even so the room felt dark, as if closing in on her.

"Is this our guy?"

"Not sure, captain. But it's looking possible."

"Evidence? What about the gun the woman pulled on you all?"

"A thirty-eight, sir. So nothing to do with Michaels and Jarvis. We're waiting on a warrant to search the Drew kid's place, as well as the woman's."

Kendal glanced at the clock on the wall.

"How long you been waiting?"

"Actually, just sent it through about half an hour ago. We sent uniforms to seal off both of their places, so we've got the time."

A long moment passed with no one saying anything before Kendal broke the silence.

"What do you think, detectives? Is this our guy?"

Helen and Hollis looked at each other. They'd had this same conversation before coming in.

"If I had to lay money on it, sir, I'd say so," Hollis

said. "There's a lot that doesn't add up yet, but with enough access we'll get there."

"Helen?"

"I'd say our main question right now is whether it was a solo effort or the two of them working together."

"If you had to guess?"

"Then I'd say it's probably the two of them in tandem. Drew just didn't seem to exhibit that much self control. For a one off, maybe, but not for both."

Kendal sat down and rubbed his temples.

"I need something to tell upstairs," he said. "How much do you want me to say?"

"Following leads?" Hollis suggested.

"Christ, Jack. That sounds like a press release. This is for the bosses. They're ready any minute to give this over to a state task force. Assuming that anything I tell them will somehow get out to the media, how much are you comfortable with me revealing?"

Hollis and Helen glanced at each other.

"Considering we have both of them in custody," Hollis said, "I'd say tell them as much as you want. It's not like the two of them are going anywhere."

Kendal leaned back in his chair.

"Okay, I'll wait a few hours. Give you time to get the warrants and get going. Then I'll put out the basic facts, and anything else they ask for. But get all the squad together and get this nailed down. One way or another we have to have something to tell the media in the morning."

"Okay, sir."

As the two of them turned to leave, Kendal spoke up again.

"Detective Lipscomb, I need a moment with you."

****

The door closed behind Jack, and Helen turned back to the captain.

"Yes, sir?"

"Take a seat, please."

Helen sat, wondering what kind of shoe was about to drop on her now.

"How's Turner holding up?"

"Sir?"

Kendal gestured toward the computer on the desk.

"I've been reading up on the squad. I may only be here for a short duration, but as long as I am, you're my people. So I've been learning about you guys."

"Okay." Helen worked to keep confusion from showing on her face.

"This is the first time Turner's been involved in an incident like this. From all accounts, at least the early ones, she did okay. Is that true?"

"The same as any of us," Helen said. "I actually was kind of impressed by how well she kept her cool."

"And we were lucky that no one actually had to fire. Lucky on all counts. But it still was a tense situation, right?"

"Of course," Helen said. Then, after hesitating for a moment, "Have you ever…"

Kendal shook his head. "I'm not quite the desk jockey everyone seems to think, but no, I've never had to draw. I know Whitmore has a couple of times in his career."

"Yeah," Helen said. "Lou handled himself okay."

"And of course you and Hollis had that–incident– last year."

Helen grimaced. "Incident" seemed a rather mild

word to describe your partner being gunned down in a hallway and yourself held captive by a serial murderer. Indeed, despite the fact that she was the professional, Helen figured it at fifty/fifty that she'd still be alive were it not for a civilian, a murder suspect no less, blundering into the situation.

"True, " she said. "we've all had some experience."

"Except for Turner," Kendal pointed out. "This is her first time at bat."

"Excuse me, sir, but what's your point?"

Kendal smiled and leaned back in his chair.

"My point, detective, is that I'm not sure how close you and Turner are, but I'd like you to check with her, make sure she's okay."

"Sir?"

"She's young. And,"—he pointed to his computer—"has a promising career ahead of her. Talk with her, please. Just make sure that she's handling today okay. We've all got some long days ahead of us yet. I haven't heard from the chief for several hours, but I'm sure that by this time tomorrow the case will be handed over. So keep an eye on your colleague, detective. Make sure she's taking today's events in stride."

"Yes, sir," Helen said as she stood. "Is that all?'

"For now."

Helen turned to leave the office.

"Oh, and detective…"

She glanced back at the captain.

"Good work today."

Nodding, Helen turned and left.

CHAPTER THIRTY-NINE

"You don't have enough," ADA Kristi Miller told them around eleven that night.

The day had wound down. Three detectives on the graveyard shift were off chasing a lead on a case. Two of the temporary transfers were sitting at some of the extra desks writing up reports.

Regular police work, after all, had to continue.

The rest of the regular shift, including Janey, were long gone. Helen had wanted to talk to her, per Kendal's request, but when she'd finally found the time, Janey had already taken off, hopefully to meet her latest crush and forget about police work for a while.

Miller, a slim brunette in her early forties, had shown up wearing sweats and a pink headband. She'd grimaced upon entering.

"Three kids," she'd muttered. "Only time I can work out is after hours."

The detectives who'd greeted her, Hollis, Helen and Lou, had barely noticed. After the day they'd put in, they didn't exactly look fresh and well scrubbed themselves.

Now, some twenty minutes later, with the four of them situated around a table in the rear of the squad room and a cup of coffee in everyone's hand, she hit them with what they didn't want to hear.

"Come again?" Lou's deep, baritone voice sounded almost injured.

"Nothing physical, at least so far, to tie either of them to the murders. Had it not been for your little encounter today, and by the way kudos to keeping that from becoming a conflagration, you would probably have questioned the kid and let him go."

"Maybe," Hollis said, "but we also would have kept an eye on him to see what developed."

"Which you can still do," Kristi pointed out.

"Not anymore," Helen pointed out. "He knows we're looking at him, so both of them will be on their best behavior."

"I'm sorry," ADA Miller said, "but you have what happened this morning, and if you want I can get creative and easily rattle off about fifteen different charges to bind them over on. But at the moment there's nothing, outside of their aberrant behavior and the familial connection, to link either of them to the murders of Michaels and Jarvis."

Helen and Lou slumped their gazes, while Hollis drummed his fingers on the table.

"Best guess, Kristi. How long can we keep them in lockup?"

Miller snapped her briefcase shut.

"Considering their probable financial situation, plus the drugs and weapons charges, I can't see a judge letting them out on less than a six-figure bail. After all, they did throw down on about half the city's police force. That buys you some time to dig some more."

She stood, shook their hands, and headed out.

Lou and Hollis slumped back in their seats while Helen got up and went to the coffee machine. She turned back and cocked an eyebrow at her colleagues.

Both men shook their heads.

After filling her cup and stirring in a moderate amount of cream and sugar, she returned to the table. "So what now?" she asked.

"Long day," Hollis said. "I'm sure the captain wouldn't mind us knocking off for the night. It's not like our two guests are going anywhere, and right now I can't think what the hell else to do. Primary be damned. If anyone has any ideas of where to go from here, I'm all ears."

"Where'd Janey go to?" Helen asked.

"She had a deposition to give down at the courthouse. It got kind of bogged down and she didn't get out until seven or so. She called in but, hell, by that time we were already searching Drew's apartment, so I told her to head on home."

Lou picked up a pencil from somewhere and started tapping it on the table.

"So we've got two of our own dead, a handful of nine mm casings but no weapon to match them with, some muddy half prints that may or may not belong to our guy, and two druggoes taking a short vacation from their day jobs at our expense. That about it?"

"That's it," Hollis said. "Plus a commanding officer who's plunked down in his chair just waiting for the phone call to take all of that away from us."

"Are we sure," Whitmore asked, "that we wouldn't mind someone taking this cluster over?"

Hollis gave him a look.

"Sorry, man. Just rambling out loud."

Helen yawned, then took a sip of her drink.

"Christ, Helen, go home. We've got nothing more to do before the morning."

"Hell," Whitmore chimed in, "even come morning

we've got nothing to do. No leads, no clues and damned few options."

"If you say so." Helen stood up and drained the last of her coffee, suddenly wondering why she'd bothered when she was heading home to try to sleep.

"Who knows," she said as she picked up her coat from the back of her chair, "maybe in another few hours we'll get that magical piece of the puzzle that will pop it all into place."

But as she looked at the downcast faces of her two colleagues she figured they didn't believe her words any more than she did.

CHAPTER FORTY

Once again the buzzing of her cell, positioned on her nightstand before she dropped off, tugged at Helen, doing its best to claw her out of slumber. But her mind resisted, doing its best to hold her in the deep, dreamless state she'd somehow managed to acquire.

The buzzing continued. Not consciously aware of the struggle, she would only reflect later that her subconscious, or at least some small corner of it, knew what the buzzing phone represented and was trying to protect her, to hold her in the cocoon of safety sleep represented.

Even so, the call couldn't–wouldn't–be resisted. Finally she came half awake, fumbling for a few brief seconds before grabbing at the instrument.

"'Lo," she muttered.

"Helen? Wake up. Now!"

Lou Whitmore's voice, and Helen felt that she had never heard anyone so frantic, so frenzied.

"Lou," she said, struggling to full awareness. "What is it? What's up?"

"You need to get out here, Helen. Kendal put out the word for everyone, all shifts."

"The station?" By this time, she'd managed to focus on the clock on the nightstand.

3:05.

What the hell?

"Naw, not the house. You need to get to…to." His voice trailed off, and Helen began to feel the first cold of true fear.

"Where, Lou? Where do I need to be?"

A pause, and in the background she could hear muttered speech, the opening and closing of doors and, once, the whoop of a siren.

"Lou?" she repeated, the terror now with a firm grip on her.

"Janey's." The word came out as if he'd been strangled. "We need you at Janey's."

Helen shut her eyes and, although she knew it was senseless to ask, spoke involuntarily.

"Why?"

"They got her, Helen. Whoever these sons of bitches are, they got to Janey."

CHAPTER FORTY-ONE

Another early morning crime scene.

Another home, surrounded by the flashing lights of emergency vehicles.

Another set of ambulance attendants, twiddling their thumbs off to the side because there was no hurry anymore.

Another dead colleague.

How many, Helen wondered as she approached the area. How many crime scenes had she approached during her career?

Not old by any means, she'd been on the force for fifteen years, eight of them as a detective. In that time, the number of crime scenes, from petty theft to homicide, must easily reach into the hundreds. In terms of just homicides alone, considering the rate of violent crime in this city, the number would be high as well, though not quite in the triple digits.

How many had she visited?

Here and now, the question of how many faded away, to be replaced with the question of how she could possibly get through this one.

A young patrol officer, either not knowing or not recognizing her in the weirdly-lit night, began to turn her away. But with a quick gesture toward her badge clipped to the front of her jacket, the yellow barrier tape was lifted, allowing her to walk through.

Janey lived in a condo in one of the city's suburbs, not one of the more affluent, but still a nice neighborhood. The condo itself, in muted earth tones and with a double-car garage, was probably a bit much for Janey's salary as a detective third-grade. On the other hand, she hadn't had any children, yet, and with her record she had a bright future in the department.

Had *had* a bright future, Helen reminded herself. Because the presence of all the tech people, along with an ambulance crew standing idly by their vehicle, told her the forensics work was not yet done, and Janey's body probably still lay inside.

As Helen climbed the steps to the condo's front door, she noticed several neighbors, of both genders and a variety of ages, standing around just outside of the barrier tapes.

Not an affluent neighborhood, by any means, but one that didn't have much familiarity with violent crime.

On the porch, standing off to the side and with hands in pockets, slouched Frank Matthews, a gray-haired veteran in his early fifties, on loan from East Division.

"How many are here?" she asked.

"At least ten of us, either in the house, around the yard or on their way."

"Where's Whitmore?"

"Inside."

The front door had been left open, and Helen glanced inside to see the normal sort of scurrying activity that accompanied a major crime scene. From her vantage point, though, she couldn't see Janey's body.

"Where'd they find her?" she asked.

"Right in the front room. There's a couch off to the far side, and when a neighbor came in he found her slumped there. Two through the head."

Even though his words came across as dry and clinical, Helen could hear a bit of a catch in his voice.

"Neighbor?" she asked.

"Yeah. Notice how these condos have connecting walls? Guy next door was asleep and heard some sort of banging sound, he says. Guess he's a friend of Janey's 'cause he had her phone number. When he couldn't get an answer, he came outside and found the door hanging open."

Helen frowned, remembering the current assumption that their killer was using a silencer.

"Did he hear the shots?"

"Not sure. Hollis was the one who talked to him. Way she's arranged, he could have just heard her falling down."

"So he went in?"

"About three steps. Far enough to look inside and see what there was to see, then beat it out of there."

"Was her boyfriend around?"

"Boyfriend?"

"She'd started seeing someone recently. Anyone else around the place?"

"Not as far as I know."

Helen frowned. She'd gotten the impression that Janey and her new guy, in the flush of early days, had been spending nearly all their nights together.

Then again, considering everyone's work hours as of late...

Helen tried to think of something else to ask, knowing that she was merely forestalling entering the house, but was saved by Hollis and Captain Kendal stepping out onto the porch.

Hollis nodded at her, while Kendal gave her a kind of absent-minded look.

Behind the two men, she could still see the flurry of motion inside the house.

"This way," Kendal said, gesturing to a patch of ground several yards off, currently free of people or equipment. Helen, Hollis and Matthews trailed behind.

"So what happened?" Helen asked, doing her best to keep her voice level.

"We're not quite sure, yet," Kendal said "except that it was a head shot, same as the other two."

"Nine?"

"Looks like, but you know the drill. We've been through it enough the last few days."

"Shouldn't have to wait long," Matthews said.

"No. I called the chief as soon as I heard, even before I got out here. I would imagine every single member of the brass, not to mention the entire city commission, is out of their beds already. This is probably what they mean by crossing a Rubicon."

"Sir?" Helen asked, the sudden shift throwing her off.

"You know. A point of no return. Well, we're sure as hell there right now."

"How long you figure we have, captain?" Hollis asked.

Kendal sighed and rubbed his neck.

"Hours at the most. It's taken a lot to keep them from reassigning up to this point. Now, I'd honestly be surprised if they gave us until noon. More likely by the time we get back to the station it'll all be over."

Hollis grimaced and reached a hand toward his jacket pocket, arresting the motion about halfway. Helen knew that, up to about three years ago, he'd been a heavy smoker before quitting cold turkey.

"So what do we do in the meantime?" Helen asked.

Kendal looked her way.

"What we would ordinarily do. Work the case. Jack, this is still yours, at least nominally. Stay here on scene and cover it like you would any other. I'll leave about three others on site to assist. Frank, why don't you head downtown and start going through Janey's files for any possible suspects."

"Captain, that's a waste—"

"I know it's pointless, Frank. But it has to be done anyway. Especially now, we can't overlook anything, no matter how remote."

"Gotcha."

"Let's assemble in three hours at the max. I should have some word from the chief by then. Until then, we handle things by the book."

Hollis and Matthews headed off, Hollis back into the condo, which Helen still had not entered, and Matthews off to his car.

Kendal turned to Helen.

"I've got a few things to take care of here, detective. Then I'll be back downtown. I want you in my office in thirty minutes. Clear?"

"Sir, I don't understand—"

"Half an hour, detective."

Without another word he headed back into Janey's home.

His body language made it pretty clear that Helen wasn't supposed to follow him, so she didn't.

But as she turned to go to her car, she noticed a young man standing toward the front of the crowd, almost pressed against the yellow barrier tape.

She hadn't seen him when she'd first walked up to the house, just minutes before. He was dressed in casual clothes, gray gym pants and some sort of windbreaker. Not nearly enough clothing to guard against the early hours in a late March morning. A black baseball cap crunched low obscured most of his face, but with all the strobing lights around she could make him out to be no more than late twenties.

On a hunch, Helen walked over his way.

The uniformed officer, a young Asian woman, guarding that particular part of the perimeter looked at her curiously but didn't say anything.

"Hello," Helen said as she approached the bystander. She pointed to her badge.

"Hi," the man said, his voice deep but shaking.

Standing close to him now, Helen noticed his face, drawn and pale except for red smudges around the eyes.

He stood something just under six foot, but had a trim waist and fairly broad shoulders.

"My name's Helen," she said, "Helen—"

"Lipscomb," he cut her off. "I pretty much figured that. You look about how she described."

Helen nodded, her assumption confirmed.

"And you are?"

"My name's Adam," the young man said. "Adam Thorson. I am-I mean, I was-uh…"

As he tried to speak, the kid's face tightened even more, and his eyes squinted up.

Helen ducked under the barrier tape and took him by the arm.

"Come on, Adam," she said. "I think we need to talk."

As the two of them walked off, Thorson casting glances back at Janey's house as they left, Helen realized she was, at least nominally, violating the captain's orders to head back to the station.

Hell with it, she silently mused. *It's about time I did something right*.

CHAPTER FORTY-TWO

"I should have been with her," Adam said as Helen steered her car along the Interstate. She'd suggested going somewhere, maybe finding a diner open late and grabbing a cup of coffee, but the kid had only wanted to drive. Helen figured that the sense of constant motion could somehow work to keep him from falling apart all the way.

"What do you mean?" she asked. Her window, despite the March cold, was cracked open about an inch. Enough to let some fresh air in but not so much that conversation, at their speed, would be impossible.

"Just that," he said, looking out his window, instead of at her. "I was supposed to come over tonight. We've been—you know—seeing a lot of each other lately. But she was working, and had some errands to run, and I have a project that's due at work in a couple of days. So when she called to tell me she'd gotten home I took a pass, decided to stay home."

He stopped talking, and Helen thought she heard a bit of a choking sound.

She decided to leave him be until he wanted to talk again.

They continued zipping along the Interstate, almost deserted at this early hour, except for the occasional trucker. As they passed the exit for a rest area, she noticed a fleet of semis, motors idling and faint puffs from exhaust pipes, their drivers no doubt still asleep in the sleepers.

A few minutes later, with Helen still having no specific destination in mind, Adam turned to her.

"I'm probably a suspect, right?" he asked.

"Say what?" she glanced at him, then turned back to her driving.

"Don't you always look at the boyfriend? Or the husband or whoever? Doesn't that make me your main suspect?"

Helen grinned, though she wasn't quite sure why.

"Don't worry about that, Adam. Ordinarily, you'd be right. But not this time. You keep an eye on the local news?"

"Sure, but what…" It took a second for the kid to get it, and when he did Helen could have sworn she actually heard him gulp.

"Wait a minute. Are you talking about those cop killings? The two guys killed over the last week or so."

Helen, gripping the steering wheel tighter, nodded.

"Are you saying that whoever did them killed Janey, too? That this was a–what would you call it–a serial killer?"

Helen took a deep breath and consciously shifted into cop mode. It was a way of thinking that she'd pretty much abandoned about the time she and Adam had hustled away from Janey's place.

The kid was right, at least as far as he'd gone with it. Even though knowing deep down that he probably had nothing to do with Janey's murder, Helen should have taken him right down to the station, placed him in an interview room and gotten everything she could out of him. That would have been the correct thing to do.

But as she'd silently expressed to herself earlier, at that moment she'd been more interested in *right* than in *correct*.

"Here's how it's going to work, Adam. I'm turning around and heading back to Central. We are going to have to talk to you, get some background info, but that's it."

"Do I need a lawyer or something? You know, I didn't know Janey all that long."

Helen shook her head, searching the morning gloom for the next turnoff.

"No, you don't. I shouldn't say this. It's a complete break of protocol, but I can almost guarantee you that you're not suspected of anything."

"'Cause this ties in with those other guys, right?"

"Yeah," Helen said, flicking on her blinker out of habit, even though there were no other vehicles within sight. "Janey ties in with those other guys."

Even as she spoke the words a cold, dead feeling settled deep within Helen's being.

It's time, she thought.

Time to forget Lori Michaels, or any cases shared by Roy and the boss.

No doubt about it now.

We're all targets.

And for a moment that cold feeling got even colder, as she wondered if Tim Johnson had been right.

Was it possible, she wondered, that she herself had brought all of this on her friends?

THE AVENGER–AFTER THE THIRD

For the first time ever, he became sick after a job.

Barely making it back to his hotel, thankful that so late at night there was little traffic, he pulled into the hotel's parking garage clenching his teeth, mentally commanding his stomach to hold tight. But as he climbed out of the rental car he knew that he wouldn't make it to his room.

Again grateful for the lateness of the hour, he rushed to a far corner of the garage, bent over and disgorged his stomach.

A long, continuous, and muscle-wracking expurgation left him exhausted, pale and sweating on the concrete garage floor.

This had never happened before.

After taking in several deep, soul-cleansing breaths, he managed to climb to his feet, sweat dripping from his face and leaving blotches on the gray concrete. He took off his jacket, wiped his mouth with his shirt sleeve, then put the jacket back on. Nice and clean in case he bumped into anyone on the way to his room.

But he didn't, managing to cover the expanse of the garage to an empty elevator, and an empty hallway when he exited. He'd barely made it to his room a minute later when the torment came on him once again.

This time it only took the form of dry heaves, though ones so deep and painful that he imagined death would feel better.

Eventually, and once more, the Avenger had no notion of how long it took, the spell passed him by, and he fell to the floor, his back against the bathroom wall.

His heart raced, the clamminess of fear washing over his frame.

A job had never affected him this way. From the first one, all the way back in L.A., the Avenger had never felt any sort of compunction or discomfort. For him, in the beginning, with the Company's blessing, or at least their tacit approval, killing (never murder, there was a difference) had been merely a job, one to be handled with as much dispatch as possible.

Then, after the Director's death, he'd split from them, and his work had become more of a calling.

But never, in either iteration, had it given him this sort of problem.

He wondered if it had to do with the fact that this time he'd targeted a woman. Actually, more of a girl, not even yet thirty years old.

Closing his eyes, he placed his palms together and sent himself down the tangled skeins of his memory, plucking out isolated strands, trying to place whether he'd ever killed a woman before.

The task was made more difficult by the fact that, and he well knew this, his mind wasn't what it had once been. As the mélange of faces, names and places raced before his vision, he was well aware he couldn't trust that all of the scenes were true. Some no doubt were. Others may have shades of veracity to them. While some were surely completely imaginary.

As far back as he could search, he held no memories of killing a woman. So that may have been what caused such a violent physical reaction.

Or maybe, as he walked to the mini bar and poured himself a tall Scotch, his internal conflict stemmed from not targeting the right woman.

As the liquor eased its way down his throat, bringing a small amount of surcease, The Avenger considered that as the true problem.

He had not killed the right woman.

The one who had caused all the trouble.

The one who'd brought him, practically beckoned him, to this city.

He nodded, drained the rest of his glass and suddenly felt his old self.

Like smoke clearing from his eyes, The Avenger now saw his mistake. Unlike the other cities, where several people had been at fault for their actions, in this situation there was one main perpetrator.

And so far, he'd let that person skate.

No more. The time had come to deal with her directly.

Placing his empty glass down, The Avenger turned to the window, shocked to see sunlight spiking through the lower panes.

He'd done the hit at night, and it had still been dark when he'd left the parking garage and gotten to his room. How long had his fit in the bathroom lasted?

He shook his head, wondering just what was happening to him. Had the accumulated stress of his missions finally manifested itself? Was he in danger of losing his mind within his calling?

Standing there, basking in the sunlight steadily rising into the room, sudden hunger pangs assailed him. He craved nourishment in a way he never had before.

His body responding, he told himself. Working to fight off whatever devils tormented him by demanding food.

He was fine, nothing to worry about at all. Physically, mentally and spiritually, with his focus now complete and inclusive, he was ready to resume his mission.

After some food, and a long, long sleep.

CHAPTER FORTY-THREE

Helen wheeled her car into the parking garage next to Central. Even though they were in her private vehicle, she could have pulled rank, so to speak, and driven to the upper level reserved for police vehicles. But it was early enough in the morning, the sun just beginning to peep itself above the horizon, that she basically had her choice of slots and levels.

She showed her badge at the entry kiosk, to avoid paying the nominal fee, then proceeded to twirl her car up and up through the various corkscrew ramps.

Beside her, Adam Thorson had been silent for several minutes.

Occasionally, on the ride over, she'd glanced his way, each time seeing him staring straight ahead, face clenched and drawn, eyes unblinking. She didn't know anything about the kid, but if he was decent enough for Janey to have become interested in him, barring any false fronts he may have put up, this was probably his first experience with someone he cared for dying violently.

So Helen had left him alone.

While not going all the way to the top, she did take her car far enough up that they could exit through one of the side doors and cross a covered walkway into the station. Like most structures of this sort, it had a low concrete retaining wall, which offered an open-air view of the surrounding area.

Helen had parked on the side of the garage facing the station, and as she and Adam got out, she glanced over in that direction.

Her skin tightened all over.

In cop terms, this was the deadest of the dead times. Ordinarily at this point in the morning, the graveyard patrol shift had not yet returned, and the day shift officers would be trickling in. As they arrived, the first shifters would head either to their lockers or the roll call room, both located in the basement.

So most days the building would appear, at least from the outside, almost deserted, with maybe one or two stray lights left on somewhere, and hardly any people or cars within sight.

But not so on this morning. As Helen gazed toward the station, nearly every window in the building was lit up, and in at least half of those windows she could see, even from the distance, people moving back and forth.

Outside, down by the entrance, a swarm of media people had camped out. From her vantage, Helen counted four television vans and at least as many radio vehicles. Two women, one local anchor, and another who Helen didn't recognize, were doing stand-ups literally on the steps leading into the station building.

But as she turned her gaze upward, to Central's roof, she began to get a sick feeling in her stomach.

An untrained person wouldn't have spotted them at all. They were hidden so well, but several years back Helen and Jack Hollis had taken a short crash course on SWAT tactics, just in case the special teams ever needed to recruit new members on an emergency basis, and she could easily spot at least three snipers positioned along the perimeter of the roof.

"Is something wrong?" Adam asked behind her.

Helen, realizing she hadn't moved for several seconds, turned to the young man.

"Huh?"

"You were just kind of staring off into space. Is everything okay?"

Even as he said the words, the kid's face twisted a bit, as if realizing the irony of his question considering the circumstances.

"No," Helen said, "nothing…"

She glanced behind her at the brightly-lit station, such an unusual sight this early in the morning.

"It's just…this place just doesn't seem the same anymore."

CHAPTER FORTY-FOUR

Helen deposited Adam in a holding room on the second floor.

"Don't worry," she said. "I'll send someone in soon to take your statement, and then you should be free to leave."

As she spoke, she worried it might not quite work out that way. Were she or Hollis running the investigation, they wouldn't even consider this kid a suspect. But the amount of activity in and out of the building, including the rooftop snipers guarding over the building, pretty much confirmed that, as of Janey's death, someone higher up had finally stepped in.

Even so, she couldn't see any possible linkage between Adam and either Michaels or Jarvis. Were it a matter of Janey's murder only, someone she'd recently begun dating would be an automatic suspect, but surely he was in the clear here.

As she signed a couple of paper forms, signifying she'd brought the kid in as a witness in the case, Helen remembered another time when, simply due to the law of averages, she'd automatically assumed a lover of a victim was a killer. She'd been wrong that time, almost criminally wrong as it turned out.

As she headed out of the holding area and toward the stairs that lead up to the squad room, she pulled out her cell phone and checked it for messages. Since the other day in Kendal's office, she'd tried three times to reach out to Ron Green. Each time, she'd been vague as to the subject matter, merely asking him to contact her right away.

Each time, she'd deliberately put more urgency into the message.

Still, when she now checked, no return calls from him.

There were, however, two messages, the first logged in nearly an hour before and the other within the last fifteen minutes.

Both from Tim Johnson.

Sidling around a corner and looking both ways, she keyed up Johnson's first call.

"Hey, Lipscomb, it's Tim. Just heard about your friend, and I'm on my way to the scene now. I know this is lousy timing and all, but hey, we all have our jobs, right? I'd like to get some words from you as to Turner. Maybe give me something that will humanize her for the story? And as far as the other thing we were discussing the other day…well, I think I may have been off base on that. Give me a call when you can, and I'll explain."

Helen shook her head. Johnson wasn't bad, at least as journalists went, but she really felt no inclination to sit down and spill anything personal about Janey.

What would she say? Janey was a young cop with a future? She had grown up out of state and moved here after college? Or that she had a new boyfriend who'd had his entire life knocked off kilter a couple of hours ago?

She could just see herself spilling all that out to the world.

She tapped again, figuring Johnson's second call would be just a rehash of the first but wanting to make sure.

"Hey, Lipscomb. I know you're probably busy as all hell, but in case you get this before it hits the fan my editor's killing me for some sort of inside scoop. It's going like batshit crazy around here. Probably not as nuts as it is there at Central, but still pretty bad. Ed wants me on a flight to Canton this afternoon. Guess who to see? I'm trying to argue him out of it.

"Scratch what I said the other night. I think Green's a dead end. We've got a newbie here who's been bending my ear about something going on when she lived in California. Don't feel too special, kiddo. You're not the only one I'm yammering at, but I'll take anything I can get from an official source. Even if it doesn't jibe with the official story, if you know what I mean. Dammit, call when you get a second."

Making a face, Helen turned her phone off. She wasn't sure if Johnson was just being a self-centered prick, or if he'd had other people around and was trying to get a message to her.

The reference to Canton bothered her, seeing as how that was the town where Ron Green had ended up. But she didn't understand the California reference.

At the moment, though, with Janey dead only a few hours and Adam Thorson downstairs waiting on someone to come get him, she had more immediate things to worry about.

At the top of the list, they'd probably expected her back in the squad room long before now.

Squaring her shoulders, Helen turned the corner and went through the door to meet up with the rest of the squad.

And walked right into the middle of Hell on Earth.

CHAPTER FORTY-FIVE

The squad room looked busier than Helen could ever recall. Even during the last mayoral inauguration, things hadn't been so chaotic. People, both plainclothes and uniforms, running in and out; nearly every computer on the floor tapping away; and those not on computers moving to and fro with smart phones pasted to their ears.

From the section toward the back holding the interview rooms came some sort of cacophony, leading Helen to believe that an assortment of suspects, for who knew what crimes, had been left to sit idle while more important business came first. The door to the captain's office was closed, as usual, but it kept opening and reclosing as strangers moved in and out.

Even more unsettling, a large number of the people bustling around were unknown to her, though here and there she picked out a couple of state police investigators she'd run into from time to time.

So it had already begun. Janey's murder being the final straw setting things in motion.

In the midst of the swirl of madness, Hollis sat at his desk. Calm, nearly motionless, he appeared merely surveying everything going on around them.

She sidled over his way.

"What's the latest?" she asked, keeping one eye on the captain's door.

Hollis looked up, and Helen nearly took a step back.

Under the harsh, fluorescent lights of the squad room, she saw a mass of new wrinkles on his face she could swear hadn't been there the day before. His hair hung limp, and she could see more red in his eyes than white.

She couldn't help but wonder if, the next time she got a chance to look in the mirror, her face would resemble his.

Helen snagged a chair from a few feet away and sat down next to him.

"Talk to me, Jack."

For an instant, the big, tough cop she'd known for so many years took on the appearance of a frightened little kid.

"Did I get her killed?" Hollis asked.

"What?" Helen shook her head. "Did you do what?"

"Did I get Janey killed? I was the primary, right? The one supposed to be in charge, at least until they showed up." He tossed his head toward the captain's office.

Helen wasn't sure who "they" were, but she had a pretty good guess.

"It's not your fault, Jack."

"Who else's, then? I've been sitting here ever since getting back from her place. They practically shoved me out of there, by the way." The mysterious "they" again. "And I've been going over the whole thing. Ever since we got the squeal on Roy. What did I miss? What wasn't I cop enough to see?"

Helen wanted to reach out to her colleague, grab his hand or squeeze his shoulder, but she knew such a gesture would only make things worse. She recognized the particular species of guilt plaguing him.

She'd struggled with the same sort of guilt several

months before. After last year's serial killings had been resolved, with the culprit gunned down by herself and Hollis, it had taken no time at all for the Monday morning quarterbacks to start up.

Most of the news and opinion coverage over the following weeks, not to mention the discussions during city council meetings, focused on the fact that had Helen seen things more clearly early on, at least a handful of people would have been spared. That her single-minded (never mind it was never like that) pursuit of Green caused her to overlook clues and information, which would have allowed an earlier apprehension of the true killer.

Never mind that none of the critics could point to a single piece of evidence or information, could never provide any specifics. The general possibility was taken, pumped up and allowed to run wild.

So much so that, after a while, Helen began to believe it herself. At one point, in a moment of overwhelming self disgust, she'd almost turned in her badge. At the time, none of the reassurances of her fellow cops, those best in a position to know what had actually gone down, helped to assuage the near-paralyzing guilt she'd felt.

Now, sitting next to her friend and partner, she could see the same torment running through him. And from experience, she knew nothing she said or did would get through.

He simply had to deal with it on his own.

Still, she wanted to keep him talking.

"So are we out of it now?" she asked.

"Yeah," Hollis said. "Some of these people running around that you don't recognize? They're from the troopers. Kendal came out and announced it earlier, then ran back into his office with a couple of the top ones."

Helen stood and gazed around the room. Now that she'd been here a while, she could see the chaos was actually a bit more controlled than it had first appeared. Most of the people navigating about were new, while the regular squad members, for the most part, sat at their desks, trying to look buried in paperwork.

"Johnson called me," Hollis said.

Helen turned back to him. "What?"

"Tim Johnson. The guy from the paper? Said he'd been trying to get ahold of you but you weren't answering your phone. Where'd you run off to, anyway? Kendal was pissed that we all weren't accounted for."

Helen shrugged. "Adam. Janey's boyfriend? He and I went for a ride, kind of a calming down type thing."

"The kid know anything?"

"I didn't talk to him much," Helen said. "Beyond assuring him he wasn't a suspect. He's seen enough TV and movies that it had him worried. But he managed to put two and two together and realized Janey wasn't a one off."

Hollis frowned.

"Still," he said, "that may not have been the wisest thing to do. We're assuming the three of them are connected, but what if they aren't? Janey could have been a one off, or maybe this kid heard about Roy and Pete, put it together, and decided to take advantage of the situation."

Now it was Helen's turn to grimace.

"Maybe so, but I went on instinct. And my gut told me he's not in on it. And if by chance he is involved, all I did was allay his worries. So if anything it's a plus."

"So where is he now?"

"Downstairs. I put him in a holding until someone can take a statement." She looked around at all the strangers rushing around and her own people sitting at their desks. "I guess that could be any one of us."

Hollis sighed, a facial tic beginning. Helen had the unsettling feeling he had more to say.

"Kendal wants to see you. As soon as you got here, he said. He and Jorgenson are waiting in his office."

Helen glanced toward the closed office door.

"Who's Jorgenson?" she asked.

"Lt. Jorgenson. I'm guessing from the Drug and Crime office of the staties. All we know for sure is that the man is now firmly in charge of this investigation."

"What the hell then? Why don't the rest of us just say screw it and go home? After all—"

"Easy there, partner," Hollis interrupted. "We knew this was coming sooner or later, and despite what we may think of the chief, it's the right call. There's no way we can go on with this. Especially since any one of us may be the next victim."

And there it was. The thing Helen had been avoiding for the last few hours. She'd known it as soon as Hollis had called her, or at least as soon as she was awake enough to process his words.

This was no longer a matter of finding out who had it in for Michaels, or if some connection existed between him and Jarvis.

It was now about all of them. Every single person on the squad, and possibly extending beyond, to the West and East divisions.

Somebody was gunning for them.

For all of them.

Her cords suddenly cut, Helen collapsed into an empty chair next to Hollis's desk. Placing her palms on her thighs, she stared down at the floor between her knees.

"Has the lab—"

"Rushed like you wouldn't believe. Obviously, the PM hasn't been done yet, though from what I gather they shoved all the other customers back and put Janey at the front. So it's possible they're going over her as we speak."

A faint wave of nausea ran through Helen's gut. No way to shake, and for some reason she really didn't want to, the image of her friend and co-worker stretched out on the slab. Helen had attended enough autopsies herself over the years to know the routine by heart. Hell, some days she felt she could actually pick up the tools of the trade and do the procedure herself.

But such knowledge, guided by long experience, now served as a detriment. Even with her eyes open and focused on the room around her, the scene of what they were right now doing to Janey's form over in the ME's building caused her a sort of queasiness she hadn't experienced in several years.

She looked around the frantic squad room, suddenly noticing something out of place.

"Where's Lou?" she asked.

Hollis grimaced.

"Rottenest damned luck. You remember that suspect they went after for Roy? The Pinon guy?"

"The one they found dead?"

"Right. This morning, just as he got here, Lou got a call from West. Seems they picked up somebody last night in connection with that. Off a tip or something. Lou went over there to look into it."

Helen shook her head.

"That's not good, Jack. He was as close to Janey as any of us. This isn't the time for him to go off and—"

"Believe me, I know. But he was out the door before anyone knew. Smith over there saw him get a phone call and we traced it back to West and got the story. He's over there right now."

Before either she or Hollis could say anything more, the captain's door opened.

Kendal stood in the doorway, shirt rumpled and hair mussed.

"Detective Lipscomb, could you join us for a moment?"

CHAPTER–FORTY-SIX

As Lou Whitmore exited the elevator and stepped into the squad room of West Division, a gray-haired Latino man got up from a desk and walked over to him.

"Whitmore," the man said, holding out his hand.

"You must be Smith," Lou said as they shook.

"That's right, Steve Smith."

Lou cocked his head and stared at the man. "We've got a Smith on our squad. Doesn't look anything like you."

The other man grinned. "Name from dad, looks from mom," he said.

Lou grinned back, but even as he did so he figured his face looked something like a death mask.

Smith sobered and stepped closer.

"Sorry, guy. Probably not the time for levity. I know you've got other things on your mind, but—"

"Nothing I can do at the moment but sit around and mope," Lou said. "Way it looked when I left, the damned thing's being taken out of our hands. Not just my squad, but all of us."

"Yeah." Smith nodded. "That's what we're hearing. So let's deal with something we can control."

Smith turned to a cross hallway next to the door, and Lou followed. They walked down a corridor toward a cluster of holding cells.

"Name is, if you can believe it, Tyrone Jesus

Wallace. And he'll make sure you know about the middle name, believe me."

"So what's his deal?" Lou asked.

"Mainly small time. Spends a lot of time dealing the parks, mostly at night. Turns out he had a loose connection with your victim of the other day, this Pinon guy."

"How'd you get onto him?" Lou asked.

Smith glanced back, his face lighting up for a second.

"How do you think?"

Lou shook his head.

"Jailhouse?"

"That's right. You ever stop to figure that if the public found out how much of our work is done by cellmates wanting to cut a deal, they'd vote to cut our salaries?"

Lou guessed that Smith was talking in such a jocular way to ease his tension, and while he appreciated the thought, it really wasn't working.

"Here we are," Smith said as he stopped beside the farthest cell on the right. He worked the keypad alongside the door frame, and the two of them stepped inside.

The young black man in the cell had moved the single chair away from the table and scooched it against the far wall. He leaned against the wall, poised on the chair's two rear legs.

"Meet Tyrone Wallace," Smith said as he shut the door.

The prisoner, his gaze locked on the black and white tiled floor, replied without looking up. "That's Tyrone Jesus, cop. I done told you that."

"My apologies, Tyrone," Smith said as he turned and winked at Whitmore.

Now the prisoner looked up at the two of them. "Who's this guy? Another cop?"

"My name's Whitmore," Lou said.

Tyrone roamed his gaze deliberately up and down Lou's frame. "You the muscle that beaner boy here brought in to soften me up?"

Smith sighed, shook his head and, arms crossed, leaned in a corner of the wall.

"No," Lou said, "I'm not the muscle. Not much. I'm the guy who's looking into the murder of Luis Pinon. You happen to know him?"

Wallace tensed a little, but managed to keep most of his slouch.

"I heard around that Lu got it done to him good. Nothing to do with me."

Smith sighed again.

"Cut the crap, Tyrone. Okay? Detective Whitmore, how was your guy killed?"

"Some sort of blunt object. ME wasn't sure, but said it could have been a ball peen hammer."

"Well, there you go. We just happened to pick up Tyrone *Jesus* here at his girlfriend's place, and there was a ball peen in his bedroom, stuck under his mattress. Not the brightest of moves, huh, Tyrone?"

The prisoner tried to stare them down now, but his eyes jiggled the smallest bit. Both Lou and Smith kept their faces straight.

"I don't suppose there was any evidence on the head of the hammer?" Lou asked.

"Nope. Looked like it had been scrubbed clean."

Now Wallace's eyes took on a cocky glaze.

Kevin R. Doyle

"'Course," Smith continued, "it helped that the object in question had a wooden handle. They're testing it right now." He turned his gaze full on the prisoner. "Now, as a bright man of the streets you may not know this, but either Detective Whitmore or I could tell you it's damned near one hundred percent impossible to clean material out of a wooden object. So way I see it, you've got two choices. Isn't that right, Detective Whitmore?"

Lou nodded, but didn't say anything.

"I want a lawyer," Wallace said. "I got a lawyer call to make. Let me make it."

Smith and Lou looked at each other, and Lou shrugged.

"Looks like he made his decision."

Smith grimaced and ushered Lou out.

"Stay cool, Tyrone. We'll get someone in here to chat with you."

"That's Tyrone Jesus, goddammit. And I don't want just somebody. I want a fucking lawyer!"

The two cops shut the door on the shouting man.

"What do you have for motive?" Lou asked.

"Rumor so far. According to the cellmate, the two fell out over the splits of a deal. Tyrone came over to Pinon's place to talk things over and, well, there you have it."

Lou rubbed his face, every muscle in his body feeling both tight and exhausted at the same time.

"So you were looking at Pinon for the Michaels' deal, right? Back when it was just Michaels?" Smith asked.

Lou nodded.

"Which is kind of a moot point, now. My only

problem is…" He faded off, suddenly too fatigued even to keep talking.

Feeling a hand on his shoulder, he opened his eyes.

"How about this," Smith said. "My load's pretty light at the moment. Technically, Pinon is your case, of course. But if you've no objection, I'll take it from here. Run it through, and if it comes to a culmination I'll give you a buzz."

Lou hesitated. He didn't like the thought of willingly handing over a case, especially a major crime. But he didn't have any idea what would be going on when he got back to Central. The State folks might have taken over the whole thing and shoved the local squad to the side, or they could be planning on using them to do all the gopher work. All Lou knew for sure was that for the next few days his mind definitely wasn't going to be on some dead scumbag.

Not when he had so many of his own dead to mourn.

"Sounds like a deal, Steve. Keep it in the bank, and I'll reciprocate some day."

"You got it."

The two men shook hands, and Lou moved on down the corridor, heading toward the doors and out of the station.

Back to his own dead to mourn.

CHAPTER FORTY-SEVEN

When Helen entered Kendal's office, she saw another man standing at the window.

Tall, around six two or so, and blond-haired, in profile the stranger looked somewhere around his mid-thirties. Wearing a navy blue suit, which even from the distance she guessed as solid wool, he was dressed a step or two up from most cops she knew. She wondered for a second if he were a lawyer, but over the years she'd met most of the criminal lawyers in town, and this man was unknown to her.

"Take a seat," Kendal said, an odd tone in his voice. Weariness?

A hint of fatigue, maybe?

As Kendal sat behind his desk, the blond man turned to her.

"You've really fucked us up, detective."

Helen's fists clenched, but caution kept her quiet. She couldn't peg the guy. She had a guess as to his identity, but for the moment, until she knew more, decided to hold her tongue.

"Helen," Kendal said, "this is Lieutenant Jorgenson, from the State Patrol."

Helen nodded, keeping her face impassive, at the same time a slight worm of uncertainty wriggled through her insides.

"As of a few hours ago," Kendal continued, "the

lieutenant and his people are in charge of investigating the murders of our colleagues."

"A task which you've done a pretty good job of complicating the hell out of, by the way."

Helen stared at Jorgenson, not wanting to appear antagonistic, but refusing to back down.

"I don't know what you mean," she said. "What have I done that's hindered you at all? So far this morning, I showed up at the latest scene when requested and escorted a potential witness into the building. Nothing else."

"Keep it up, Lipscomb," Jorgenson said, and now a distinct note of tension had crept into his voice. "Keep it up and you're lucky if you get out of prison sometime in the next five years."

Helen half rose out of her chair, only to have Kendal wave at her to sit back down.

"I doubt it's that serious," the captain said.

"The hell it isn't." The tension in Jorgenson's voice edged toward flat-out anger. "What do you think she's looking at for obstructing an ongoing felony investigation?"

"Obstructing?" This time, Helen ignored Kendal when he tried to placate her. She stood up and, moving about a foot away from the desk, took a position facing the state cop. "What the hell are you talking about, mister?

"As if you didn't know."

"Kurt!" Kendal broke in.

Jorgenson turned partially from Helen.

"Frank, I understand that you were just given this gig, but how the hell is she still walking around with a badge?"

"For Christ sakes," Helen snapped. "What are you two talking about?"

"Green," Jorgenson said, "as if you didn't know."

For Helen, that tiny feeling of anxiety had now begun to expand into something definite.

"Green?" she parroted.

"Helen," Kendal said, "Ronald Green's attorney contacted the city attorney late last night. There's talk of a harassment suit against the city."

Helen sat back down, her jaw clenched so tightly she almost broke a tooth.

"Harassment suit?"

"That's right," Jorgenson interposed. "Seems that Mr. Green was given a heads up to the possibility that he could become a suspect in the deaths of Michaels, Jarvis, and now Turner. Now tell us, detective, where would he get that idea from?"

Helen couldn't remember the last time her mind had worked so quickly. But every possible response she could think of would only get her in deeper.

"Last year," Kendal said, "there were some who thought you'd suggested to Green that he think about a lawsuit. Now it seems he may take you up on that."

"Which really isn't the problem," Jorgenson said.

"I realize that," Helen said. "Any possible surprise advantage we would have had is shot."

"So I've got a question for you," Kendal said, "and I'd better get a straight answer. When's the last time you had contact with him?"

Helen paused, looking for, but not finding, a way out.

"Detective?" Kendal prodded while Jorgenson glowered behind him.

"I haven't spoken to him since he left town last year," she said.

Kendal and Jorgenson stared her down for a moment.

"But I did try to call him several times in the last few days."

Time seemed to stop in the office.

"You what?" Kendal finally asked.

"I tried to call him. More than once."

"Why?"

Helen scrambled for some excuse that wouldn't make her sound beyond incompetent.

In the end, she concluded the only possible way out was to come completely clean.

"I'm positive he's not involved in this, and I wanted to—" She trailed off, searching for the best word.

"You wanted to warn him, right?" Jorgenson chimed in.

"I wanted to give him a chance to—"

"You wanted to warn him," Kendal said.

"No, sir. But I figured that if I reached out we could see where things stood and—"

"And this was after I specifically told you to have nothing to do with the Green angle?"

When Helen had first entered the office, Kendal had seemed willing to hear her out. But now, the rise in his voice and clenching of his face didn't bode well for her.

"I realize this looks bad, sir. But I'm telling you, Green isn't involved."

Jorgenson and Kendal looked at each other, and the state cop shook his head.

"Two things about that, detective. One, you don't know that. Just because you were wrong about him

271

before, that shouldn't cloud your judgment now."

"I just wouldn't want to make the same mistake again."

"I get that. But it's not your mistake to make, so to speak. Which leads to the second thing you were wrong about. Frank?"

Kendal stood up, and that sinking feeling in Helen's gut accelerated.

"Detective Lipscomb, this is straight from the chief's office. As of now, you're suspended, with pay, until this goes through the PRO. Green's attorney is coming into town sometime today, and we hope to have this ironed out by tomorrow at the latest. But until then we need you away from this squad and this department. And even if somehow you're cleared, I'm going to have to give some serious thought as to whether or not you come back here."

"I never spoke to him," she protested.

"No, but if you were calling him, harassing him, he probably figured out what it was about. And he's a smart enough man to guess we were at least suspecting him. That's probably enough right there, if I decide to push it, to get you bounced from the department for good."

"Everyone says you're a smart cop, Lipscomb," Jorgenson said. "But right now, you're looking pretty damned dumb. It won't take much for me to make this a charge of obstruction of justice. Were I you, I'd get the hell out of here as quickly as possible, and stay as far away from my investigation as you can."

Helen stood up, her focus now squarely on the state cop.

"In the last two weeks, I've seen three of my friends killed. Do you think for even a minute that if I thought there was even a chance that Green was involved I would have warned him off?"

"But that's the point," Jorgenson snapped. "It wasn't your call. Not only were you going on emotion instead of investigation, you weren't the primary. If nothing else, your contacting Green should have been run by Jack Hollis first. Or was it?"

"No," Helen said, silently thanking God that she'd called Green on her own. "Jack had nothing to do with this."

Jorgenson turned back to Kendal.

"I'd say it's time to wrap this up, Frank. Wouldn't you say?"

Kendal held his hand out to Helen, palm up.

Sighing, she slipped her badge holder out of her jacket pocket and her gun out of its holster. She handed both of them over to Kendal.

"I'll keep them here for now," he said. "Give it a couple of days, and I hope we can get this behind us."

Silently, Helen turned and went to the door. With her hand on the knob, she looked back at Kendal.

"Nothing personal, captain. But a few minutes ago as I was standing up in the parking garage, looking over this way, I had the thought that the station looked strange, almost like a place I'd never been before."

Kendal slipped her badge holder and gun into his desk drawer.

"And?"

"And now," she replied, "it looks even more so."

CHAPTER FORTY-EIGHT

Los Angeles

"Send him in." Lawrence Sears clicked off his intercom at the same time he used a remote to mute the television recessed into the wall on the far side of the office.

He barely had time to get up from his desk and slip on his suit jacket before Morton walked in, flanked by two of his men.

On this morning, Mr. Morton wore a light tan poplin suit with dark blue shirt and a pink and blue tie. The two other men, faceless behind their Ray-Bans, both wore dark gray suits, white shirts and black ties.

It occurred to Sears, something he'd never noticed in all his time dealing with the man, that while Morton wore a variety of clothing, on duty his employees only wore gray suits, white shirts and black ties. Except for the color of their ties, the men could have been mistaken for IBM employees.

"Good morning," Sears said, wondering if Morton had noticed the television still on across the room.

More than likely, seeing as how the man seemed to notice everything.

"Mr. Sears," Morton said, walking up to his desk but not sitting down, "there was an incident in the Midwest last night."

Sears nodded and gestured toward the TV.

"I know. I've just been watching the news. Only took a few hours for the media to get all over it."

"Understandable, seeing as it's the latest in a string."

"All plainclothes officers," Sears said.

For a moment neither man, watching the silent screen, said anything. It showed a young blonde reporter, no doubt from one of the local stations, doing a standup in front of the city building downtown. A rotating, blue and yellow box in the corner of the screen flashed the words "News Alert" while in the upper right corner an insert box showed the head shot of a young woman, long brown hair and no older than thirty at the most. Even on Sears's large, flat screen set, her name "Det. Janey Turner" was barely visible at the bottom of the insert.

"Is it him?" Sears finally asked.

"I'm still acquiring information," Morton said. "The murder happened something like ten hours ago, but we're moving as fast as we can."

"Give me your gut, Mr. Morton. Is this Andrew's handiwork that we're looking at?"

Morton squirmed, just the slightest bit. Sears knew full well that the man hated using hunches and guesses, preferring instead hard info.

"If I had to guess, Mr. Sears, I'd say this is the most likely of the three areas we were looking at. If I manage to get absolute confirmation do you want me to proceed as usual?"

Now it was Sears turn to hesitate. He looked over at the television screen, now showing three insert boxes side by side, with three head shots and profiles in them.

"I'm not so sure the usual procedure will get us much," he said. "After all, how many times have we done the usual?"

"Four by my count, sir."

"So maybe it's time to try something else."

Morton glanced over at Sears, a frown on his face.

"Did you have something particular in mind?"

Sears walked around his desk and went over to a wet bar against the east wall. He mixed himself a strong Scotch, no ice, then turned back to the other men.

Morton made an elaborate show of checking his watch.

"I know," Sears said, "but, dammit, this thing's tearing me apart."

"We could do something really radical," Morton said.

"Such as?"

"Turn everything over to the authorities. Let them deal with it."

Sears frowned and took a gulp from his glass.

"You know we can't do that."

"Because?"

"You know damn well why not!" Sears gulped, even more this time.

Morton sighed.

"It could be in our best interest," he pointed out. "Sooner or later, Andrew's going to be found out. Might be better to get out in front of it."

Now it was Sears's turn to frown as he thought that over, though finally shaking his head.

"She'll never go along with it. I've tried before to talk her into more stringent measures, and you know how that's ended up."

One of Morton's men shifted a bit as a new scene showed up on the still-silent television, and his motion startled Sears. Morton's people, both male and female, were so damned faceless that it didn't take too long for you to forget they were even in the room.

"Okay, then," Morton said. "I'd say right now we're at about a ninety percent certainty, and I should have some more information by midday. How about I go ahead and head out there and assess the situation personally?"

Sears nodded and drained the rest of his drink. For a minute he stared into the empty glass.

"Sir?" Morton's voice broke him out of his reverie. "We'll bring him back. Any changes in protocol can be discussed once the situation's contained."

"Three cops," Sears said. "What the hell can be running through his mind?"

"Probably the same thing as always, just amped up more than usual."

"But how much worse can it get?" Sears asked. "What happens when we hit a point where it can't be contained?"

Morton gestured to his two automatons, who turned and headed out of the office, leaving the door open behind them.

"How much worse?" Morton said as he turned to leave himself. "I guess that's really up to Mrs. Sears."

CHAPTER FORTY-NINE

Leaving Kendal's office, feeling Jorgenson's glare stabbing her in the back, Helen stopped at the desk she'd been temporarily using. Leaning over and attempting to act as if rearranging items, she began speaking to Hollis, sitting at his own desk a few feet away.

"Talk to me, Jack. Just don't make it obvious."

"Huh?"

"They just sacked me," Helen whispered.

Hollis's arm muscles clenched up, the only reaction he showed. No one even a couple of feet away would have noticed anything.

"You got fired? For what?"

"Not fired. At least not yet. But Kendal took my badge and told me to go home. At least for now."

"That bastard!" Hollis began to stand up, but Helen made a slight shushing gesture in his direction.

"Don't lose it on me, buddy. I need you to keep it together. We all do."

Straightening herself up, swiveling her head around the squad room, still frenzied chaos all around, she settled her gaze on her now-former partner.

"The parking garage," she said, "row twelve, this side. Meet me there as quickly as you can."

Just for show, in case any eyes were observing from the once again closed office, she held out her hand for Hollis to shake.

Then she threw her coat on, picked up a few things from the desk, and headed out.

Several people watched her leaving, but she figured they'd get the story in no time at all.

Rather than take the elevator, she went out the side doors that let onto the stairwell.

The squad room doors shutting behind her sounded odd.

They sounded, in fact, kind of final.

****

Hollis frowned, his eyes narrowed to slits. Not entirely, Helen figured, because of the cold.

"You shouldn't have done that," he said, "not behind my back.'

"I'm sorry, Jack. It was a reactive kind of thing."

The two of them were huddled against the exit door leading to the stairwell, about ten feet from her parked car.

Helen had just relayed to him what had gone down in Kendal's office.

"It's my case," Hollis protested, "or at least it was until a few hours ago. You went behind my back by calling Green."

"I know, and it was a mistake. But do you honestly think he had anything to do with this?"

Hollis considered it, his arms crossed against the early morning cold. April only a few days away, and they still had frigid temps.

Helen decided to jog him along some. "What'd the lab have to say about Janey?"

Hollis shrugged.

"The usual. Found two shell casings, nine millimeter, right off. Jansen down in ballistics confirmed

279

they match the ones found with Pete and Roy. "

"The bullets themselves?"

Hollis looked a little sick.

"Passed right through her and ended up in the couch. Still not sure how whoever it was got inside her house. The lab folks are still working on that one."

"Think about it, Jack. Whoever it is is smart enough to get the drop on more than one experienced cop. You wouldn't imagine Janey just blindly opening up her door to someone, especially at night. But this guy, or guys, must have things planned out to a T. Does that sound like Green to you? A business teacher?"

"We don't know what he's been up to in the last year or so," Hollis replied. "Maybe he's been planning this ever since last summer. We always knew the guy was smart."

"But not smart like this. He's book smart, not like the streets."

"This isn't a street type crime, and you know it."

Helen nodded vigorously.

"That's my point. We've got something here beyond just the normal thug or psycho. Something really bad."

"Correction," Hollis said. "We don't. It's out of our hands now."

"I know. I met Jorgenson there in the captain's office."

"But before you showed up Kendal made it clear. We're to go back to our regular cases. At the most, the states may allow us to do their scut work for them, but any real investigation is going to be done at their level, not ours."

"What about the protection?" Helen asked.

"You mean the boys up on the roof?"

"Yeah. They'll be fine as long as folks are inside, but what about when you leave. Hell, as far as that goes, what about me? The chief may have suspended me, but whoever's out there gunning around doesn't know that."

"They haven't said anything about that, may still be working on it. Look, Helen, I'll see if I can talk to the captain. Maybe he can convince the brass to ease up on—"

"Don't, Jack. You say anything about this, and they'll start wondering if you were involved. They're saying I may have obstructed justice, and in hindsight they're probably right."

"But you can't just take the fall for this."

Helen shook her head, wondering just how to get through to the guy.

"Jack, three of us are already dead. Jorgenson and his people may have the skills, and the political pressure, but that's it. And Kendal, who the hell knows how involved he wants to get."

"You saying that the troopers won't want to get it solved? That's nuts, Helen."

She shook her head again.

"What I'm saying is that the pressure's going to be to wrap this quick. Now we have a third cop killed? And a cute young girl at that? You tell me what the odds are that they'll go for the quickest, easiest collar, just to say they made an arrest."

"And that would be Green? With a possible lawsuit already staring them down?"

"Him or someone else. What I'm saying is it's going to be all blow and show till they collar someone. Anyone. With all the cop-related issues around the country the last few years, they're going to want to put this one away quickly."

"And while they do so…" Hollis began.

"Exactly."

The two of them, colleagues and often partners for so long, stood and stared at each other.

"So what are you going to do?" Hollis finally asked.

Before Helen could answer, her phone buzzed. Taking it out, she glanced at the number and message. She read it over again, her mind racing.

Then she slipped the phone back into her coat pocket.

"Right about now," she said, "I'm going to let a man buy me a late breakfast. Then, one way or another, I've got to get ahold of Green. I'll call you later, at home. Not here."

Hollis nodded.

"Be careful out there."

Even as he said the words, Hollis grimaced.

Helen chuckled, though it came out rather forced.

"My dad used to love that show," she said as she slipped into her car and turned the key.

Pulling out of her parking slot and heading down the exit ramp, Helen glanced up in the rear-view mirror.

Hollis hadn't yet gone back inside, and she wondered if he was watching out for her for as long as he could.

It took three more loops around the ramp before she lost sight of him completely.

And as she glanced one more time in the now empty rear-view, she felt completely alone.

CHAPTER FIFTY

They met shortly after nine at Smitty's Doubles. Pretty much a dive bar just north of the downtown area. At night, Smitty's was usually frequented by blue-collar workers, retail people and nurses from one of the main hospitals, located about a block away. But the mornings were much more eclectic.

No one was really sure about the meaning of the word "Doubles," but it may have had something to do with the split nature of the bar. Along with its regular nighttime business, Smitty's opened up each morning around six or so and stayed open until eleven. By general consensus, they had the best greasy spoon breakfast in town. Despite, or maybe because of, its dive reputation at night, in the mornings one would often see a banker in a thousand-dollar suit sitting at the counter, elbow to elbow with a meat packer still in his apron, blood spatters and all.

Smitty's was that kind of place, but not the sort of establishment you went to if you wanted your picture in the paper. Rumor had it that once, at some indeterminate point in the past, a local reporter had tried to snap a photo of a city councilman sharing a booth with the owner of a local pawn store, one who reputedly doubled as a fence. Smitty, who at six eight had to stoop to enter the doorway of his own establishment, supposedly broke the reporter's camera, along with his arms, to the cheers of

283

his patrons.

At Smitty's Doubles, everyone minded their own business.

When Helen entered, she spotted Johnson right off. Sitting in a back booth, he looked up and waved her over.

Helen slid into the opposite side of the booth and glanced at his plate, literally mounded with bacon, eggs, biscuits and gravy. So much so that the food slopped over the edges of the plate.

At Smitty's, this was the smaller version of their full breakfast.

"Ravenous?" she said, gesturing toward his meal.

Johnson grinned, though he didn't put a lot of mirth into it.

"You bet. It's been a long night. Though probably not as long as yours."

A waitress came over and Helen, not really wanting anything but knowing she needed some kind of nourishment, ordered an orange juice. Once the woman had moved off, she turned back to Johnson.

"So what's so urgent? I've got a lot on my plate, so to speak."

"Come on, Helen. Don't try to pull one over. I heard they've sacked you over at the PD."

That set her back for a moment.

"You must have some amazingly fast, or desperate, sources."

Johnson grinned and shoveled a spoonful of eggs into his mouth.

"Gathering the news at the speed of light," he said.

Helen shrugged and did her best to look nonchalant. "I wouldn't exactly call it a sack. At least not yet. I should be back on the job soon. Just need to clear a few things up."

Johnson stared at her in such a way that Helen figured he knew she was downplaying the situation.

She shrugged again.

"Off the record?"

Johnson hesitated, then nodded his acquiescence.

"I need to hear it, Tim."

"Okay, okay. Off the record, but I may have you changing your mind in a few minutes."

Not sure what he meant by that, Helen decided to let it pass.

"So it's bad," she said. "Not exactly life threatening, but pretty serious. I'm sure if you don't know all the gory details yet, you will soon enough.'

"So you think you're off for good?"

Helen stayed silent as the waitress appeared with her juice, then spoke up after she moved off.

"There's a good chance of that, sure. Actually, if I was just fired I'd probably be getting off pretty easy."

Now Johnson grinned again, though with a lot more energy to it than before.

"Maybe not. I may just have your 'Get Out of Jail' free card."

He reached down to the seat beside him and brought up a manila file folder.

"I've got this on a flash drive as well. But I thought you'd want to see a hard copy first."

As Helen reached over to slide the file her way, their waitress came by with an order for another table. After she walked past, Helen flipped open the file.

Johnson stayed quiet for the ten minutes or so it took her to skim the material. When she finished, she closed the folder, leaned back, and took her first sip of her now-warm juice.

"Is this a joke?" she asked.

Johnson shook his head.

"No joke. I'm not saying I'm a hundred percent certain, but it's pretty interesting, don't you think?"

"How'd you come upon this?"

"Gal named Tracey Wright. She's a new hire, spent some time working on one of our sister pubs on the West Coast. About the time your lieutenant got killed she started paying attention to my articles. Finally, after Turner, Tracey said she needed to talk to me. She gave me the basic thing that was bugging her, we put our heads together and did some digging, and there you are. Interesting huh?"

Instead of answering, Helen opened the file and skimmed through it again. About halfway through, she closed it.

"If it turns out on the level, you've got a hell of a story here. So why bring it to me? Why not just run it down and go with it?"

Johnson grinned and took a big forkful of the mess on his plate. He chewed slowly and thoroughly before answering.

"Maybe I'm looking for two stories instead of one," he said, wiping his mouth with the back of his hand.

"It's obvious what the one is," Helen said, tapping the folder. "But what's the second?"

"Call it sort of human interest. A decent person, good at their job, personal downfall, then redemption. What I'm thinking is—"

Helen stood up, the tops of her thighs bumping into the table. "We're done here."

As she started out of the booth, he reached out and

grasped her wrist.

"Helen—"

"You want to use me as a subject," she hissed, noticing in her peripheral vision a few people looking their way. "Don't you think I've had enough of that to last a lifetime? I'm trying to move past it and you want to dredge it all up again? What are you angling for? A raise? A promotion?"

"Helen, wait a minute."

He still had his hand on her arm, but when she glared down at it, he pulled back.

"We're done," she repeated and turned to leave, but only made one step when he kept talking.

"Don't you want to get him?"

Helen froze, her muscles tensing up.

"Whoever this guy is, he's taken out three of your people so far. Right?"

"What about it?"

"And now the state cops have come in, and you all are being shunted aside. You most of all, right?"

She still hadn't turned back to face him. Mired in place, she noticed a few more people looking at her.

"I took the wrong approach," Johnson said behind her. "Okay? But this could be important, and you know it."

Helen sighed, turned back, and sat down again.

The folder was still where she'd left it.

"So tell me what you're thinking," she said.

Johnson gestured toward the file.

"Most of it's in there. When I started working on the Jarvis story, I had a kind of deja vu feeling, but I couldn't pin it down. Then Tracey came along and set me on the right path. She didn't get it with Michaels, but as soon as

Jarvis was put down she began to put it together."

"Put what together?" Helen asked.

"In particular the 9mm shots to the head. That was the main thing that popped for her."

Helen took a swallow from her mug. The beverage, entirely flat and warm, by now, went down without her even noticing it.

"So you didn't just come up with this yesterday?"

"Not at all. We've been working on it for a week or so now, Tracey and I."

"And came up with how many?" she asked.

"Three for sure. Chicago last year and San Francisco before that. And, of course, L.A. There's a couple of other possibles, but they don't exactly follow the exact pattern."

Helen took a deep, tense breath.

"And you didn't think it necessary to bring this to the attention of the police? You realize that between then and now whoever it was murdered another cop?"

"Think for a minute, Helen. If we'd called you guys up, what would the reaction have been?"

Helen looked down and saw she was gripping her glass so hard that it could break. She eased off and tried to collect her thoughts.

"Hollis would have listened to you," she finally said.

"Look, you're going through some heavy-duty stress right about now, but try to think it through. When has it ever happened that the cops took pointers from the press? Short of when some killer has written letters and confessed?"

"But no one else has seen any connection? How can that be?"

"Probably because the victims and numbers are all

different. With L.A., where it seems to have started, there were three people who worked for the city government, basically clerks. In San Fran, they lost four major business leaders. In Chicago, a total of three doctors. The only commonality being the 9mm and the head shots."

Helen opened the file and flipped through it again, more carefully this time.

"But the police in the individual cities caught on to something, right?"

"They did. Especially in Frisco, but in both cases, just as publicity began to ramp up, the killings stopped."

She looked up at Johnson.

"Never solved?"

The waitress came back their way, but when she was within ten feet of the booth Johnson waved her off.

"Never solved. And according to Tracey, after a while the cases just kind of faded away."

"There's no guarantee this is our person. And it's a long way from doctors and bankers to cops."

"But you can't deny the similarities. And what if they are all connected?"

Absentmindedly, Helen took a last swig of her juice.

"Okay," she said. "So let's say you're on to something here. Why me?"

"Like I said, I'm looking for two stories for the price of one. Can't you see this as your redemption?"

Helen shook her head. "There's got to be more."

Johnson sighed and flagged the waitress down. When she came by, he asked for the check. The girl glanced at Helen, who shook her head, then went off.

"Okay," he said. "Let's say, just for the sake of argument, I'm onto something here. I sure as heck can't investigate on my own, don't have the resources. And if

I go into the police station and say I've got a track on the cop killer, they're going to laugh me out. But—"

"But if you are onto something, it would be awful to let it slip away, right?"

Johnson grinned, leaned back and crossed his hands on his lap.

"So why not give what you've got to someone with access to resources," Helen continued, "but who has nothing to lose in terms of reputation."

The reporter nodded.

"Which is me," Helen said.

"Sorry, kid. But facts are facts, right? It's an open secret that ever since the Green debacle they've been looking for a way to get rid of you. So like you say, what have you got to lose?"

"Except I don't have access anymore. They took my badge this morning."

"And you're going to let that stop you?" Johnson asked.

Helen contemplated him for a moment, then placed her hand on the file.

"You said you had this on a flash drive?"

Johnson grinned, reached into his pocket, and slid the drive across the table.

"Keep the hard copy, too. I've got my own."

"You know I'll have to get a couple of others in on this."

"You going to take it to those state yutzes?" Johnson asked.

"I'll have to find some way. I'll pursue it, but there's no way I can do it alone."

Johnson shrugged. "Fine by me, but that gets us to what I want out of it."

Helen frowned.

"I thought you said you wanted the story."

"True. But the question is, how do I get it?"

Helen thought for a moment.

"I can't be giving information about an ongoing investigation to the press, Tim. Whether I'm involved or not. Not even to the press that gave it to me in the first place."

"I know," he said, spreading his hands out on the table. "All I ask is that you give me a heads up before any major action goes down."

"It could get dicey," she said as she stood and shrugged on her jacket. "I've got one thing I have to do first, a loose end to tire up before I deal with this. When I do, I'll give you as much of a lead time as I can."

CHAPTER FIFTY-ONE

One definite advantage to being shoved halfway out the door, Helen reflected, was having plenty of time on her hands. One downside, not being able to expense the cost of the flight into Akron-Canton airport, or the rental car she used to make the short hop into Canton.

After one or two wrong turns and a bit of squabbling with a fidgety GPS, Helen finally pulled up outside of Wendell L. Oliver High School.

It had kind of surprised her that she actually enjoyed driving around the town looking for the school. To a lot of people Canton, with over 70,000 residents, would seem like a fairly mid-sized city, but to Helen it felt like a small town. The mid-day traffic was fairly light, and there was a decent amount to see.

She even took a few minutes to drive by the pro football Hall of Fame. She'd never been much of an aficionado, but her dad had been, and she still remembered the number of Sunday afternoons as a little girl, stretched out on their couch and nestled in the crook of his arm as they watched the Rams play. That had all ended, of course, one night when her dad suffered a massive cardiac attack at work.

He'd been dead for years now, but her memories were still as fresh as ever.

Helen pulled the rental Celica into a section of the parking lot marked "Visitors," turned off the engine, and contemplated her next move.

She had the man's home phone number, but her messages had gone unanswered. She only knew his workplace due to a web search. She'd known Canton, known a high school, but there were three in the town. Fortunately, most schools these days had their faculty listed on their web sites, so even a suspended cop had found it easy to track him down.

Hopping on a plane hadn't taken a whole lot of thought or courage, but now that she sat here, yards away from the man, she wondered if she wasn't embarking on round two of the biggest error of her career.

She mulled this over for several seconds before, realizing her procrastination for what it was, she opened the door and got out.

After all, how much worse could she make things?

****

The atmosphere inside was relaxed enough that they didn't have a full-blown public safety officer, i.e. a city cop assigned to patrol the school, but a uniformed security guard met her in the front lobby.

Things would have been easier, though not much, if she still had her badge to flash. But her shield still rested, she assumed, in Kendal's desk drawer, and besides, it was questionable how much an out-of-state badge would have helped. Instead, she identified herself as a friend of the man's from out of town who needed to see him regarding a family emergency.

She liked to think she hadn't lied so much as really stretched the truth. She was from out of town, for sure. And while he probably wouldn't greet her as a friend, he at least would recognize her on sight. And you could consider the reason for her visit as something of an emergency.

The guard ushered her to the front office, where they allowed her to wait in the faculty lounge.

A smallish area, at least considering the size of the school, the lounge held two circular tables and ten chairs. A refrigerator in one corner had a door that didn't quite seal, and along the far wall stood a shelf arrangement of mail slots, each with a name pinned below.

Helen thought about sitting down, but didn't want to appear too casual when he showed up, so opted to walk over and look out the windows, staring intently at a parking lot.

She'd only held that pose for about five minutes when the door opened, and she turned to see Ronald Green.

She didn't gasp, which was good, but did feel a distinct tightening in her chest.

Green looked different, very different than he had the last time she'd seen him.

"I'd like to say I'm surprised," were his opening words, "but I'm really not. Did you come back for another try at me?'

While Helen hadn't expected the vehemence in his tone, she could understand it. The last time they'd spoken, she'd thought they'd parted on terms of, if not friends, at least understanding each other. Then again, he'd had several months to dwell on things, and one could see that the last thing he wanted was to be reminded of the shambled life he'd left behind.

"No, Ron. I'm actually here to give you a heads up."

Green, at least twenty pounds lighter than a year ago and with a pale, drawn look to his face, stayed silent.

"I know you probably don't want to see me or

anyone connected with last year, but I figured I had to come out."

"Are they really going to come after me again?" he asked.

Helen nodded, as if something had been confirmed.

"I heard your lawyer's already contacted the department. But what I don't understand is how you heard about…"

Sighing, Green pulled out a chair and sat at one of the tables. He looked up at Helen, who now felt awkward and out of place. After a moment, he raised his right hand and gestured to another seat.

As Helen sat, he began talking.

"I got a call a few days back," he said. "From a reporter."

Helen nodded. "Tim Johnson."

"Right," Green said. "Imagine my surprise. Since– since I left I haven't really paid attention to much from back home."

"Do you ever see your kids?"

"Not as much as I'd like to. This job's a heck of a lot harder than teaching at the university. Plus, two states in between don't help a whole lot. And I'm still, you know, trying to get things together."

Helen figured he meant in financial terms. She'd never specifically asked before, but had assumed that the loss of a good job, plus the dissolution of his family and whatever legal fees he'd incurred the year before, had to have left him in some sort of monetary bind.

"Do you go back home or do they come out here?"

She held her breath waiting for the answer. If Green had a habit of returning to his former hometown, that could supply the possibility of opportunity for the crimes.

"We meet halfway," he said. "I usually get a motel room in Indianapolis, and their mom drops them off there. So tell me, Helen, like I asked a minute ago. Are you here to finish the job?"

She paused. Although she'd rehearsed all of this on the plane ride up, she felt practically speechless.

"I'm not," she finally said, "but some others may be coming behind me."

"So either way, I'm screwed, right? Why the hell don't you people just leave me alone? Goddammit, just leave me the hell alone!"

His voice cracked on the last syllable, and his hands shook. Helen realized she was sitting with a broken man, someone in no way capable of one murder, let alone three.

She considered telling him of her own changed circumstances, but realized that it would probably come off falsely, as if she were trying to get on his good side.

"So what did he say?" she asked.

"Huh?"

"Johnson, when he called you. What did he say?"

"And just why the hell should I say anything? Don't you think I learned my lesson the last time around?"

"Ron—"

"Aw, screw it." A deep breath and exhausted sigh later, he stood and began pacing the length of the room. Helen wondered just when classes began and ended, and if anyone else would barge in on them before she found out as much as she needed to.

"So what'd you come out here for, Lipscomb? I mean really?"

"Believe it or not, to warn you."

"Warn me? You mean there's more?"

"No, not more. It's just–listen to me. The state troopers have taken over the case."

"You're not on it?"

Helen laughed, the sound coming out as more of a harsh bark.

"Not only am I not on this one, I'm not going to be on any cases for a while. If ever."

Green stopped his pacing.

"Meaning what?"

Second by second saw Helen changing her plans. So she gave him the cliff's notes version of recent events, ending up with her suspension.

"So Johnson was just spinning a guess when he called me?"

"He was. Though as it turns out, the trooper in charge is thinking along the same lines. I hope your lawyer's as good as he needs to be."

Now it was Green's turn to chuckle.

"He couldn't possibly be for what I'm paying him. But he's a brother-in-law of another teacher here, and considering circumstances, he's taking me on a contingency."

"Huh? What sort of contingency could there be in a…" She paused, her mind snapping to the obvious answer.

"You're the one who first suggested it," Green said. "Or had you forgotten that?"

She most emphatically had not. Helen would never forget her last face-to-face with Green. And while she hadn't come right out and suggested that he sue the city for what he'd gone through, she'd strongly implied it.

But things were different now.

"I'd probably steer clear of that, Ron. You don't know what—"

"Actually, I don't know what I'm doing talking to you. If you came all the way out here to give me a heads up, thanks, I guess. And if you came out here to look me in the eye and try to figure out whether I'm your killer, well, you've had your look. Now just do me a favor and go back home. I'm done talking to you people."

Green stood up, sliding his chair back about a foot, and walked out of the lounge, leaving Helen sitting there feeling like an idiot.

He had a lot more animosity than before, but she figured that was understandable. When they'd last met, his life had been in shambles, and he'd been pretty much in shock about how quickly, and badly, everything had fallen apart.

Now, he had a baseline to compare his old and new life with, and as she looked around the cramped, Spartan teacher's lounge, Helen knew he had to face daily reminders of everything he'd lost because of the police.

Because of her.

And now it could get worse. Because Jorgenson would be coming for him, sooner or later, and start dragging him through the mud all over again.

Unless Johnson's new theory was correct, and there was someone else out there deliberately stalking detectives.

And unless she could somehow prove it.

If neither of those two things played out, the strong possibility existed that Green's second life, much like his first, would be ripped to shreds.

Suspended or not, Helen figured she had to track that person down, or at least assist. If for no other reason than to spare Green any more pain or humiliation.

She felt in large part responsible for his personal crisis before, even while acknowledging Green himself had helped contribute to his problems.

But she was damned if she was going to let it happen again.

CHAPTER FIFTY-TWO

It was closing onto midnight of Friday night when Helen pulled up outside of Hollis's apartment. In his mid-thirties, the guy easily made enough money to afford a decent house, but like a lot of single cops, including Helen herself, he stuck to renting an apartment.

It was a phenomenon she hadn't thought much about as a young cop in her mid to late twenties. But as she grew older, it had gradually occurred to her that so many of her colleagues, especially of the unmarried variety, preferred the simplicity of renting.

And every now and then, in her more morbid moments, she contemplated how maybe, just maybe, the thought process was, in the event of sudden death, rental property would be easier to dispose of, one less loose end dangling out there.

Helen could never quite bring herself to speculate if such a motivation applied to herself, but considering the events of the last month it wasn't that far of a stretch.

Hollis's lights were off, naturally, but with all of them quite literally under the gun, Helen didn't see any possible way of letting this wait till morning. Even with two plane flights and the meeting with Green crammed into twenty-four hours, she had to keep going.

It only took two knocks before the entryway light came on and a darkness slid across the peephole.

The door opened, and Hollis stood there in a pair of

ratty gym shorts.

"Helen," he said, "what the hell?"

"Sorry, Jack. But we need to talk, and it couldn't wait till morning."

He rubbed sleep out of his eyes.

"And you couldn't call?"

"I didn't want..." she paused, knowing she hadn't called for fear he would put her off. "I didn't think. When I had time to go over this I only thought of coming over."

Hollis glanced down at the folder she held under her arm.

"Really serious?" he asked.

"Pretty much. I think I have a line on our killer."

****

"So let me get this straight," Hollis said about fifteen minutes later. The two of them were seated at his dining room table, two hastily prepared cups of coffee in front of them. Hollis had gone to his bedroom to don a pair of faded blue jeans, and while he'd been back there Helen had heard muffled conversation.

"Lisa?" she'd asked when he'd come back from the bedroom.

He'd nodded and went to make the coffee.

"Sorry," Helen said, at the same time trying to remember the last time there'd been a visitor in her bedroom. It depressed her to realize she couldn't remember.

"So what you're saying," Hollis said, "is that there's a possibility our killer has operated in other cities? Based on the type of wound and ballistics? That's awful thin, Helen. These other victims weren't even cops."

"No, they're not. And that had me for a minute. But there's a couple of things to consider. First, Johnson's only for sure about San Francisco and Chicago. But there's a few others that he suspects, and one of them caught my eye."

She opened the folder to a particular page and tapped her finger on it. Hollis, raising his mug at the same time, bent down and read the page.

"L.A.?" he said, looking back up. "What about it?"

"Let's assume, just for a minute, that Johnson's on to something. What do all the victims, no matter where, have in common. Bankers. Lawyers. Cops here. And, if L.A. happens to be one, civil service workers."

Hollis's brow puckered as he thought that through.

"They all can control others," he finally said.

"Just what I was thinking. Now, again, let's assume for a second that all of these are tied together. What's significant about the L.A. killings as opposed to the others?"

That one didn't take him any time at all.

"L.A. was the first," he said.

"Bingo."

"But all of these, including L.A., just stopped. As far as your buddy found out, there were never any substantive arrests."

"Which means one of two things," Helen said.

"Yeah, for instance, it's all a cloud of smoke, there's nothing tying them together."

"Maybe. Or…" she hesitated, hoping Hollis would get there on his own.

"Or there's a third element in the mix somewhere, something that's influencing events."

"Just what I was thinking. And the fact that the pattern, if there is one, began in L.A. could mean that's where the killer lives, or lived."

Helen finally took a drink of her coffee, the set muscles in his face telling her Hollis was going along with her, at least for now.

She just hoped the two of them were enough, at least for a start.

CHAPTER FIFTY-THREE

Saturday morning, Helen got to work.

Fortified by three cups of coffee and intermittent bouts of troubled sleep, she sat down with her laptop and started in. The flash drive Johnson had given her held a fairly complete file on the various spates of killings. She added some information Hollis had e-mailed a few hours before and, a fourth steaming cup on the table beside her, dug in with an intensity she hadn't experienced in some time.

She held no illusions concerning the tenuousness of her plan. Despite the suspension, she was still nominally on the force. But if they discovered her conducting an unauthorized parallel investigation, she could most likely kiss any hope of reconciliation goodbye.

By noon, she'd pieced together a fairly complete timeline of the L.A., San Francisco and Chicago events. She thought about adding in those from Kansas City, another suspicious series of deaths Johnson had mentioned in his notes. The previous year, over the course of several weeks, three judges had been gunned down.

It would have seemed reasonable to include the case, even without the legal connection, due to KC's proximity to their own municipality. However, all three judges had, at the time of their slayings, been involved in a linked series of trials involving gang members, and the KC cops had pursued that angle with certainty.

On the other hand, as of Johnson's most recent information, no arrests had been made in the cases, so Helen had marked it down as a possible, then continued on.

She had also made a list of people she wanted to contact for information and a catalog of forensic questions she needed to dig back into.

By this time, it was around eleven o'clock on the West Coast, so she made the call she'd held off on.

Someone picked up on the second ring.

"Robbery Homicide, Ruiz speaking."

"Hello, I'm attempting to contact a detective named Raymond Candle. Would he happen to be there?"

"Who's calling please?"

Helen provided her name, departmental rank, and badge number, realizing as she did so that she was taking one more step across the Rubicon.

"Just a second, detective."

Ruiz was gone for longer than a second, actually closer to five minutes, when another man, one who sounded older and more weary, came on the line.

"Detective Lipscomb? I'm Lieutenant Rankin. May I help you in some way?"

Helen smothered her irritation at what felt like the beginning of a bureaucratic runaround.

"Yes, sir. I'm working on a case we have out here, and I've come across some information that may tie into an old case of Detective Candle's. So I was wanting to touch base with him and pick his brain for a few minutes."

"Hmm, well I'm sorry, detective. But Ray retired last year. Could I possibly help?"

"Maybe," Helen said, and proceeded to give him a basic rundown on what she needed.

When the lieutenant spoke again he sounded slower, more guarded.

"I do remember that one. And I'm sorry to tell you this, but I think you're heading down a dead end."

"Sir?"

"There was quite a bit of division in the squad concerning all that. Candle was convinced we had a serial operating, but most of us considered them as one offs."

"All the victims were civil service workers," Helen pointed out.

"Yeah, all three of them. You have any idea how many city and county employees we got out here? Three's just a drop in a drop in a drop in the bucket."

"What about the fact that all were killed with nine millimeters?"

"Again, Lipscomb, think of our community. We probably have more nines floating around town than you have citizens in yours. Speaking of which, your name's kind of familiar? Have we ever met?"

"What about the casings?" Helen asked, wanting to head him off before he remembered anything about her from the media. "Was there ever a match on the various shells?"

"Christ, detective. This was four years ago. I'd have to go back and check, but off the top of my head I'd say there either was no match or we never bothered to find out."

"How can you be so sure if it was so long..." Helen trailed off, mentally kicking herself for her stupidity.

"How much experience do you have in this kind of

thing?" the lieutenant asked. "If we'd done a match, we'd have known right away whether they were connected. Since we ended up treating them as different cases, obviously we never matched anything up."

"Except for Candle," she said.

"Right. It got to be a real bugaboo with him. Even after we'd more or less closed it, Ray kept working at it. Kept insisting that he was going to crack the thing wide open. Got so ridiculous about it that the higher ups kind of eased him out of the important work, gave him the crap cases and, well, you know how it goes."

Helen closed her eyes for a minute, the lieutenant's recital cutting a bit too close to home.

At the same time, she thought something sounded a bit off. Population density aside, she couldn't quite believe that most experienced cops wouldn't see the possibility of a connection between three such similar killings.

She wondered if there was something Rankin wasn't telling her.

"So detective Candle retired, you say?"

"Yeah, about a year or so ago."

"Is he still in the area?" Helen mentally crossed her fingers, hoping the cop hadn't departed to some other city or part of the country.

Or maybe even down to Mexico.

"Was as of about six months ago. I ran into him at an Angels game back in October."

"You wouldn't happen to have—"

"Sorry, detective. We weren't that close. Besides, fellow officer or no, I'd feel a little awkward giving out Ray's personal number without a bit more background, if you know what I mean."

"Of course," Helen said.

"But if you want, I can meet you halfway."

"How so?"

"I'm sure either our commander or the HR office will have a fairly current phone number for him. When I get a minute today, I can try to give him a call, lay out the situation, and see if he wants to talk to you."

Helen thanked him and rattled off her cell number. They spent a few minutes talking general shop before hanging up.

Off the phone, Helen paused, wondering if Rankin had merely found a polite, conflict-free way to blow her off. For all she knew, he had no intention of passing her message along to Candle. Even if he did, who knew what sorts of things would happen during the course of his day that would assume more importance than tracking down a retired colleague to help someone almost two thousand miles away.

A new experience for her, working outside the lines like this, and she wondered just how many mistakes she was making without even knowing it.

CHAPTER FIFTY-FOUR

Amazingly, Candle called her around four thirty that afternoon.

After the introduction and initial pleasantries, she got down to the matter at hand.

"Sure, I remember that case," Candle said. "It's the main thing that got me shunted off to the side and eventually out the door. So what can I do for you, detective?"

Candle didn't really sound like a cop, even a retired one. He had a rather high-pitched voice interspersed with soft sibilants. But she'd learned long ago not to measure people by first impressions, and Lieutenant Rankin had described a tough, tenacious man.

"Did anyone else buy into your theory about a serial?" she asked.

"Oh, one or two considered it, but when the rubber hit the road, no one would go out on a limb with me, if you'll pardon me mixing clichés. If I'd been smart I would have probably just nodded my head and went along."

"And you never solved any of those cases, correct?"

There was a pause on the other end. Helen stayed quiet and waited the man out.

"No," he finally said, "never officially solved."

She caught the little tell in that sentence, but wanted to get to it in a roundabout way.

"Did you ever have any serious suspects?"

Another pause, longer this time, and Helen began to get an odd feeling in her gut.

"What exactly did you say this is in reference to?" Candle asked.

"We've had three police officers killed out here, all with nine millimeter shots to the head."

"Our victims weren't cops," he said.

"True, but it's come to my notice that in a handful of cities there've been similar murders, at least similar in style and weaponry. And in each case all of the victims, depending on the location, shared similar occupations."

Again, she felt that odd sensation of going where she didn't belong. She hadn't told Candle of her current status. She felt beyond dishonest, but she'd gone too far now to turn back.

"Sounds kind of thin to me," Candle said.

"Maybe. But it's a pattern, and at the moment I don't have anything else. So, did you ever have any serious suspects?"

Another silence, one that felt like it lasted a minute or more, before a hollow, whispery rattling came through the phone.

"I'm retired, Detective Lipscomb. Made it through more or less whole and healthy and have my pension to boot."

Helen, sensing the man was talking more to himself than to her, didn't reply.

"And I don't have much, but what I do have I'd like to keep. I'm too old for departmental politics, and too damned vulnerable."

He stopped talking, and again Helen refrained herself from saying anything.

Several more ticks of the clock went by, before Candle resumed talking.

"You understand what I'm saying?"

Helen nodded, even though the ex-cop couldn't see it over the phone.

"I think so."

"I'm sure you do Detective—Lipscomb did you say? That name actually sounds kind of familiar."

"Are you trying to get me to admit to something?" she asked.

The man in California chuckled. "Yeah," he said, "that's what I thought. I read about you in the news last year."

"Didn't see them tearing me apart on TV?"

"Hell, no." He chuckled again, not quite as much warmth this time. "You spend enough years dealing with the Southern California media, and believe me you never want to watch another news show again. Still read the *Times*, though. And even our paper out here covered your problems there pretty extensively."

"Don't believe everything you read," Helen said.

"Damned straight. The editorial pages, even all the way out here, made you sound like some sort of incompetent renegade."

"What did you think?" Helen asked, genuinely interested in the veteran's view.

"Well, you had to read through their bias a bit. But it sounded to me like you were a hero. You stopped a serial after all. Pretty much on your own."

Helen hadn't even been close to being on her own. She wouldn't be alive if not for a wrongly-accused civilian, but she decided not to go into the intricacies now.

Something in the man's voice, a mournfulness that hadn't been there before, made her catch her breath.

"You didn't stop yours, did you, Ray?"

Another pause then, long and ponderous, before he answered.

"No, I didn't. I probably could have, but I didn't get the chance."

"Can you tell me about it?"

The seconds dripped by as the old man thought that over.

"We're off the record here," he said. "You got that? If you ever attempt to lead this back to me I'll deny we ever talked. Okay?"

"Okay."

"I mean it, lady. Don't even think of trying to ever haul me into a court, or any kind of evidentiary process. Got it?"

"I got it. All I'm after is a place to start, some kind of trail."

"You have any idea what it feels like to be forced out of your job?"

Helen took a deep breath.

"Truth be told, Ray. They've got me halfway out the door already."

"Pretty bad?"

"Pretty much." She paused, making one of the quickest decisions in her life. "Up front, before you go any further. I've been suspended. I've got no official standing at all. To be talking to you or doing anything else."

"So why are you bothering?"

Even as Candle asked the question, Helen had the feeling he knew the answer.

"They were my co-workers," she said, "my fellow cops. And someone gunned them down."

"If I give you the lowdown, you've got to promise me one thing."

"Which is?" Helen asked.

"That no matter what, I mean no matter at all, you finish the job I couldn't."

Helen's palms became damp.

"You've got it, Ray. No matter what."

"Then I hope you've got plenty of time, Detective Lipscomb. 'Cause have I got a story for you."

CHAPTER FIFTY-FIVE

The sun had gone down some time past, and Helen stood at her sliding doors, looking out on her balcony, with a glass of wine. It wasn't her first of the evening, though she was far from drunk. The day, for this time of year, had been fairly sunny and now, with the stars out, the sky looked as if it belonged in May, rather than the tail end of March.

Her apartment, on the eighth floor, had quite a view, and in the distance she saw the flashing lights of a patrol car. The faint wail of the siren came to her through the closed doors, and for a second she thought back to the old days as a rookie on patrol, which hadn't, at the time, seemed all that good.

Her desire, her only real goal, had been to become a detective, mainly because after a while she got tired of cleaning out the interior of the patrol car. Especially after weekend nights, when at the end of a shift the inside had usually smelled like a combination between a toilet, a still, and a collection of used gym socks.

The climb had been hard, and not quite as long as she'd expected, but she'd made it. Received her detective's shield and begun the second phase of her career. The thought of the shield now resting in a drawer downtown, waiting on the paperwork from higher up to be decommissioned, should have caused her something close to grief.

Instead, she felt nothing. She wondered if the recent deaths of her colleagues had begun to numb her in some way.

She'd turned off the interior lights, but left her laptop open and on, its glow being the only illumination inside her apartment.

Candle had given her the leads, enough that she'd then spent the early evening chasing the trail through her computer. Between Candle's info, the material supplied by Johnson and the other reporter, and what Helen had tracked down on her own, she felt she now had the full picture.

The only problem—what to do about it.

Her natural first thought, call Hollis and Whitmore and turn it over to them, but that would be slinging them up in the unofficial web she'd constructed, and with the State people running things she doubted it would do much good anyway. Of course, she could have just slipped them the information and let them build a scenario of finding it on their own, but her calls to the West Coast, if anyone were to follow up, would prove that a lie.

And if she tried to clue Jorgenson and his people in, Helen had no doubt that her information would go exactly nowhere. Last she'd heard, before being booted out, they were all set to go after Ron Green and tear as big of a hole in his new life as Helen herself had in his old.

So that was out as well.

She twisted her right hand back and forth. She was holding her cell phone. From the beginning, she'd known who she was going to call and more or less how she was going to go about things.

She just had to firm up her resolve.

While talking to Candle, the cliché of crossing the Rubicon had flitted through her mind. But that conversation, in hindsight, had been merely taking a step.

Wading, if you will.

Now, she was about to go all the way, and she knew, beyond doubt, that there would be no turning back.

She needed to bargain, needed to get them to listen. And she had only one thing to bargain with.

Turning the phone over, she called up her menu.

A second later, the phone was ringing.

"Hello?"

He sounded tired, worn down.

After only a few days on the job.

"Captain," Helen said into her phone, "it's Helen Lipscomb. I need to speak to you."

THE AVENGER

He felt his time here drawing to a close.

They were coming for him. He could once more feel all the old symptoms that told him the Company was closing in.

Not just the appearance the other day of the two operatives in his hotel room. Obviously, that indicated they had tracked him down. But even without that occurrence, he sensed them coming.

For the last day or so his skin had felt tight, as if shrinking in on his frame. His vision had begun to blur, and he often found himself breathing faster and shallower than normal.

As if he were a target, his body sensed itself in someone's crosshairs.

But his work wasn't finished yet. He still had more of them to get, one of them in particular. The ones who had brought him here, whose actions last year had set off a blazing signal, which drew him here from halfway across the country, had not yet paid in full.

And they had to.

They still had to pay.

It had taken a while for him to dispose of the two operatives. The Avenger didn't know this city as well as he should have, and at first he didn't know where to begin when it came to getting rid of their remains.

But he had money. And a computer.

And in any town, anywhere, money would eventually do the trick. It just took him a bit of trolling to narrow down the possibilities.

Twelve hours later, he'd managed to remove all traces of the operatives, leaving him free to once again resume his work.

He'd considered moving to a different hotel, his location now known to, if no one else, the three men who'd taken care of his little problem. There was a chance, of course, that they would turn him in, but he doubted they'd want to incriminate themselves like that.

The more likely possibility would be them deciding to return and help themselves to more of his funds, but these men were professionals, recommended by a professional, and he had no doubt they recognized a fellow professional in The Avenger.

Still, he figured as he walked back into the bedroom, a little extra precaution wouldn't hurt anything. Grabbing his suitcase from the closet, he began folding and packing his clothing. As he did so, he composed in his head the excuse he would give when he called down to the registration desk to ask for a different room.

He knew they were close. The first two he'd disposed of wouldn't be the last.

The old woman and Lawrence were moving in on him again.

This time, though, he vowed would be different.

This time, he'd had more than enough.

Whether he completed his work here or not, he would not, simply would *not*, allow them to take him home again.

He was his own man, and it was time now to prove it.

Not just to the folks back home, but to everyone.

CHAPTER FIFTY-SIX

Straight up six the next morning, Lt. Kurt Jorgenson, in a blue suit with no tie, strode into the squad room. Behind him walked three people: a young, fairly tall black woman and two men, neither of them looking over thirty. Helen guessed Jorgenson had been working nearly around the clock for the last few days, but even so he came in with shoulders straight and posture firm.

A man in control of his emotions and his environment.

Until, that is, he looked toward the group of people clustered in the corner next to the squad's smartboard and saw Helen standing there.

"What the…?"

"Come on over, lieutenant," Capt. Kendal said. "We've got some new information for you."

Jorgenson came over, his subordinates at his side.

"What new information?" he asked.

"It's like this," Kendal said, "we may have cracked the case."

Jorgenson's eyes darted back and forth, finally resting on Helen. She suppressed the urge to smile at him.

"We've got the investigation under control, Frank" Jorgenson said, "and last I knew this person was on suspension."

"She was," Kendal said, "well, technically still is.

But I'm letting her sit in on this because I think she's earned a spot here."

The state cop's neck turned red.

"What she's earned," he said through gritted teeth, "is losing her badge. And I'm willing to bet your chief agrees with me."

"Quite possibly. But until I hear different, I've reinstated Det. Lipscomb, mainly due to the work she's done in the last twenty-four hours."

Jorgenson threw up his hands and seemed to begin breathing again.

"Do whatever you think necessary, Frank. But keep in mind that this is a state investigation, and you and your people are at our disposal, not the other way around."

"Understood, Kurt." Kendal grinned. "But for right now, will it hurt anything to hear what Helen has to say?"

"I guess we've got the time. Green's lawyer is coming by around nine, and I'm guessing that after they arrive we'll be too damned busy to listen to nonsensical—"

"For God's sake, Jorgenson," Helen couldn't resist interrupting, "Ronald Green isn't your killer. He's a school teacher, pure and simple. And this case goes far beyond our three people. It even goes beyond this state."

Now the tall black woman spoke up.

"Meaning what?"

Helen gave her a look.

"Tammy Metcalf," the woman said.

"That's Sergeant Metcalf," Jorgenson butted in. "She's my second on this thing."

Helen shrugged.

"Well, it's kind of patchwork, but I spent a lot of time on this and, pretty much, I think I may have our killer."

Helen was careful to frame the argument around only herself. This had been a matter of heated discussion an hour or so earlier, with Hollis and Whitmore wanting to help carry the load. Even after Helen had pointed out that the whole thing could blow up, her two partners had wanted to be included.

But when she'd pointed out that the two of them had a lot more to lose, whereas her lot had essentially already been cast, they relented. Albeit reluctantly.

And now it was show time.

She picked up the remote for the smartboard, clicked it on and scrolled up the first screen.

Here we go, she thought.

CHAPTER FIFTY-SEVEN

Los Angeles

Early Sunday morning, she stormed into his office while he was conducting a meeting with three sub-directors. Meetings at this time of the week weren't the norm, but Lawrence was leaving the city that afternoon and was uncertain when he'd return. So he'd made a few phone calls and was spending the morning conducting some business face to face before his trip.

His secretary hadn't bothered to buzz that the old lady was on her way, and from the look on her face, Lawrence figured she'd brushed past the secretary before she had a chance.

"What the hell do you think you're doing?" she barked as soon as she'd closed the door.

Lawrence glanced up, sighed, and leaned back in his chair.

"That will be all," he told the three other men in the office.

They quickly snatched up various papers and reports spread out on a round table in the middle of the office and scooted out.

"Lois—" Lawrence began, but didn't get far.

"You found him. Don't try to deny it. You found him and weren't going to tell me."

"I would have, just as soon as I'd ascertained—"

"Bullshit, Larry!" The old woman's eyes narrowed, and she began trembling. "You already sent Morton out. You know exactly where he is, and you're planning on heading there yourself. All without a word to me."

"So what?" Lawrence snapped back. "Either I'm in charge of things around here or I'm not. It seems as if you're well inclined to let me run things, at least until you don't like it. When the old man was alive, he left me well enough alone."

"Don't you dare bring him into this. And don't change the subject. You found my son and didn't tell me. Now, you're getting ready to go out and bring him back. Right?"

Lawrence leaned forward and placed his forearms on his desk.

"Morton called you?"

"As his plane was taking off," she replied.

"Well, he shouldn't have done that."

"He works for me," she hissed.

"He works for the company, which at the moment is run by me. If you wish to change that, then do so. You'd be well within your rights. But as long as I'm in charge…"

Lois leaned forward herself, placing both palms on the desk, then lowered herself over the surface. Their faces were barely ten inches apart.

"You can run this firm however you want to. I don't really care because, frankly, we're too goddamned rich for you to possibly screw it up. But when it comes to Andy, you let me know everything, all the time. Or you will find yourself out on the sidewalk looking in. Got it?"

They locked gazes for several heartbeats before Lawrence Sears looked away.

"Got it," he said, hating the whine in his voice.

"So when are we leaving?"

Lawrence paused, then his shoulders slumped in defeat.

"A few hours," he said. "You're coming along?"

"I am. And we're going to bring your brother back home. For good this time."

CHAPTER FIFTY-EIGHT

"His name is Andrew Sears."

The portrait of a young man, no more than mid-thirties, with sandy blond hair and rather dull-looking blue eyes, stared back at the people assembled in front of the squad's smartboard.

Of the seven others, only Hollis and Kendal knew exactly where Helen was going. Before Jorgenson's arrival, they'd had time to fill Whitmore in on part of it.

Neither Jorgenson nor his people looked too happy at being here so early, but Helen had made Kendal swing it, insisting she wanted to unveil her info with as few prying eyes and ears as possible.

If the info she'd acquired from Candle, not to mention Tim Johnson and his colleague at the *Trib*, were true, the fewer who knew the better.

"Sears?" Jorgenson said. "That name sounds kind of familiar."

"Sure. There's a department store named for him," cracked one of his subordinates.

Jorgenson frowned.

"I don't mean like that, Carl. I mean—"

"Actually," Helen interposed, "it's not so much his name you're familiar with as possibly hers."

She slid her finger across her I-Pad and a new face popped up. Female, well-cared for, anywhere from mid-fifties to late sixties, still-brunette hair with flecks of gray here and there and the faintest traces, at least in the reproduction, of wrinkles.

"This is Lois Sears. Maiden name Lois Andrews. She was a small-town girl from Connecticut who headed out to California in the early sixties to get into movies."

"Wait just a minute," Jorgenson butted in, "what does this possibly have to do with our case?"

"Give it time, Kurt," Kendal said. "Helen will make it all clear."

"As I was saying, she was the absolute cliché. Unfortunately, she didn't get discovered at a soda counter. Instead, she made one or two low-budget drive-in movies, not quite porn but what they called back then soft core, and that was it for her acting career.

"Except that she did manage to meet and marry George Sears, who worked as a broker in a small real estate office."

"Okay, now I get it," Carl, the junior officer said. "I've heard of George Sears."

"I haven't," Metcalf put in. "Who is he?"

"Was," Helen said. "By the time George passed on, he'd managed to build his own little fiefdom that included retail malls, oil refineries, real estate, construction companies and then more real estate. He passed away about five years ago, mark that date, and at the time of his death his *personal* wealth was figured somewhere around five or six billion. The actual worth of all his companies is supposedly well upward of twenty billion."

Helen held up her hand to stifle a yawn. She'd spent nearly an hour on the phone with Candle the afternoon before, then even more time collating his information with what the two reporters had given her. Considering the time spent preparing this presentation and bothering Kendal in the early morning, she had nothing but fumes left.

"Okay," said Carl, "so several years back a rich old man died in southern California, so what?"

"Simple," Helen said. She swiped her finger again, and the screen returned to Andrew's picture. "About six months after George Sears died, his son executed three civil service workers in L.A. Shot in the head with a 9 millimeter handgun."

No one stirred in the room, it hardly sounded as if anyone was breathing. All eyes focused on the picture up on the board.

"Come again?" Jorgenson said.

"Four years ago three different civil service workers in L.A. county were murdered, over a period of about three months. Two men and one woman. One worked in the medical examiner's office; another was a clerk for a judge who specialized in probate; and the third was a veteran of the county records office, in the branch that deals with real estate transactions."

"Where are you getting this all from?" Jorgenson asked.

Helen glanced at Kendal, who kept his face impassive.

"Give me a minute," she said. "After Sears's death, there were some problems with the estate. In fact, seeing as it was only a few years ago, there still are. Something as large as his holdings isn't taken care of in a thirty-day probate."

"Other family? Other than the wife and son?"

"Youngest son." Helen swiped and a new face appeared. Either late forties or early fifties, and about as nondescript as one could find. "This is Lawrence Sears. Current age forty-nine, so quite a bit older than his brother."

"Same mother?" Hollis asked.

Helen nodded. "From what I can gather, Andrew was something of a middle-aged surprise for his parents."

"Gather from where?" Jorgenson cut in again. "Seriously, Lipscomb—"

"Just a few more minutes. When a third civil service person showed up killed in exactly the same way, even from a staff as large as L.A. has, it caught attention. A special team of detectives was assigned, and they began going all out to catch what they believed to be a serial killer in their midst, one with a grudge against a particular type of person."

"Something this town's familiar with," someone muttered.

Helen did her best not to glance back, but kept on going.

"However, within two months into the investigation the killings seem to have stopped, and no one was ever prosecuted for the murders."

These were a bunch of sharp people in the room, but they'd all been on edge for days on end, and it was still early in the morning. Through the slatted blinds against the far wall, the crimson of early morning sun was just beginning to seep in.

But then, one by one, they began to get it.

"Now hold on a second," Jorgenson said. "You say those murders were never solved?"

"Correct."

"Then why are you showing us these pictures? Why

are you telling us about the Sears bunch?" At this point, the sergeant ignored Helen and turned to Kendal.

"What's going on here, captain? This woman's not even supposed to be on this case, so what the hell—"

"I have it on very firm, though unofficial word," Helen butted in "that Andrew Sears was the murderer of those three people in L.A."

Jorgenson had no choice but to turn back to her.

"Unofficial word?"

"An informant," Helen said, "an extremely confidential informant has conveyed to me that at least a handful of people out west became convinced that Andrew Sears was their killer."

"Confidential is for outside of the investigation. Who is this CI of yours?"

Helen took a deep breath, hoping Kendal would back her up as promised.

"Sorry, sergeant. But I can't tell you. In exchange for this information, I swore to the person that I wouldn't reveal them. If it's right, we'll be able to find enough that we can nab him anyway."

"Unacceptable." Jorgenson turned toward Kendal. "Captain, I'd suggest that you get your person in line and explain to her—"

"I'd suggest," Kendal interrupted, "that you let Detective Lipscomb finish. Either that, or you and your bunch can just pack up your stuff and get the hell out of here."

Jorgenson glared, but turned back to Helen.

"Okay, let's see what else you got."

"From what I've managed to piece together," Helen said, "by the time of the third killing the L.A. cops had culled about ten suspects, of which Andrew Sears was one. Turns out each of those murdered people were in some way involved, though in very minor roles, with the Sears family. One was the coroner's assistant who signed the death warrant; another was a clerk in the probate office who, through luck of the draw, signed off on his will; and the third had overseen the 911 dispatch center the night the call came in on Mr. Sears. It was merely through happenstance that the cops out there managed to put that together, but when they began to investigate, word came down damned quick that Sears was hands off."

"Because?"

"Because, primarily, of his family's influence. The family owns something like half of southern California, and goes to the same clubs and parties as the people who own the other half. So it was made clear, very clear, that Andrew Sears was not a suspect in the killings."

"Sounds like your source is a cop out there."

"Could be." Helen refused to be baited by the man. "Or a reporter with the inside track, or someone in the medical examiner's office or a secretary in the city steno pool. Can I continue?"

Jorgenson waved his hand.

"What's interesting for our purposes is that as soon as the pressure to lay off Sears developed, the killings themselves stopped."

"Which could be for any number of reasons."

"True. However, at the same time, there's a record of Andrew Sears entering the Sisters of Hope, a rehab institution north of L.A."

"Aren't records of those places usually confidential?" Kendal asked.

"They are, sir. Again, for now you just have to trust

my info."

"So you have three murders over four years ago on the other side of the country," Jorgenson said. "So what?"

Over the course of the next twenty minutes, Helen took them through the rest of the schedule. A year after the L.A. killings, the deaths of four major businessmen in San Francisco, all of whom, in one way or another, had dealings with the Sears family. A couple of years later, the doctor murders in Chicago.

"And the connection there?"

"Not entirely nailed down yet, but the three of them were specialists in Huntington's disease, which was the cause of death of the Sears patriarch. Granted, it's thin, but if we're dealing with a madman, the loosest possible logic could be enough for him."

"If you say so, though this is sounding more and more like cotton candy all the time."

"In each case," Helen continued, ignoring that jibe, "9 mm to the head. For a while, there was a plausible thought that the two California cases were connected, but in each case the killings stopped just as abruptly as they started."

"Which has what to do with this Sears person?"

And here's where it got tricky for Helen. If they questioned her information too closely, she'd have to reveal Candle's name. In which case, he would deny everything. On the other hand, if she could at least convince them they would come up with evidence independent of Candle, especially as he'd made clear that his involvement ended with his revelations to her.

Still, she'd made a promise to the man, and if anyone could, she could relate to being hung out to dry by the powers that be. Fortunately, much of her information had come from the *Tribune* reporters as from Candle, so she should be able to obscure things that way.

And once they caught, if they caught, Sears the source of original information wouldn't really matter, no matter what some defense attorney may claim.

"It took some digging, and it's still preliminary," she said. "But it appears that in each case, plus a few others, shortly after the murders stopped Sears entered a new rehab program."

"Now wait just a minute," Jorgenson broke in. "What exactly is the motivation here? You say he's acting like a Lord High Avenger? Okay, it's a stretch, but I can buy that, if the guy's nuts enough. But there's something I still don't get. You're talking some little rich kid who's pulling off a series of damned near professional hits. In the most recent case against trained cops. How's he doing that?"

Helen paused, well aware this was the weak spot in her scenario.

"To be honest, lieutenant, I'm not sure. It would make more sense, but not by much, if Sears was hiring hit men to do these jobs. Far as I can see, that's one of the things we'll have to find out when we catch him."

Jorgenson frowned.

"That seems like a pretty big hole in your theory, detective. As just one example, Miss Turner was murdered inside of her house. So you're trying to sell us that an untrained man somehow managed to enter a police officer's home and take her down."

Kendal moved forward, as if to speak up, but Hollis gestured him back. Helen made a point of not looking in their direction, but later she'd be sure to thank Hollis for his faith.

"As I said, it's a problem, but everything considered not an insurmountable one."

"Far as that goes," Hollis put in, "with his money and resources, he could have hired trainers. Or who knows what kind of people he may have run around with out in L.A.

"With family money like that they surely have bodyguards and military types all around. Pilots, if nothing else."

"Sounds like a stretch," Jorgenson said.

"But it'll work until something better turns up."

"Okay, so let's move on. You've listed several sets of crimes in various cities, but so what. What does that have to do with out here? Why would he come so far from home?"

Helen, Hollis, and Kendal had talked that over before the others showed up, and the three of them came to the same conclusion. It wasn't a comfortable one to consider, but the best they had.

Helen glanced over at Kendal, who nodded his head in encouragement.

"We think," she said, "and we won't know for sure unless we get to talk to him, that he picked our town for his next target because of the publicity."

"Publicity?" Tammy Metcalf broke in. "What publicity are you..."

She trailed off as Helen saw the realization dawning on her.

Jorgenson got it almost as quickly.

"Oh, shit," he said. "Tell us you're not suggesting what I think you are."

Helen nodded, though the truth was almost too

shameful to face.

"We think it was because of the Green case. As you know, it wasn't the murders themselves that made the news. Hell, for the longest time we didn't know we had a serial in our midst. It was the, in hindsight, wrong-headed pursuit of Green that all the cable shows and radio hosts glommed onto."

"And you believe it was that seeming–injustice–that made this Sears person decide to come out here?"

"Until we have more info," Kendal broke into the conversation, "it's the most likely theory."

For an instant there, everyone in the room focused on Helen. She could imagine what they were thinking, mainly because the same thoughts had been uppermost in her mind for several hours now.

If they were right, if it turned out that the pursuit of Ron Green had drawn another killer into their midst, then in a way Helen was directly responsible for the murders of her three friends.

It was an uncomfortable feeling, and one she knew she'd have to face and deal with eventually.

But not just now.

Now she had a job to do. Some way or another, she had to convince the state people of the validity of her theory.

And she still had her ace to play.

"You mentioned this guy's been in rehab more than once. Rehab for what?" Jorgenson asked. "Drugs? Alcohol? What?"

Helen hesitated. She didn't want to lose them at this point, but there were gaps in her understanding of the case.

"That part's unclear," Kendal jumped in for her. "At

the moment, all that we've managed to track down are entrance and exit dates. It seems that, in the instances we've found so far, within three months of his release from an institution, another round of killings starts up in another city."

"This is beyond circumstantial," Jorgenson pointed out. "Have there ever been any ballistics comparisons done between the various murders? Any sorts of composites? Anything beyond this fantasy that Detective Lipscomb is spinning?"

Helen took a deep breath. Now was the time to pull out her trump. She knew that so far what she'd laid out could be explained half a dozen different ways. But she had one more piece of the puzzle to put down.

She looked over at Hollis, who gave her a quick nod.

"No," she said to the state cop, "so far there isn't any hard evidence, at least that we can access, to tie Andrew Sears to anything. However, we have a possible ace in the hole."

A swipe of her finger, and a new face appeared. A middle-aged man with a thick mane of black hair and a darkly-tanned face.

"This is Trevor Morton. He's the president and founder of Morton Confidential Investigations, LLC. His company specializes in service, including body guarding and 'damage control' to most of Southern California, but primarily Hollywood."

"So?" Jorgenson drummed his fingers on the arm of his chair.

"So twenty years ago Trevor Morton began his business with a private loan he acquired from George Sears. And while to the world his company provides a variety of services to the L.A. elite, the Sears family is his first and foremost customers."

"Again, so? Could we please get to the point?"

"Of course. Only a few hours ago, Trevor Morton arrived in town. A call to his home office revealed only that he was 'out of the office'. But a quick check of airline records shows him arriving with two of his employees by United."

Jorgenson started to say something, but Helen cut him off.

"And on February 24th, three weeks before Roy Michaels's murder, Andrew Sears finished his latest stint in rehab. He was spotted around his regular haunts for all of five days and, according to my CI, hasn't been seen in L.A. since."

CHAPTER FIFTY-NINE

"This is only temporary," Kendal said in his office a few minutes later.

Reaching into his desk, he pulled out Helen's badge case. When he handed it to her, she slipped it into her jacket without even looking at it.

"You have the authority to return it?" she asked.

Kendal grinned, though with a strained quality.

"Been busy around here, kind of like you've been. Just didn't have the time to messenger it over. But as far as the top floor's concerned, you're still on suspension."

"Unless Jorgenson's on the phone to them right now."

Kendal sat behind his desk and motioned Helen to sit as well.

"I kind of doubt that. I've known Curt for a while, worked with him from time to time, and I think he's willing to give this a go."

"You think he believed me?"

"I think he's a good cop who's investigating the deaths of other good cops. Despite your initial experiences with him, he's not going to move aside from a lead just because he doesn't like the person who brought it to him."

"This is more than a lead," Helen said.

"Speaking of which, I've gone out on something of a limb here myself. How about telling me who your sources are?"

Helen hesitated. She figured it within the boundaries of their agreement to give Johnson and his colleague to Kendal. But when it came to Ray Candle, she hesitated. Considering her own experiences with higher ups, she wanted to protect the retired L.A. cop as much as she could.

So she laid out the background of her contacts with the two reporters.

"Amazing that they've put it together, but haven't published anything yet," Kendal said.

"Johnson has a bit more of a moral center than you would think. It's my guess that he figures any publication would cause the man to jump, and with his resources who knows where he'd end up."

"Maybe," the captain said, "But I'm also guessing that you've got some kind of deal with him?"

"First crack at the story. I know it really wasn't in my authority to give it, but—"

"It's okay. I think we can work something out. Far as that goes, I'd rather somebody local get it than those morons down there."

He made a brief, dismissive gesture toward the office windows, which looked out onto the plaza area in front of the building, where reporters, producers and sound trucks from various cable stations had been encamped for several days.

"But we do need to discuss the original source. I'd say Curt had it about right in there when he said your information sounded like it came from a cop."

"Captain—"

"Dammit, Helen, I'm sticking it all out here. You were right a second ago. I don't have the authority to give you back your badge. In fact, if it hadn't been for our past history I would guess that Curt would be on the phone right now to the chief. The fact that nobody's yet come through that door and kicked my ass out tells me he's holding off. But you know as well as I do that when it comes time to actually build a prosecutable case, we may have to have the name of your informant."

"I'm hoping when we nail Sears there will be enough already there to make it unnecessary."

"And it may work out that way. Just understand that if it doesn't, I'll be coming to you for more, and if you refuse to give it, I'll be the one taking your badge away. For good, this time."

Helen nodded.

"So how are we going to do this?" she asked.

"I've got Hollis coordinating surveillance teams on Morton. Jorgenson's leant some of his people, and together we should have at least six pairs of eyes on him at all times."

"So if Sears is in town and Morton finds him, we'll have him as well."

"That's the plan."

"And can I be in on it?"

Kendal smiled, the move actually erasing some of the stress from around his eyes.

"You're designated as our central hub. Any action on Morton's part, and the various parties call you, and we go from there."

"That's why returning the badge?" she asked.

"Exactly. If this turns out to be gold, you deserve to be in on it, and I don't want any ambiguity out there in the field."

CHAPTER SIXTY

Helen's cell buzzed shortly after three that afternoon.

"It's Lou," Whitmore's baritone echoed in her ear. "Our boy's on the move."

"Headed where?"

"North on the Interstate. If I had to guess, I'd say he's going to the airport."

Helen felt a slight clawing in her gut.

"Alone?" she asked.

"According to Lattimer. He didn't see anyone in the passenger or back, and it's a mid-sized rental."

"So he may be going to pick someone up?"

"Could be. Or could be that whatever business he had in town is over with."

"Keep on him," Helen said. "I'll fill everyone in on this end."

****

"He could be heading home, job finished," Kendal pointed out.

"But finished in what way?" Jorgenson asked. "There's been no trace of Sears."

"Maybe our assumption's wrong," Helen said. "Maybe Morton isn't the one who takes him home."

"Meaning what? That he just spots the guy and then has someone else come in and do the heavy work?"

"It's possible," Hollis said, "but why don't we just

hold on and see what happens."

****

Forty-five minutes later, the next call came in from Whitmore.

"Okay," he said, and this time they had him on speaker, "it was definitely the airport, but this isn't quite what we expected."

"Is he heading out of town?" Helen asked.

"Not even close. Our guy actually swung by here to pick some people up."

"Come again?"

"He parked in short term and made it straight to the South-western gate. Waited around for about twenty minutes until a flight came in from California."

"California." Helen made it a statement, not a question.

"Correct. And guess who came off the flight and hooked up with him?"

"Wait a minute," Hollis said, "someone from back west?"

"Two someones," Whitmore replied. "To be precise, if the photos in our info pack are correct, Lois and Lawrence Sears. Mother and brother of our suspect. Looks like Helen's CI was on the money."

Everyone in the squad room at that moment turned and looked at Helen.

"I'll be damned," Jorgenson said.

CHAPTER SIXTY-ONE

"I would have thought those two would have a private plane," Helen said.

She and Hollis were in a department car, Hollis driving and heading toward the downtown hotel where Morton had been staying. A total of four cars had headed out, all but theirs containing one city detective and one of Jorgenson's people. Whitmore himself, during his stakeout, had been accompanied by Tammy Metcalf and Hal Smith.

"Maybe their plane's in the shop," Hollis said.

"Or maybe they're trying to be as inconspicuous as possible," Helen returned.

Hollis's shoulders hunched.

"So what the hell are we talking here?" he asked. "Some sort of intervention? Mommy and big brother coming to take the bad little boy home? That doesn't make a whole lot of sense."

Helen stared straight ahead for a minute.

"What I'm about to say doesn't go beyond this car," she said after a minute.

Hollis flicked a glance her way as he narrowly squeezed through a yellow light. They were running without lights or siren.

"Okay."

"I mean it, Jack. Kendal's been pushing me, but so far I haven't even told him. I've got to keep this as close to home as possible."

"Because?"

"You heard the info about the Sears family wealth. My guy has managed to stay under their radar, more or less, but he's scared that if he comes to their notice it will end badly for him."

"I'm guessing, like everyone else during the briefing, that the guy's a cop."

Helen nodded, and briefly explained to him about Candle back in L.A. and his role in the whole thing.

Hollis didn't say much, merely nodded when she was done.

Over the next few minutes, they got lucky in having three green lights in a row. Damned near a miracle for downtown in the late afternoon.

Helen kept glancing behind them and to the sides. There were supposed to be three other cars converging on their quarry, but she couldn't spot any of them.

"So like I said," Hollis said, "you think this is like an intervention or something?"

Helen considered the possibility.

"You mean like little Andrew gets out of treatment, or whatever, after a while goes off on another spree, and mom and big brother came back to take him home?"

"It would seem to fit."

Their luck ran out when they hit a red light. Hollis whooped the lights and siren for one cycle, and the car ahead of them scrunched enough to the side to let them get by.

"But it seems too dangerous," Helen said. "If we're right, this guy's killed over a dozen men over the last few years. What's to make his family think they can control him when they find him?"

They glanced at each other for a heartbeat.

"Morton," Hollis said, "is probably more than just a locator."

Before Helen could reply, their car radio squawked.

"Hey, Hollis, you there man?"

Helen picked up the dash mic.

"What's up, Lou?"

"They're on the move again."

"What? When did they arrive?"

"Not ten minutes ago. Morton drove right in to the garage, the three of them got out and they lit up the elevators. We pulled in here and parked. Metcalf went on to the lobby to try to track down their room, and not five minutes later here they're coming out."

"Does Morton have any luggage or anything?"

"Nada. But they've got somebody with them."

Hollis took his eyes off the road long enough to glance Helen's way.

She keyed the mic again.

"Andrew?" she asked.

"Looks like from here. How far out are you guys?"

Hollis mouthed the word "two."

"Two minutes if traffic holds," Helen said. "Lou, what's it look like to you?

"Pretty much what we figured. They're doing their best to keep him under wraps and get him out of here"

"All units," Helen said into the mike. "Converge on that garage as quickly as you can. Lou, is Metcalf back yet?"

"Just came off the elevator. She's coming at them from the other direction."

"Keep them from leaving. Move in if you have to, but don't let them get out of that hotel. We're almost there."

A chorus of affirmatives came over the frequency. Helen bracketed the mic and leaned back.

"Jack?"

"Couple of seconds," he said, not taking his eyes from the road. "Right about...now!"

A sharp turn of the wheel took them up the ramp that led to the Broadmore garage. A plywood barricade barred their way, but Hollis didn't even seem to notice it. He crashed through, and in the rearview Helen saw another of the chase cars coming up right behind them.

She took out her gun and gripped it firmly in her hand. As Hollis sped through the twists and turns of the garage ramps, she took three deep breaths in an attempt to compose herself.

Michaels, Jarvis, and Turner. If anything went even halfway right, in a few split seconds they'd be on the tail end of dealing with the killer of three cops. Not to mention all those other people around the country.

Hollis took the last turn to get them up to the third level, driving one-handed now to grasp his own gun, and they came within sight of the tableau spread out before them.

They saw Whitmore, big as life and crackling with energy, standing in the middle of that level, throwing down on four people backed up against a rental car, Smith slightly to his left. Behind him and to his right stood Metcalf, tense and rigid as she held her own weapon out.

Hollis screeched to a stop, the other car doing the same right on their tail. Behind them, Helen thought she heard the other two cars arrive.

It was one of those moments, the kind that Helen had

fortunately only experienced a few times in her career. Everything protracted, drug out into slow motion, as car doors opened and shut, people moved into position, and the four who constituted their quarry moved backwards as they saw even more foes move into place. Even the sounds slowed down, becoming more of a background hum, as Helen set herself into the classic stance, with Hollis on the other side of the vehicle, as her peripheral vision caught everyone else in their places.

Fine. Just a few seconds now and it would all be over, suspect acquired and bystanders neutralized.

Then she heard a kind of snap coming from the cluster of folks against the wall, and it all fell to hell.

CHAPTER SIXTY-TWO

With her first sighting of Andrew Sears, Helen could tell the man was deranged. Even from halfway across the parking level, he exhibited a jerky, spasmodic movement that gave serious evidence of a problem.

But in the next instant she realized the fallacy of her interpretation. Sears was attempting two feats at one time. Jerking himself in such a manner as to shield himself behind the other three people, an old woman, a middle-aged man and Trevor Morton, while at the same time pulling something from his clothing.

Oh God, she thought as once again everything seemed to slow down around her.

Helen and her colleagues had spread out, arranging themselves in a sort of half moon configuration, as Sears grabbed his mother around the neck, pulling her to him body-to-body, and leveled the gun in his left hand.

Flame started sparking from the barrel as Helen set herself in a lower stance. All of the detectives, both city and state, were wearing bulletproof vests, so that wasn't an issue.

Until Sears leveled his gun and began firing at their heads.

Helen shifted to the side, attempting to draw a bead on him through all the shifting bodies. The older man, Lawrence, had fallen to the asphalt in panic, while Morton had spun off to the side and seemed to be tugging a weapon from his jacket as well.

The old woman, amazingly, appeared the most composed of the lot, merely standing there allowing her younger son to use her as a shield.

Either shock, Helen thought, *or motherly love to the ultimate*.

Then Helen had her bead, and she squeezed her trigger, as she did so knowing with a calm instinct that her bullet would find its mark.

But before it could, another bullet impacted its target, and to her left she saw Hollis's head jerk to the side.

No time, she thought. *No time to deal with it. Get the man down, dammit, get him down*.

A chunk flew out of Sears's neck, and Helen thought that was hers, but there wasn't time to worry as he jerked to the side with another bullet smashing into his left shoulder.

Now the mother began screaming as her son's blood sprayed over her. One more bullet impacted, as close as Helen could tell right between the eyes.

And that was either the best damn shooting imaginable or the luckiest shot possible.

Morton had finally extracted a weapon from his clothing, but it was all done. He stood off to the side, waving his gun for a minute before someone's shouted command made him drop it.

All of this was beside the point for Helen, and as soon as she saw people converging on the three against the wall, she turned to Hollis.

She knelt by his side, instinctively reaching out to cradle his head, now a mass of blood and blackened tissue.

He jerked and writhed for all of about six seconds, then relaxed, an empty glaze sweeping over his eyes.

Vaguely, as if from a distance, Helen became aware of the activity around her. She didn't know how long it took, a second or an hour, before a large black hand clasped her shoulder.

"Helen," Lou's deep bass was now the mildest of whispers, "it's time to get up."

Wiping her eyes to clear her vision, Helen looked up and saw a team of paramedics with a stretcher, their ambulance about sixty feet off, blue, red and yellow lights silently flashing.

"Sears?" she asked, not sure if the words actually made it out of her.

"Andrew's dead. Won't know till autopsy, but I'm guessing it was Metcalf who nailed him. We need to get you up now. Kendal and Jorgenson are about a block out."

Helen climbed to her feet, but did so without taking her eyes from Hollis's recumbent form. She realized that her stomach, her heart, her entire being felt hollow, and she wondered if she'd ever feel full again.

As she stood upright, Lou took his hand off her shoulder.

"Okay to go?" he asked.

Helen nodded, and not touching him, but not straying too far from his side either, she walked away from her friend.

CHAPTER SIXTY-THREE

Three days after the throwdown in the parking garage, Helen Lipscomb sat in one of the plush red chairs that dotted the reception area right outside of the chief's office. She'd come alone, though common sense dictated she should have an advocate with her, but she figured there would be time enough for that once she saw how things would unfold.

She didn't know for sure who all was sequestered in the chief's office, though she could hazard some fairly accurate guesses. She could also assume that, when it came right down to it, she didn't really have to sit around waiting for them to call her in.

After all, she had a pretty good idea of what they would say. She just hoped they'd get it over with.

Jack Hollis's funeral was in less than an hour.

One of the chief's three secretaries, young and pretty with long brunette hair, entered the reception area and seated herself behind a desk against the far wall. Chief Rodgers had three secretaries, and Helen wondered where the other two were.

The young woman glanced at her, and if she took note of Helen's black skirt, blouse and jacket, she showed no reaction.

Helen continued staring straight ahead, deliberately not looking at the door that led to the inner office, and doing her best not to look at the time either.

351

Jack's funeral.

Even with everything that had transpired over the last month, all the colleagues she'd lost, she still found it almost impossible to fit those two words together in her mind.

Yet, as with everything else, she would sooner or later have to force herself to accept this new reality.

The inner door opened up and Bill Henrickson, the deputy chief in charge of public affairs, stepped out.

"We're ready for you," he said. As she stood up, smoothed her skirt and headed into the office, Henrickson turned to the secretary holding vigil.

"No interruptions," he said.

When she entered the office, Henrickson shut the door behind her and took up a position leaning against one of the walls.

"Take a seat please," Chief Rodgers said from behind his desk.

Only one empty seat remained in the room. Besides the chief and Henrickson, three men and one woman occupied the office. In front of the chief's desk, but angled in such a way that he could look over the whole room, sat one of the city councilmen. In another chair on the other side of the desk was Louise Felburn, another deputy chief, in charge of the detective division. In a chair toward the back of the room, she spotted Captain Kendal, his face pinched.

And the last man, of course, was Jorgenson.

Helen worked to keep from frowning. In the last few days, the local media, via a push from Rodgers, had damned near lionized Jorgenson. All five local television stations had run profiles on the man, touting him as the one who'd finally brought the cop killings to a halt. After all, up until the end he'd been the one officially in charge of the investigation, so who better to give the credit to?

Even Tim Johnson over at the *Tribune*, despite having written three separate articles on the affair, had barely mentioned her role. And Helen couldn't help but wonder what sort of pressure had been put on him to keep on the bandwagon.

Well, she thought, *the gang's all here, so let's start the game.*

She sat in the empty seat.

"We have something of a problem here, wouldn't you say, detective?" Rodgers opened.

Coming in, Helen had noticed that she was the only person in the department not in uniform. All the rest, even Jorgenson, wore their dress uniforms, with black covers over the badges.

She couldn't decide if she felt under or over dressed.

"Yes, sir," she said, "I guess you do."

The chief frowned a bit at her pronoun shift, but he didn't miss a beat.

"I'm assuming that, like all of us, you'll want to attend Detective Hollis's ceremony, so we'll make this brief."

Helen had started to grip the chair arms, but she forced her hands to loosen.

"Yes, sir."

"Lieutenant Jorgenson, and by extension the State AG, have lodged some pretty serious allegations against you."

Helen nodded.

"I'm aware of that, sir."

"In fact, I had quite a lengthy discussion with the AG this morning as to whether or not you should be brought up on obstruction charges."

Helen's heart began racing, but she forced herself not to show any reaction.

"I don't follow that, chief. I may have cut a few corners, but we managed to stop a murderer and arrest his accomplices."

Rodgers scowled and steepled his hands on top of his desk.

"That's true. And at the moment that's the only thing that may possibly pull you out of this. The lieutenant here has already written his report, making it very clear you deliberately defied both departmental policy and direct orders by conducting an independent, unaccountable investigation. And as part of that investigation of yours, you flew out of town and consulted with a person who was a prime suspect in the case. Do you deny that, detective?"

Helen breathed deeply, working out how to respond. So this is what it came down to. It wasn't so much getting ahead of them all on Sears. In the end, it had worked out. Hell, as far as she was concerned, Jorgenson and his task force could keep all the credit.

But this meeting wasn't about that. It was still, always and eternally, about the leftover feelings concerning how she'd handled Ronald Green, both now and in the past.

And, in a perverse way, she could see their point. With Sears dead, they'd probably never know the truth for sure, but Helen felt fairly confident it was her pursuit of Green last year, and the publicity that accompanied the fiasco, that brought Sears to town.

Thus, in a fairly direct way, making her responsible for her colleagues' deaths.

"I did go out to Ohio, yes. But I only wanted to—"

"I don't care what you did or didn't want to do, Lipscomb. The fact is, someone of your years should have known how that could play in court. And beyond that, you simply had no business having anything to do with the matter. Let alone getting most of your information from the press. Just how much more reckless could you have been?"

Helen could imagine Jorgenson smirking behind her, but she wasn't going to give him the pleasure of even noticing him. Kendal was behind her too, and he'd come through when it came time, but she couldn't count on him to do the same now.

The room had narrowed down to just her and the chief.

For the moment, she decided to keep quiet and see how it played.

She didn't have to wait long.

"You jumped the gun," Jorgenson spoke up. "You decided to cowboy the damned thing and cut corners. And the result was a shootout."

Now she turned to face the man.

"You went along with it."

"Only because we had no choice. You already had the media roped into the affair, plus who knows who else, and I had no option but to contain the damage as much as possible."

"Go to hell," Helen muttered.

"Chief," Jorgenson turned to Rodgers. "Is this the kind of insubordination you tolerate? This detective jammed herself into our investigation, and you see how it turned out."

"How it turned out is that the man who killed four

cops, plus a hell of a lot of other people around the country, is dead," Helen said. "On top of that, his accomplices are in custody."

"Not necessarily," Rodgers put in.

Helen, her stomach feeling hollow, turned back to the chief's desk.

"Excuse me?"

"There's some question as to whether we can keep the Sears family and Mr. Morton in custody."

Helen stood up.

"You're letting them go?"

"Sit down, detective," Rodgers said.

"But—"

"I said, sit down!"

Helen took a deep breath, then sat back in the chair.

"Now then," Rodgers continued, "I'm taking this meeting right now, and I don't want anyone to interrupt me."

Looking around the office, he must have seen acquiescence, so he continued.

"Detective, you're going to have charges filed concerning insubordination, flouting of procedure and interfering with an active investigation. Captain Kendal approved to some extent, but that was after most of your actions occurred. Because of all this, we may or may not be able to hold the Sears family, but believe me we're going to do everything possible to do so.

"I've checked with his superiors, and Lieutenant Jorgenson and his people are going to stay on site for some time, working to tie all of this up into a nice bow. Detective Lipscomb, you are as of now back on suspension, without pay this time, and more time may be tacked on once your actions of the last week have been thoroughly reviewed."

"Chief," Kendal said behind her, "I don't think—"

Before he could finish, Helen cut him off.

"Sir, action like that has to come after a formal hearing. It can't be arbitrarily decided."

"Don't worry, detective. There will be a formal hearing, and you'll be notified of the time to appear. But believe me when I say that this is how the committee's decision will come down. So we might as well begin now."

Helen couldn't see Kendal's reaction, but in her peripheral vision Jorgenson was smirking.

"And when you leave this office," Rodgers said, "you'll probably head straight to a union advocate. Feel free to repeat this conversation verbatim, if you wish."

Sensing things wrapping up, Helen stood.

"No, sir. After I leave, I'm heading right to Jack's funeral. After that, I may or may not call my advocate. After all, you've wanted me out of here for nearly a year now. So it looks as if I've given you the perfect opportunity."

"I resent the implication, detective, but if you feel there's some personal animosity here, feel free to take it up at your hearing."

Helen tried to think of a comeback, but nothing came to mind.

"That's all, then. We'll see you at the funeral, and even though on leave you need to be available for any interviews or statements the sergeant may require. Are we clear?"

"Is that it, sir?"

"That's all, detective. For now."

She scanned the room, locking gaze with each

person there.

"Okay, then."

And she turned and walked out.

CHAPTER SIXTY-FOUR

It had been over for nearly half an hour, and by now almost everyone had left.

Almost.

Helen and Lou sat together, shoulders touching, on two of the folding chairs that had formed one end of the first row.

A red-haired woman, who Helen was pretty sure was the same one she'd glimpsed in Hollis's apartment a few weeks back, sat in the middle. She didn't look to either side, her gaze set on the two cemetery workers methodically filling in the grave site.

They'd been silent for nearly the entire time, when Whitmore suddenly spoke up.

"So they're going to keep riding you?"

"It's how they made it sound," Helen said. "Not sure how long it's going to last though."

"Got to admit you made them all look good. I'd think they'd be taking that into account."

"Sure," Helen said, "but at what price?"

Lou rubbed his hands along his thighs. "Maybe you need to take some time to think it all over."

"Not sure if that'd be a good thing. We've lost a lot of friends over the last few weeks. You ever find yourself thinking there may be a better way to live?"

"Dammit, Helen, I think that at least once a week. But if I hung it up, or if you did, what would we do?"

In unison, the two gravediggers lowered their shovels and stepped back. One of them reached into his hip pocket and brought out a red bandanna. He began wiping the sweat from his face.

"It's going to be summer in a few weeks," she said. "Right about now lying on a beach somewhere and letting the sun bleach my brain sounds like something to do."

The red-haired woman stood up, smoothed her black skirt and walked past them to leave. She nodded at them, and Lou nodded back in return. Helen wanted to say something, but couldn't think of any words.

"Got to get back to the shop," Lou said, heaving himself up. "Don't know about you, but I've still got to meet the review board over what went down in that garage."

Helen didn't look at him. Instead, she focused her gaze on the lumpy, now-filled in gravesite.

"Don't worry about it," she said. "We did good."

Lou shifted his feet. "How much time you got stored up?"

She shifted her head, figuring he could see the glisten in her eyes.

"Enough."

"Maybe you should take it. Give you a chance to see the other side, get things sorted out."

Helen nodded, turning away from him to stare back at Hollis's resting place.

Lou stood there for another minute, then squeezed her shoulder.

She reached her hand up and squeezed back.

"Take care, kid," he said before walking off.

Glancing her way, the gravediggers picked up their

shovels and headed off.

Helen decided to sit there for a while longer, in the solitude, and try to figure things out.

At least for a while.

A word about the author...

A high-school teacher, former college instructor and fiction writer, Kevin R. Doyle is the author of numerous short stories, mainly in the horror field. He's also written three crime thrillers, *The Group*, *When You Have to Go There*, and *And the Devil Walks Away* and one horror novel, *The Litter*. Recently, he's begun working on the Sam Quinton private eye series. The first Quinton book, *Squatter's Rights*, was nominated for the 2021 Shamus award as Best First PI Novel. The second book, *Heel Turn*, was released in March of 2021. More information can be found at kevindoylefiction.com.